DRUG
RELATED

Also by roy glenn

Is It a Crime

MOB

Payback

Outlaw

Crime of Passion

Body of Evidence (October 2007)

Anthologies

Girls from Da Hood

Gigolos Get Lonely Too

Around the Way Girls 4

DRUG RELATED

By roy glenn

www.urbanbooks.net

Urban Books
1199 Straight Path
West Babylon, NY 11704

ISBN-13: 978-1-60162-034-7
ISBN-10: 1-60162-034-9
First Mass Market Printing March 2008

10 9 8 7 6 5 4 3 2 1

*This is a work of fiction. It is not meant to depict, portray or
represent any particular real persons. All the characters, incidents and dialogues are the products of the author's imagination and are not to be construed as real. Any references or
similarities to actual events, entities, real people, living or
dead, or to real locales are intended to give the novel a sense of
reality. Any similarity in other names, characters, entities,
places and incidents is entirely coincidental.*

Submit wholesale Orders to:
Kensington Publishing Corp.
c/o Penquin Group (USA) Inc.
Attention: Order Processing
405 Murray Hill Parkway
East Rutherford, NJ 07073-2316
Phone: 1-800-526-0275
Fax: 1-800-227-9604

Chapter One

"Okay, Nick, you're free to go," Detective Kirkland said.

I stood up and looked at my watch. For the last seven hours I had been in the interrogation room with Wanda, answering all of the questions that Detectives Kirkland and Richards had to offer. Kirk opened the door for Wanda and they walked out of the interrogation room together. I followed them, thinking.

"It's really not necessary for you to walk me out detective," Wanda said and looked back at me.

"These halls are filled with dangerous criminals." Kirk always did have a thing for Wanda, so he had to escort her out of the building.

Dealing with Kirk was nothing new to her. "I've played this game with Kirk before," Wanda said once we were out of the building. "So, don't worry. I got this."

I wasn't worried. I'd known Wanda Moore since

I was eleven. She was a good lawyer, and like she said, she'd played this game with Kirk plenty of times during his attempts to make a case against Mike Black. Ten years ago I was an enforcer for Black. He controlled a profitable gambling, prostitution and number running business. But that was then. Now Black is semi-retired and living the good life in the Bahamas. "Thanks for hanging in there with me," I said as I started to walk away.

There were still too many unanswered questions that I had to have answers to. The most pressing of which was how I got to be the only suspect in four murders.

I needed to think, retrace my steps, do something, anything to get myself out of this. Or maybe I'd just go straight to the airport, and catch a plane to the Bahamas to become Black's new permanent houseguest.

"Not so fast, Nick." Wanda grabbed me by the arm. "You're coming with me. You need to tell me everything. Not those covert Army, need to know, bullshit answers you just fed Kirk. The whole story."

I looked at Wanda, thinking about giving her some covert Army, need to know, bullshit answer, and hailing a cab.

But I knew she was right.

Wanda led me to her car and we drove to her house in the old neighborhood. It had been ten years since I'd driven through these streets. A strange kinda chill came over me that started me thinking about the old days.

"Black know about this?" I asked Wanda, but I already knew the answer.

"Of course he does. Who do you think put up your bail? You know anybody else with a million dollars? He wouldn't turn his back on you when you need him. Even though you ran out on him when he needed you. First Jamaica, then you."

"Lighten up on me, Wanda. I've been draggin' around that burden for the last ten years."

"I'm sorry, Nick. I didn't mean to go there. I just—"

"It's okay, Wanda."

"What happened, Nick?"

"There must be something I missed."

"What is it?"

"I don't know."

"Start at the beginning, Nick. Don't leave anything out. Even if you didn't think it was important at the time."

"It started when Mrs. Gabrielle Childers sat down in front of me. No. That's not right. It really began two weeks before when Uncle Felix called and said he had a job that required our talents. A simple job, he called it, and it was.

"You see, Wanda, until about a year ago, I'd been a part of a special operations unit. Things went wrong on our last assignment, and only three of the members of our unit got out alive: Jett Bronson, Monika Wynn, and me. We were flown back to Fort Bragg, where we were promptly debriefed and processed out. Uncle Felix approached us the day after. He recruited us to do jobs for him that required our skills. Jett's specialty is electronic surveillance, computers, and all that high tech stuff. Monika's specialty is munitions. The girl really gets a rush out of watchin' things blow up. Me, my specialty is weapons, commando tactics."

"Commando tactics?"

"You know, Wanda, the killer."

"Oh. Go on, Nick."

"At Felix's request, I convinced Jett and Monika to come with me back to New York. Felix set us up in a front business as private investigators. To maintain our cover we actually did some surveillance jobs. Some insurance jobs, a few skip traces. Nothing major, but it paid. Besides, the real money was in doing those little jobs for Uncle Felix."

"Whose uncle is he?"

"What?"

"Uncle Felix. Whose uncle is he?"

"Nobody's. That's just what he said to call him."

"Okay," Wanda said and rolled her eyes. "Where did you run into him?"

"When they processed us out, Felix walked up on us at a bar. He said that General Peterson recommended that he talk to us. Felix told us just what we wanted to hear."

"What was that?" Wanda asked.

"He was talkin' real money for doing the same things we'd been doing—hack into computer systems, some light demolition and the occasional termination. We would do the jobs that couldn't be done through normal channels."

"What was the job this time?"

"Just acquire the target, a guy named Norman Vogel, and deliver. A walk in the park. And it was. A simple surveillance to get his pattern down and decide when to snatch him. Jett installed a remote video system in his house. Once it was installed, the system used standard phone lines that provide transmission and monitoring in real time at 28.8 kbps."

"In English, Nick."

"Sorry. It operates at high speed, so the transmission provides clear color images at up to fifteen frames per second over a single phone line."

"Thank you." Wanda said.

"I'll try to keep it simple." Wanda let out a little laugh. "What's so funny?"

"Nothing," She laughed. "I just remember when you could hardly read."

"Yeah, well, things change."

"Go on, Nick."

"It went off just the way it was planned. We picked him up at his house, and then Monika blew it up so there wouldn't be any trace. She made it look like there was a gas leak that caused the explosion. We made sure that the house burned to the ground so there wouldn't be too much looking for a body. Then we left him alone, as instructed, in a car on Pier 17 off of Fulton Street."

"Did he explain why he wanted the guy brought there?"

"Nope. And we didn't ask. It was a mission like any other."

"No questions asked."

"Right. We were soldiers, Wanda, trained to follow orders."

"So, the three of you kidnap this man and deliver him to whoever. What happened after that?"

"The next afternoon, I went by the office to type up my report for Felix and get out of there. But I was tired, so I sat back in the chair and before I knew it, I was asleep. I had been asleep for at least an hour before I opened my eyes, and there she was, standing in the doorway."

I went on to describe my first meeting with Mrs. Gabrielle Childers.

Thursday, July 9, 3:47 PM

"I'd like to hire a private investigator." Her voice was deep.

"That would be me. Come in. Please, have a seat."

In my dimly lit office, it took my eyes a minute to focus while I shook off my nod. She walked toward me. From my vantagepoint, I could make out only that she was very well dressed, tall and slender, but not skinny by any definition I'd ever heard. She had the type of legs that I'd probably enjoy watching when she walked out, but I couldn't tell much more about her. "Tell me, what I can do for you, Miss?"

"Mrs.," she said with attitude. "Mrs. Gabrielle Childers. And I'd like to hire you to find my brother."

I started to tell her that I don't handle cases like that.

But I didn't.

With my eyes now focused, I could see her face. I wanted her to stay. *Mrs.* Childers, huh?

The way she said it, with so much attitude about it, so I decided to have some fun with it. "How long has he been missing, *Mrs.* Childers—"

"About two weeks."

"Any possibility that he could have just gone out of town? Took a vacation and not told you?"

"It's possible, Mr.?"

"Simmons, Nick Simmons." I liked the sound of her voice. It was soothing. "Please, call me Nick."

"Okay, *Nick.* It's possible, but it's not like Jake to be gone like this. Neither my sister, Chésará, nor I have heard from him. Jake is kind of . . . well, anal. You know, everything in its place, all about details."

"Have you gone to the police, *Mrs.* Childers?"

"No. I haven't gone to the police."

"Mind if I ask why?"

She looked at me for a while. She had pretty eyes, but they weren't soft. They were cold and distant. But there was something enchanting about the way she smiled. She shifted around in her chair and crossed her legs.

She dug around in her purse and pulled out a pack of cigarettes. "You mind if I smoke?" she asked, almost as an afterthought.

"Please, be my guest."

She lit up. "I think my husband might be involved."

"All the more reason to go to the police."

"I don't want to go to the police until I'm sure that he's involved. That's why I want to hire you to prove that he's involved in it."

"Are you afraid of your husband?"

"Yes," she said quietly and looked away. Her fear came through loud and clear. "My husband is a very dangerous man, Mr. Simmons."

"Nick. Please, call me Nick. What's your husband's name?"

"Alvin, Alvin Childers."

I laughed to myself, wondering how dangerous

somebody named Alvin could be. "What makes him so dangerous?"

"He's involved in drugs. If he even thought I was talking to you about him or his business he'd—"

"Has he hurt you before?" I asked, and she dropped her head a little. I had taken notice of the dark circles under her eyes that her makeup didn't quite hide.

"I don't see what that has to do with anything." The fear in her voice quickly gave way to attitude.

But I like a woman with a little attitude.

"Look, you want me to prove that your husband is involved in your brother's disappearance, and prove it to the police at that. You have to tell me everything."

She took a deep breath. "All right. What do you want to know?"

"Answer my question."

"Yes, he's hurt me before."

"Once, twice, daily?"

"More than once, and let's leave it at that," she said quickly and defiantly.

"All right, Mrs. Childers. Tell me about Jake then. Where he lives, where he works, his girlfriends, who he hangs out with."

"He has an apartment on Bronxwood." She wrote down his address and handed it to me.

"You got a key?"

"No."

"Know of anybody who does?" I asked.

"Jake is too particular about his things to let a lot of people have a key."

"He have a girlfriend?"

"Lisa Ellison," Mrs. Childers replied. I could tell by the way she said it that she didn't like her.

"What about her? She got a key?"

"I don't know."

"You know if she's heard from him?"

"I don't know."

"You ask her?"

"No."

"Why not?"

Mrs. Childers rolled her eyes. "I don't like her." At least she was real about it.

"What about friends? Anybody he hangs out with?"

"I don't know," she said quickly. Then she said, "He's got a friend, Rocky. He grew up down the block from us in Philly. Him and Jake hang sometimes, but not that often."

"Do you have a picture of Jake?" Mrs. Childers reached in her purse and handed me a picture. "Looks like the bomb party. What's the occasion?"

"Jake's last birthday. We never had birthday parties when we were kids, so we really make a big thing of them now."

"How old is he?"

"Jake's thirty."

"He the oldest?"

"Yes."

"Who's that in the picture with him?"

"That's our sister, Chésará."

"Him and Chésará close?"

"Yes." She sounded offended by the question. "All of us are very close."

"How old is your sister, Mrs. Childers?"

"Chéz is twenty-three." Mrs. Childers leaned forward and went cleavage on me. "Are you trying to find out how old I am . . . Nick?"

The way her voice dropped when she said my name . . . *Nick*. It overcame any objection I still had about taking her case.

Since I was trying to find out how old she was, I asked. "How old are you?"

"I'm twenty-seven."

That sounded good too, but not as good as *Nick*.

"When was the last time you saw Jake?"

"About two weeks ago. He came by the house. He told me that Chilly had been looking for him."

"Chilly?"

"My husband."

"Go on. What did your husband want to see him about?"

"He wouldn't tell me. But Chilly wantin' to see Jake was unusual. Jake doesn't have much to do with Chilly."

"Is your brother involved with drugs too?"

"No. Jake is a chemist at Frontier Pharmaceuticals."

"Any reason to think that your brother is dead?"

"No!"

I wasn't sure what to read into the way she answered, but there was something about the look in her eyes that screamed that there were things she wasn't telling me. I knew then that this was a case I didn't want to get involved in. But still, there was something about her that cried out for my help.

"All right, Mrs. Childers, I'll look into it. Give me a day or two and I'll get back to you."

"When you need to contact me, leave me a message on my voice mail and let me know when and where I can meet you. Or call my sister. She'll give me the message. I really don't want to come back here." Mrs. Childers reached in her purse again, this time to retrieve her checkbook. Without asking what my rates were, she wrote out a check and handed it to me. "I hope this will cover your fee, or at least get you started. Money isn't a problem, so if you need more—"

I looked at the check. "No, Mrs. Childers, I think ten thousand dollars is enough to get me started." She stood up and I escorted her to the door. As expected, I enjoyed watching her walk. "One more question, Mrs. Childers. Why do you think that your husband is involved?"

"Just a feeling. But that *is* why I hired you."

I left my office thinking. Not about the case I had just taken on, but about Mrs. Gabrielle Childers. I found her to be a very attractive woman to say the least. I was thinking about how any man could do anything to hurt someone as beautiful as her, or any woman for that matter. I thought about the way she sat there with confidence and poise, until she started talking about her husband. Then her whole mood changed. Whatever he had done to her had left her with a lasting impression.

Now I had a real missing person's case. We'd done a few skip traces, but this was different. My first thought was to tell Jett and Monika about it, but it made more sense to find out what—and who—I had gotten them involved with. Suppose Mrs. Childers was right? Suppose her husband was involved?

This could get hectic with a quickness.

Jett and Monika grew up in the burbs. They came from nice middle class families and knew nothing about the dope game. But not me. I knew the game all too well, having been a soldier for Mike Black before joining the Army two weeks after André Harmon, who ran most of the illegal activity in the area, met his untimely demise.

I drove to Jake's apartment to have a look around. I put on my gloves, let myself in, and proceeded with my search. The place was immaculate. Everything in place, just as Mrs. Childers said it would be. I ran my finger across the coffee table. Very little dust. I went into the kitchen and opened the refrigerator. The date on the milk bottle had expired ten days ago. The bathroom was next. Sink and shower were bone dry. The toilet had that blue water in it, so I flushed it. It came back even bluer. I moved on to the bedroom. There was nothing out of place in the closet. Bed was made. It was a safe bet that no one had been there in at least a week.

I went back into the living room and turned on Jake's computer. Once Windows 2000 finally opened, I went into all the items on his desktop. I used an old DOS command to show hidden directories. Then I went into Explorer and ran a search on all documents modified in the last thirty days. There was a directory filled with word document files, and a directory with spreadsheet files. There was one file in each directory whose last modified date was eight days earlier. I tried to open them, but they were both password protected. I turned the computer off and decided I would come back to the next day with Jett. I felt someone come up behind me. "Ouch!"

Chapter Two

"How long were you out?" Wanda asked. She had changed into her robe, made a cup of coffee, and settled herself on the couch.

"Not long. Ten, fifteen minutes maybe."

"Any idea who it was?"

"No."

"What happened then?"

"I could feel the blood running down my neck. That's when I realized that I only had on one glove. The right hand glove was on the floor."

"So we know somebody wanted your finger-prints. What'd you do then?" Wanda asked questions just like Kirk. Hard and fast.

"I took a quick look around the apartment and got out."

"Where'd you go when you left?"

I stood up and walked around the room, deciding how I was going to answer the question. "I drove to the Childers' house."

"Why'd you go there?"

"To get a feel for the layout. Just being thorough, Wanda."

I couldn't bring myself to tell Wanda that I went there to see if I could see Mrs. Childers again, but it was the truth. There I was, sitting outside her house in complete darkness.

I opened the trunk, got my bag and took out my camera. This gave me an opportunity to try out my new Predator night vision goggles. Jett said they would give me high performance in low light.

"These are great, Nick!" he'd said, louder than he needed to, when he handed them to me. "Check them out. They're lightweight, only 550 grams. They're powered by a single 1.5-volt AA alkaline battery. Their design is great for helicopter pilots flying night missions. But you should be able to carry out search operations under low light conditions."

Time to see if he was right.

It was a big house. I hopped the fence and walked around, looking for any security. "I hope they don't have no dogs out here." This was a great time to think of it because I hated dogs.

I got a few shots of the house. It was surrounded on all sides by trees. The long driveway led to a big garage and more trees behind it. There were six cars in there.

I walked back to the house surprised that there was nobody patrolling the grounds. The alarm system was nothing fancy. I disabled it and was inside in two minutes.

"Nice set up. These drug dealers sure know how to live," I said.

With my night vision goggles on, I walked around the house planting listening devices and taking pictures of the entire house. I timed myself as I moved from room to room, until I reached the master bedroom. I checked the closets. The really big one was hers, naturally. I can't really think of a word to describe her wardrobe, but both expensive and extensive came to mind.

I put a listening device next to the bed behind a picture of her and Chilly. "What did she see in him?"

The curtain was opened, so I looked out of the bedroom window at the trees over the garage. I bugged the phones before returning to the car to wait. It was 1:34 when she drove up in a white Porsche.

I put the goggles back on.

What am I doing?

She stopped to open the gate. I watched as she opened the car door and her leg appeared. First one, then the other. Her outfit matched the car. I wondered if she coordinated her outfits with which car she was going to drive.

After awhile, lights began coming on inside the house. She immediately closed the curtain in the front room. Ten minutes later, the downstairs light went out. I wanted to see her one more time, and then I would go. I got out of the car and went over the fence again, heading for the garage, but I was too slow. The bedroom curtain closed just as I walked up. I turned in time to see headlights stopped at the gate. I ran behind the garage and made my way back to the car. There were now four cars other than hers parked in the driveway. A sound check of each room let me know that there were eight, maybe nine people in the house other than Mrs. Childers. She was still upstairs alone. I sat there for the next ninety minutes listening and trying to place voices with names. Picking up on Chilly was easy. He was the loudest, and did most of the talking. *I don't think I like him.*

Chilly announced that he was going to bed, and a while after that, most of the people left. I got pictures of each of the players as they came out of the house. The lights stayed on downstairs, but I didn't hear Chilly's mouth. I switched to their bedroom.

"Gee, you sleep?"

"No. Just watching TV."

"What you watching?"

"Forensic Files."

"That shit again. *Forensic Files, The System, Cold Case Files,* all that Court TV shit. Why you always watchin' that shit?"

"So I can figure out how to kill you. And do you always have to turn on every light in the room?"

"I gotta see."

"I know, but why every light? All you need is one."

"Yeah, well, you'll be a'ight."

I heard Mrs. Childers mumble something under her breath, but I couldn't make it out.

"I thought you were coming to the club tonight, Gee."

"I just didn't feel like being bothered with all of those people."

"So, where you been?"

"I went by Chéz."

"What y'all do?"

"Nothing."

"Chésará didn't have nothing to do on a Friday night? That ain't possible. What y'all do, Gee?"

"I told you, we didn't do anything. We just talked."

"She's good at that. 'Bout all she good for is talk."

More mumbling from Mrs. Childers.

"I want you to do something for me tomorrow."

"I have plans for tomorrow."

"Well, cancel them. This shit is important."

"And what I have to do isn't?"

"Nope. Just more of your usual bullshit."

"It's your usual shit that's bullshit," she whispered.

"What you say?"

"Nothing, Chilly. What do you want me to do?"

"You just be dressed and ready to go by eleven."

"Yes, your majesty."

"That's right. I'm the king here. Your ass be forgettin' that shit sometimes."

There was a long silence, then, "Stop!"

"You the one that needs to stop."

"Stop it, Chilly. I'm tired."

"Come on, now."

"No, I said I was tired . . . Ouch! You're hurting me."

"Stop fightin' me—Come on now."

"All right, all right. Go ahead."

There was more silence, followed by a few minutes of Chilly grunting like an animal. Mrs. Childers made no sound. I imagined her lying under him, eyes closed, wishing it were over. Then,

"The least you could do is move, Gee."

She didn't answer.

"Ahhh!"

I started my car and went home. I was sure now. I didn't like him.

Chapter Three

I called Jett and told him to meet me at Monika's house so I could tell them about the case. When I got there, I laid it all out for them. I left out the part about me listening while Chilly forced himself on Mrs. Childers. "Come on now, Nick," Monika said. "We ain't no real private investigators. This is just a cover. What you know about finding somebody anyway?"

"It's no different than them skip trace jobs we did," I said, pleading my case.

"Sounds like fun to me," Jett said. "Besides, Monika, what else do we have to do?"

"Shut up, gray boy," Monika said, rolling her eyes at Jett. "You got a weird sense of what's fun." Monika frowned at me. "What are you gonna do now?"

"I wanna go back to Jake's apartment and have another shot at his computer. And I could use some help."

"I'll go with you, Nick," Jett said enthusiastically, which saved me the trouble of having to convince him. "Come on, Monika, it'll be a blast. Do something different for a change."

"Let's go, Jett. I want to get finished at Jake's in time to pick up a tail on Chilly around eleven."

As we started out the door, Monika said, "Y'all wait up."

"Thought you weren't interested," I said, smiling at her.

"I'm not. That don't mean I'm not part of this team," she said, grabbing her bag and joining us at the door. "Somebody has to keep you two fools out of trouble."

On the way to Jake's I filled them in on the rest of what happened there the night before. "Any idea who hit you or what they hit you with?" Monika asked.

"Don't know who it was, but I'm pretty sure it was the butt of a gun. Heavy caliber, forty-five maybe."

"You know what this Chilly guy carries?" Jett asked.

"No, but I can find out. I'll ask Mrs. Childers."

"You got a picture?" Monika asked.

"No."

"You don't have a picture of the guy you're looking for? How do you expect to find him?"

"Oh, him."

I handed Monika the picture of Jake and Chésará at the party. Both Monika and Jett looked at me like I was crazy. I thought they wanted a picture of Mrs. Childers.

"Not bad. That the client, Nick?" Jett commented as he dissected the picture with his eyes.

"No, that's the client's sister."

"What does the client look like?"

"An older version of her."

"What's her name?"

"Chésará."

"Wouldn't mind tailin' her. If you know what I mean."

"See, that's why I'm here," Monika said as we arrived at Jake's. "Nick already got his nose up one's ass. Now you dyin' to get your head up the sister's ass."

"Calm down, Monika."

"This is a serious matter. These people are drug dealers, and if they are involved, they're not gonna think twice about killin' you for stickin' your nose in their business."

"I was thinkin' more about stickin' other parts of my anatomy in her," Jett said, still looking at the picture of Chésará.

Once we got to the door, I went to work on the lock.

"Don't you have a key?"

"No, Monika. I don't have a key," I replied as I opened the door and went inside.

"That is breaking and entering. Now we're about to tamper with evidence in what may be a crime scene. How much she payin' us?"

"Ten thousand to get us started. There's more if we need it. Money is not an issue."

"Still, I don't like the way this is going already."

"Tell you what, Monika," Jett said as he prepared to hack into Jake's files. "If shit gets too thick, we'll let you blow up the building."

"Very funny, Jett." She looked around. "This place is cleaner than my house."

"Yeah. Mrs. Childers said he's kind of anal like that."

While Jett worked on the computer, Monika and I searched the apartment again. "I'll have it in no time. This is pretty simple stuff. Just hack into this password file and . . . Damn! It's encrypted."

"Pretty simple stuff," Monika said.

"Yeah, he'll have it in no time."

Monika looked in the bedroom while I went through his file cabinets and the mail. Ten minutes or so had gone by when I heard Monika say, "Well now, what do we have here?"

"What you got?"

"Safe."

"Where?" I asked, joining her in the bedroom.

"In the closet under this box. Guess you missed this, huh, Nick?" Monika started digging in her bag for something.

"What are you looking for?"

"What do you think I'm lookin' for? Something to get this safe open."

"Jett, come open this safe before she slaps some C-4 on it."

"Nah, C-4 would be too messy for a small safe," Jett said while he wrote a program to decrypt the file.

Monika gave us the customary rolling of her eyes and attached a small device to the safe. "Bet I have this safe open before you get the password."

"You're on," Jett yelled.

"Beat ya. Ha, ha."

"That wasn't fair."

"Fair? What you white folks know about fair?" Monika asked.

They were fun to work with. Although Jett thought Monika was mean, overbearing at times, and had a tendency to be a pain in the ass, and she held Jett personally responsible for the sins of the white man, they would do anything for each other. That was why we were still alive today. On our final mission, Monika fell on approach to the objective. Her ankle was broken and she couldn't continue. She wanted us to leave her, but Jett refused. While the three of us had a philosophical debate over the need to follow orders and proceed to the objective, the objective blew up. Jett got on the radio and tried in vain to raise any member of our unit. They were all dead. Jett's loyalty to Monika saved our lives.

Monika handed me some papers from the safe to go through while she examined the rest of the contents. She opened a box with a large envelope in it, containing pictures and three videotapes. "Hey, Nick."

"Yeah."

"Who's that in the picture?" she asked, pointing at the picture next to the bed.

"I guess that's his girlfriend, Lisa Ellison."

"Then who is this?"

Monika handed me the pictures. "Damn. When Mrs. Childers said he was anal, I didn't think this is what she was talkin' about."

Monika laughed. "Looks pretty anal to me."

All of the pictures were of Jake having sex with the mystery woman, in an interesting variety of positions. "I'm willin' to bet these tapes are more of the same."

"Got it!" Jett yelled.

I took one of the less intense pictures of Jake and the woman, and joined Jett at the computer. "What's in those files, Jett?"

"You did say this guy was a chemist. Formulas, looks like. And each doc. file has a corresponding spreadsheet. I'll make a copy and show it to a chemist Monika knows."

"You done, Monika?"

"Just about. I need to take pictures of some of these papers. They look like formulas too. If we can find out what he was working on, maybe we can find out what happened to him."

"Very good. Nancy fuckin' Drew here."

"Fuck you, Jett."

"Two things prevent that," Jett said as we left the apartment and headed for the car. "Good taste being one of them."

"What's the other, Jett?" I asked, expecting a snappy come back.

"It would be too much like fuckin' my sister."

It was 11:30 when we arrived at the Childers residence. We were late, but so were they. We parked the car down the street to the sound of Chilly yelling. "I ain't gonna call you no more, Gee! Get your ass down here right now so we can go!"

"Go on without me, then!" Mrs. Childers screamed back.

"You just get your ass down here right now."

"You set this up, Nick?" Jett asked.

I nodded, trying to hear the argument.

"Not bad work. A little staticy, but not bad. You set up cameras too?"

"No, but I got pictures of each room."

"We need to go over those pictures. It will make it easier to complete the set up."

"No time now. I gotta follow them. Find out what was so important that she had to go with him."

"Get your head out her ass, Nick. You go with Jett. I'll follow the happy couple."

I started to insist that I had to go, but she was right. The sooner we could go over the pictures, the sooner we'd have the place covered.

When Mrs. Childers came to open the gate, we got out of the car, and Monika took off behind the Childers. Jett and I went back to the office to develop the film. "How'd you get in, Nick?"

"Simple alarm and cheese ball locks."

For the next hour I went over the set up of the house with Jett. Once he was satisfied with my review, he prepared to implement his plan to maximize coverage. "Where are you going?" Jett asked.

"To see Lisa Ellison. Then I thought I'd talk to the sister."

"Not without me, you're not."

"Jett, you heard what Monika said, and she was right. I know these people. Some of them I probably know personally. They will kill us for involving ourselves in their business."

"Come on, Nick. We can handle them."

"I know you're a tough guy and all, Jett, but we're outnumbered and out-gunned." *The way I left Black.* "We need to be a step ahead of them all the way," I said as I armed myself. I did know these people, and when the guns started coming out, I wasn't about to be the last one to pull his. "We need to stay on task, so I'll go talk to the sister. And you get your head out that woman's ass and set up the surveillance."

Chapter Four

"So you and your partner are strung out on these women," Wanda said.

"I wasn't strung out on her, Wanda. I thought she was a very attractive woman, but I think strung out is a little strong." Maybe it was, maybe it wasn't. But one thing was certain; I was very interested in Mrs. Gabrielle Childers. More interested than I'd been in any other woman in a long time.

"Okay, Nick, whatever you want to call it."

"Wanda, I—"

"Anyway, Nick. You left Jett, and you were on your way to talk to Lisa Ellison."

"Yeah, but I was thinkin' that we were gettin' ready to go up against Chilly and his crew. Other than Mrs. Childers' *feeling*, I had no other reason to suspect him. That wasn't good enough. If I was gonna play private investigator, it was time I started investigating. I had to consider the possibility that Chilly wasn't involved. I still thought covering the house was a good idea, just in case he was."

"That was a good idea. So where did you go after that?"

"To see the sister."

"What's her name?"

"Chésará Rollins."

Chésará lived on Manhattan's Upper East Side. None of that suburb shit for her. When I arrived at her building, a doorman met me. He announced my arrival and asked Miss Rollins for permission to send me up. She consented to see me and I was on my way.

She opened the door wearing a blue silk robe. "Hello, Mr. Simmons." As near as I could tell, she had nothing on under it. "So, you're Gee's private detective. I've been expecting you."

"Can I come in?"

"Of course. Please make yourself at home."

"Thank you, Miss Rollins. I'll try not to take up a lot of your time. I just have a few questions to ask you."

"I'm all yours," she said, locking her arm in mine and leading me into the living room. She led me to the couch and sat next to me. "Tell me what I can do to help." She looked a lot like her sister, only her look was soft and playful, not the hard edge her sister had. Jett would be losin' his mind right about now. As a matter of fact, I was having a hard time maintaining my composure, and her hand on my thigh wasn't helping.

"When was the last time you saw your brother, Miss Rollins?"

"The week before last. He was on his way to Gee's house."

"He come by here often?"

"Often enough. Maybe once or twice a week."

"Jake like to travel much?"

"Jake, no. He never went anywhere. Unless you call going to Jersey traveling."

"Has he ever been gone this long before without you or your sister hearing from him?"

"No. Like I said, Jake is over here at least once or twice a week, and he calls just about every day. I think Gee is right. That bastard she calls a husband had something to do with it."

"What makes you say that?"

"If you ever met Chilly, you'd know what I mean. He's an asshole. I wish Gee could get away from him."

"I guess you don't like your brother in-law much."

"That's a good guess, but hate would be more like the truth of the matter. The way he treats Gee is terrible. I wish he were dead."

"Okay. Other than that, any reason why you think Chilly is involved?"

"When Jake left here, he said he was going to see Chilly. Then he disappeared. Chilly is, well, . . . he's a drug dealer, but I guess you already know all of that."

"Your sister did mention that."

"I'm sure Gee told you a lotta stuff. I know I would tell you anything you wanted to know. You married?"

"No." I smiled and she licked her lips. "I've never been married."

"Good for you."

"Do you have any idea what your brother was going to see Chilly about?"

"No, Jake never talked to me much about what he was doing. I always thought that all those computations and calculations was pretty boring stuff.

I like things, and men, that are a bit more exciting in my life."

"Just what excites you, Miss Rollins?"

"One day, when you have some free time, I'll have to show you just what excites me." She smiled at me and stood up. The sash on her robe came free. "I'm going to get a drink. Can I get you something?" she inquired as she took her time retying it.

"Johnnie Walker Black, straight up." I was wrong. She had on a blue bra and panties under the robe, but they were see-through. She turned and walked over to the bar. "You know Jake's girlfriend, Lisa Ellison?"

"Yeah, I know her."

"You talk to her much?"

"We speak when I see her. Which isn't very often."

"Are they close?"

"If you're asking me if she was the only one he was seeing, I couldn't say. Jake keeps his business to himself." She sat down and handed me my drink.

"You know who this is?" I handed her the picture.

"Ooooh, Jake." She looked up at me and smiled then she handed the picture back to me. "No, Nick, I don't know who she is. You show that to Gee yet?"

"No. But I will next time I see her."

"Rocky might know who she is."

"Rocky, that's Jake's friend from Philly. You know him?"

"Sure, I know Rocky. He used to live down the block from us. Him and Jake ran track together. He works for Chilly now."

"What does he do for Chilly, Miss Rollins?"

"Chésará, please. Chésará. Say it with me, Che-sa-rá." I smiled and laughed a little at her. "He sells dope for him. I hear he's a good earner."

"This is a very nice place you have here."

"Thank you. I decorated it myself."

"You have excellent taste."

"In more ways than you can possibly imagine," Chésará said and repositioned herself on the couch.

I chose to overlook the tone of her remark. "What do you do, Chésará? You a part of the family business?"

"No. I'm not part of the family business. Gee pays for all this. Didn't she tell you?"

"No, she didn't."

"Well, Nick. You mind if I call you Nick?"

"Not at all."

"Good," she declared and moved closer to me. "I hate to be so formal. But like I was sayin', I have no desire to be involved in their business."

"Just spend the money," I said with a smile.

"You know what they say, Nick O.P.M."

"O.P.M.?"

"Other people's money."

"You something else, girl."

"You talk real nice to me and I just might have to show you what that something is."

"You talk real nice to me and I just might think about letting you. But I have work to do first."

"Hmm. Go ahead, keep talking. I like the way you work. But I warn you, I like to talk."

"So I've heard."

"Gee say that about me?"

"No, she didn't."

"Then who?"

"I have ways of finding out things I need to. That is, like, what I do. Find things out about people." Chésará tipped her head and looked strangely at me. *Why don't you just tell her that you have her sister's house bugged and her brother in-law said that about her?* I didn't mean to say it, but it was out there now. The telephone rang.

"Hello."

Saved by the bell.

"Hi, Gee."

It was her. I sat up straight. I got excited just knowing she was on the phone. Chésará looked at me and smiled. I tried to hear what Mrs. Childers was saying, but I couldn't.

"Your private dick is here. You sure know how to pick them."

Whatever Mrs. Childers was saying to her, it wiped the seductive smile off her face.

"Bye, Gee." Chésará hung up the phone. She looked at me, the seductive smile returned just as quickly as it left. "That was Gee on the phone."

"Really, what did she say?"

"That I should stop tryin' to flirt with you and cooperate."

I smiled.

"You like my sister, don't you, Nick—"

"What makes you say that, Miss, I mean, Chésará?"

"The funny look you get on your face anytime I mention her."

"How do I look?"

She made a funny face and laughed. "You know, eyes all glazed over. Gee has that effect on men. So do I."

"I noticed."

"Once we have a man, it's hard for him to resist

us. Like this guy Gee kicked it with for a while. He just won't leave her alone."

My back stiffened. "What do you mean?"

"If Gee knew I told you this, she'd freak." Chésará repositioned herself on the couch, which only proved to expose more cleavage. She was flirting even when she wasn't. "While Gee was in St. Martin, she met this guy at the hotel bar. He was there with his wife and kids. Well, he told Gee that he was from Brooklyn. That he owned a used car lot on Utica Avenue. He gave her his card, so Gee called him and they got together a few times. Now he won't leave her alone."

"Why doesn't she want to see him anymore?"

"'Cause he can't fuck. Gee said that he couldn't keep it up long enough to do anything for her. Gee said she rocked the house two times and he came."

"Don't you hate it when that happens?"

"I'm sayin'."

"Why doesn't she just tell him that? If a woman ever said that to me, I'd stop bothering her."

"But no woman has ever told you anything close to that, have they, Nick?"

"No. They haven't."

"I bet you put on a good show." *There she goes with her hand on my thigh again.* "But I promised Gee I'd stop flirting." She didn't move her hand, though. "She did tell him that. Told him to his face that his dick was little and he couldn't satisfy her."

"How'd he take it?"

"Bad. So now he's blackmailing her."

"Blackmail?"

"That same night before she told him that,

somebody took a picture of them. But right before the picture gets snapped, this fool kisses her."

"Now he wants money or he'll show it to Chilly," I said.

"And Chilly will kill her."

"What's his name?"

"Ben Josephs."

"Did she pay him?"

"Of course she did. At first Gee threatened to tell his wife, but he didn't seem to care. Told her to go ahead and tell her, she won't believe it anyway. Besides, Gee couldn't take that chance. Chilly would kill her. So she paid him, but now he wants more."

"How much?"

"She gave him five thousand dollars the first time, and ten more last night. She just told me that he wants another twenty."

"Where would I find him?"

"I don't know where he lives, but I guess you can find him at the car lot he owns in Brooklyn."

"Why are you telling me all this, Chésará?"

"'Cause if you really like Gee, you'll take this guy off her neck."

"Maybe I'll talk to him."

"If you do, don't say anything to Gee about me telling you this. She would be mad at me."

"It'll be our little secret."

"Something we can share. I like the thought of that."

"Thanks for seeing me, Chésará." I stood up and finished my drink. "And for the drink."

When Chésará stood up her sash came free again. She didn't bother to retie it this time. She locked her arm in mine and walked with me to the door. "You come on back when you have more time. To *talk*."

"I just might."

"You make sure that you do. You'll find me to be a brilliant *conversationalist*. People tell me that I'm *very* oral when the conversation is stimulating."

"I'd be interested to see."

Wanda shook her head disapprovingly. "I see you still have a way with the women. Why didn't she just come right out and say she wanted to fuck you?"

"I don't know, Wanda. Why don't you ask her?"

"I don't think so, Nick. I learned a long time ago not to mess with you and your women."

"What's that supposed to mean?" I demanded, but she and I both knew she was talking about Camille.

Now, why she wanna go and do that?

"Never mind. What did you think of the sister? Other than the obvious, I mean."

"What do you mean?"

"Open up, Nick. I'm not Kirk. This is me, you know, Wanda. I'm only trying to help you. We go too far back for you to be so defensive with me."

"I'm sorry."

"I just wanted to know if you thought she was telling you the truth, that's all."

"I thought so. I didn't think she had any reason to lie about what she told me."

"It seemed like she wasn't all that concerned about her brother being missing. I think she was more concerned with gettin' her freak on with you."

"Whatever gave you that impression?" I smiled.

"Come on, Nick. *Very* oral. If that wasn't an invitation to come back and get some head, I don't know what it was. I'm very oral."

"Like you said, Wanda, I just have that effect on women."

"Yeah. I guess you do."

Chapter Five

The more I thought about it, the more I realized that I needed to find out who and what I was up against. I knew where to go, but I wasn't sure if I wanted to go there. Freeze always knew everything about everybody. If he didn't, he either knew how to find out or it wasn't worth knowing. It had been ten years since I'd seen Freeze. Ten years since I had tried to close the door on my past. Maybe it was time to re-open that door.

Besides, I was hungry and I hadn't eaten anything all day. I drove to Cuisine, I entered the supper club and looked around for Freeze. I was surprised at what a nice place it was. Nothing like the spots we used to run back in the day. Not seeing Freeze anywhere, I allowed the hostess to seat me at a table.

"Is Freeze here?"

"Who?"

I smiled and continued to look over the menu.

"Just tell Freeze that Nick Simmons would like to see him."

The hostess walked away.

It wasn't too long before I looked up and saw Freeze coming toward my table. "Nick! What's up?"

"You tell me. You're the man. In a suit no less."

"Fuck that shit. How the fuck are you, man?" Freeze sat down and motioned for a waitress. Two responded to his motion. "What are you drinkin', Nick?"

"Johnny Black, straight up."

"Bring me the usual. You hungry, Nick?"

"Yeah, I haven't eaten all day."

"You see anything on the menu you want? Never mind, I know you'll eat anything," Freeze said, turning his attention to the waitresses. "Tell the cook to make whatever he's best at for Nick, and you know what to bring me. You, get the drinks." And with that, both women rushed off to carry out his orders.

"Do two waitresses always come when you call? And what's up with the suit?"

"Hey, this is a legitimate, upscale supper club. I gotta look the part. But never mind all that, Nick. What's up with you?"

"I've been all right, man."

"Damn, it's good to see you, Nick. You should come around more often."

"You know what's up with that."

"That stupid shit between you and Bobby." Freeze shook his head. "You need to let that shit go."

"Has Bobby let it go?"

"Not far as I know. He doesn't talk about it. He gets all quiet and shit when you bring it up."

"Then it's still on."

Freeze laughed. "Yeah, I guess it is. But that shouldn't stop you. You and me been through too much."

Knowing Freeze was right I let it pass without comment. "How's Black?"

"Doing good. Island life agrees with him."

"When's the last time you talked to him?"

"Talked to him this morning," Freeze announced as our drinks arrived. "Black calls me every morning. He likes to keep his hand in. You know how Black is. Shit ain't changed."

"He get up here much?"

"Every once in a while. He don't like bein' away from Shy for too long."

"I can't believe Black's strung out like that."

"You ain't seen Shy."

"She all that?"

"She's worth the price of admission. You oughta go down there. Ain't like you ain't been invited."

"Black don't wanna see me. I called him a few times when I got back, but we never hooked up. Then he was gone."

"Shit was crazy back then for him and Shy." The waitress returned with our food, prime rib. I started eating it like I hadn't eaten in weeks. "You think Black is still mad at you 'cause you left?"

"Ain't he?"

"Hell, no. He wasn't mad at you—not really, anyway. He understood why you felt you had to go like that. He knew that shit with you and Bobby was gonna end with one of y'all bein' dead. What

Black couldn't understand was why you joined the Army to fight for the government when your homies was fightin' a war right here. But he respected your decision. Shit, Black respected you. Said you were the most disciplined man he ever met."

"I was a soldier even then. That's why he made me work with you. Your ass was wide-open back then. Wanted to blast everybody."

"Damn near did."

"Black thought you needed discipline. And he was right, but look at you now.

"A lot's changed since you been gone."

"I see this. This is really a step up from The Late Night."

"Damn, The Late Night. I haven't thought about that place in years. We had some good times . . ." Freeze paused and looked at me. "And some bad times." I guess he remembered the last time I was there and Bobby tried to kill me. Freeze laughed a little. "Anyway, this ain't that type of place. The Late Night was just that. A late night hang out. We are marketing to a different clientele."

"Listen to you."

"Wanda taught me to say shit like that. She's a trip, but she was right. She's right about most things. She made us all a ton of money over the years. Anyway, I know you didn't come here just to talk about old times. What's poppin'?"

"You know somebody named Alvin Childers?"

"Chilly?"

"Yeah, Chilly."

"I know him, and so do you, Nick. You remember he used to deal for André back in the day. He's the one who made peace with Black, and they set up the dead zone where nobody deals. Bitch nigga had to make peace 'cause Black was gonna blast that ass next. Now he runs most of the drugs uptown. What's your interest?"

"Business. His wife is my client."

"Gee? What Gee hire you for?"

"Find her brother."

"Didn't know Gee had a brother."

"Didn't think you would. He's not part of the family business. His name is Jake Rollins. He's a chemist."

"Never met him. Just her sister, Chésará."

"I just left her."

"She's a bad muthafucka."

"So I noticed."

"Wild as hell. Into everything."

"I could see that, yeah."

"Pussy was good, though."

"You fucked—" Freeze looked at me like I was stupid. "Never mind. She got anything to do with the family business?"

"No, Gee's breakin' her off. You think Chilly had something to do with it?"

"Mrs. Childers does."

"If Chilly did have somethin' to do with it, your job is easy. All you gotta do is find the body. Chilly likes to make his shit real public. Make a statement, like André used to. You know what I'm sayin'." Freeze laughed. "I know you do. That used to be our thing. Remember?"

I laughed. "Yeah. I remember."

"So, let me get this straight. Gee hired you to find her brother. Gee don't think Chilly's involved,

Gee knows he's involved. So, what does Gee want with you?"

"So I can prove it to the cops."

"Nick, this ain't nothin' you want any parts of."

"I see this. I'll leave it alone."

"You a lyin' muthafucka."

I got up from table. "Thanks for dinner, Freeze."

"Nick."

"Yeah."

"If shit gets wild," Freeze stood up, "I'm with you."

"Thanks."

I left there thinking about Black.

Whether he respected me or not, the truth of the matter was that I ran out on him when he needed me most. But I wasn't about to let Bobby kill me over Camille just to save face with Black. But in spite of all that, Freeze was still for me. It would make my burden just that much heavier. It started me thinking about the old days, the old crew—Black and Bobby, Jamaica and Freeze.

I thought about the first time Black told us he was going to kill André. We knew he was planning something big when he called a meeting at The Late Night. Black never had meetings. In spite of that, we were late. Waitin' on Freeze, of course.

"Now that we're all here," Black said as soon as we came through the door, "I bet you all are wondering why I got you all over here."

"The thought had occurred to me," Bobby said,

staring at me. The way he was looking, I knew then that he knew I was fuckin' Camille.

"I'm gonna kill André," Black declared.

There was complete silence in the room.

We all sat there, looking at Black and one another, until Bobby started laughing. Everybody joined him at first, until we noticed Black wasn't laughing.

"You serious, Black?" Freeze asked.

"Deadly." Black flashed a rare smile.

"How you gonna do it?" I asked.

"What you gonna do? Just walk into his office and blast him?" Bobby inquired, but his eyes were still on me. Then he slowly turned to Black.

"No. I have a plan," Black said.

"You plannin' on taking over after he's dead, Black?" I asked.

"The gambling houses and the women, yes. But I'm gettin' out of the dope game."

Nobody was really surprised by that. We'd all seen it coming. After Vickie died in his apartment smoking cocaine, Black turned totally against drugs. He even stopped smokin' weed. And Black loved to smoke weed.

"We'd be givin' up a lot of money, Black. I don't think that's good for business," Bobby said.

"Maybe. No. You're right, Bobby, it's not good for business. We'll just have to find different ways of making money. But when I walk around here and I see what it's done to the neighborhood," he looked at Jamaica, "to people, I just can't be involved in that anymore. Anybody who wants to is free to do whatever he wants once this is over. As long as you don't do business around here."

Black looked around the room.

"Bobby, you with me? I can't do this without you."

"You don't even have to ask me. You know I am," Bobby said.

"Even though it's not good for business?" Black asked.

"Business will just have to suffer."

"Anybody else?" Black questioned.

No one said a word.

"All right then. My plan is based on the fact that for every action there is a reaction. If certain things happened, I can get people right where I need them to be. Now, there are enough people who hate André to go around. Cops won't care, and as long as business doesn't suffer, no one else will care either."

"Just as long as everybody continues to get paid, you're right. Nobody will care," Bobby added.

"We have to kill Ricky. Him and André started out together. He'll try to take over. Benny and Dupree were loyal to André, so they gotta die too. And that's it. Now, if André dies, Cazzie will try to move on us, so we have to kill him too. Killin' Cazzie will be harder, but not impossible."

"Go on," Bobby said.

"All right now, everybody pay attention. Benny and Dupree are the key to it all. They make the rounds every night to collect the money from all the houses. On Friday nights there's more than a quarter of a million dollars. They start at one o'clock, and by three-thirty they'll be coming out of the last house. That's where we'll hit them. Nick, you and Freeze will be waiting for them. As soon as they get to the car, you and Freeze blast them. Nick, you cover while Freeze gets the money."

"Done," I said. Good soldier, you know.

"Now, Benny and Dupree are dead and the money is gone, what's gonna happen next?" Black asked.

"Somebody will call Ricky's punk ass," Freeze said.

"Exactly. Someone in the house will call him to tell him about the robbery. Ricky will be at his after hours spot, sitting in that office, just like he does every fuckin' night. As soon as he gets the call about the robbery, he'll call André, and they'll plan to meet at André's office. Bobby, when Ricky comes out of his office and starts to make his way through the crowd, you and Jamaica take him then."

"What about Cazzie?" I asked.

"He's the wildcard in all of this. Problem is, there's no way I can predict his movements the way I did everybody else."

"Black," Jamaica said. "Let me take care of Cazzie. I know how to take him."

Black looked at Jamaica for a long time. He knew Jamaica was off the chain with that heroin. We all did. "Okay, I'll leave that all to you, Jamaica."

"What about your boy, André?" Freeze asked.

"When he gets to his office, I'll be there waitin' for him. Now for this to work, everything has to run on schedule." Black gave me, Bobby, and Jamaica a pager.

"What're these for?" Bobby asked. "I already got a pager."

"When you complete your assignment, you page the next man. Three sevens if everything goes as planned. If anything goes wrong, you page the next man with all nines. When it's over, we all meet here. Anyone get nines, we abort and meet back here. Any questions?"

It worked out just like he planned it. Except for Jamaica disappearing, it all went off clean and easy. When he didn't show up afterwards at The Late Night, nobody really gave it much thought. We all just figured he was off somewhere getting high. Like I said, we all knew Jamaica was off the chain with the heroin since Vickie died. He and Vickie were real close. Used to get high and hang out all the time. But shit, hangin' out was all Vickie ever wanted to do anyway. I laughed out loud.

"What's so funny?" Wanda asked.

"Nothing, really. Just thinking about Vickie."

"Vickie? What brought that on?"

"Been thinkin' a lot about the old days. You know, how Vickie died and the effect it had on things."

"It affected all of us."

"Yeah, I guess, but not like it did Jamaica. How is he, anyway?"

"He says he's all right, but the last time I talked to him, I don't know, there was something funny about the way he was talking. Something about his tone brought me right back to when Vickie died."

"Where is he?"

"He's in the Bahamas. Black says he's gotten himself into a few things down there. I just hope that whatever he's into doesn't involve drugs, is profitable, and doesn't cause any of us any grief."

"You think he's back on?"

"I don't know, Nick. It would be a real shame, because he worked very hard to get himself clean," Wanda said then paused. "But Jamaica wasn't the only one who took Vickie's death hard. The one who took it the worst was Mike."

She was definitely right about that. And to be honest, I can't say I would have been any better. After all, she died in his apartment. Overdosed on pure cocaine he had there. Black never did any 'caine, but those days he would always keep some around 'cause women would do all kinds of shit for it.

That night, we were hangin' out. When Black saw André, he gave Black some pure. Black didn't get home until nine the next morning. He said he was getting ready to put a cut on it, but he was blasted and didn't feel like it, so he threw the bag on the coffee table and crashed on the couch. He had been asleep a couple of hours when Vickie came in. She had a key to all of our apartments. They kicked it for a minute, and then Black passed out again. When he woke up later and decided to get in the bed, the door, to his bedroom was locked. Black knocked on the door but Vickie didn't answer. When Black noticed the bag was gone from the table, he kicked the door in and found her lying naked on the floor with the pipe still in her hand.

After that it was like something snapped inside of him. You wouldn't know it to see him or talk to him, but that was when he really earned the name Vicious Black. The first time I really noticed it, he had called me and said, "Come scoop me up. I gotta make a run." Whenever he said that, we knew he was either going to collect money for André or hurt somebody for not paying. People hated to see Black coming, 'cause they knew why he was there, and it was all-bad. I picked Black up and we were on our way to see an old hustler named Wilson Goode.

"So, what's up with good old Mr. Wilson?" I asked.

"He owes André fifty large," Black replied.

"For what? Wilson's a pimp. How'd André get his hooks into him?"

"Says Wilson came to him wanting to borrow fifty grand. You know at twenty-five cents on the dollar André was more than happy to front it to him. When he couldn't pay, André put that ass to work. But he's been playin' André for a couple of weeks now. Cynt said that Wilson was at her spot late one night and he dropped ten grand playing poker. Said he had some young girl with him."

"Young girl and a old man, cause of trouble since the world began," I said, laughing.

"I thought it was a two faced-woman and a jealous man that was the cause of trouble since the world began."

"Whatever, Black." We both laughed.

"I know the little honey he got himself hooked up with," Black said. "She's a fine-ass bitch."

"Can I fuck her?"

"Don't waste your time. She thinks she's too pretty to move. Wasn't even worth the time it took for me to get undressed."

"I hate it when that happens."

When we got to Wilson's apartment, I knocked on the door, but nobody answered. "I know he's in there. I hear them talking." Black stepped up to the door and listened for a second or two, then he put both hands on the door and pushed it. "Move back." He took a step back and kicked it in.

Black stepped aside and I ran in with my gun out. Black followed me in calmly with his hands in his coat pockets. There was Wilson with two very pretty young ladies. Both of them were naked, and all Wilson had on was his underwear. On the coffee table was cocaine, some rock and some powder, and two or three pipes.

"What the fuck!" Wilson shouted. "What the fuck you muthafuckas doing here? And my fuckin' door! Y'all gonna fix my door."

When Black saw the dope on the table his eyes narrowed.

"Black! You hear me talkin' to you, nigga? Black! What the fuck is going on here?"

But Black didn't answer. He just stood there staring at the dope.

"André sent us," I finally said. "He wants his money."

"I'm a get him his money, Black. I just need a day or two to make some things happen. You tell him that."

"You two get dressed and get outta here," Black said to the women.

"They ain't gotta go nowhere. Y'all ain't gotta go nowhere. They were just about to leave."

"I ain't gonna say it again." And with that, both ladies got up and went in the bedroom. "Go with them, Nick." I did so gladly.

While I was in there watching the ladies get dressed, I could hear Wilson yelling at Black, but Black never said a word. Once I escorted the ladies out, Black took a gun and a silencer out of his pocket. "Search the place, Nick. Find me some money." Black put the silencer on the gun, but the whole time, he was staring at the table. I put on my gloves and tossed the place.

By this time, Wilson's whole attitude had changed. Now, with the ladies gone, he was begging Black to give him a couple of days to come up with the money.

"I found this under the mattress," I said, handing Black twenty grand.

"On the real, Black, I need that money to make this thing happen. Give me 'til tomorrow, Black. I'll make it worthwhile for both of you."

Black stood up. I started for the door, thinking that Black would just take the money and be back on that ass again tomorrow. But not this time. Black raised his gun and fired two shots to Wilson's head.

That's how it went. André would send Black to collect, and Black would kill them. After a while, André sent Black away before he killed everybody who sold for him.

Wanda yawned and got up from the couch. "I'm going to get some coffee. You want some?" she asked.

"No, Wanda, I'm fine."

"I know," Wanda whispered.

She turned away and walked into the kitchen. I watched her walk. Although we had spent the last nine hours together, this was the first time I noticed how pretty Wanda was. Not the tall, skinny girl we used to tease as kids. Before yesterday, it had been ten years since I had seen her. And I probably wouldn't have called her if I weren't in this trouble. I felt pretty selfish. She had spent the night fencing with Kirk. I knew she was tired, but she had no plans for sleeping until she had the whole story. Black posted a million dollars to bail me out. They were my family, and I would never turn my back on them again.

"Sure you won't have some?" Wanda asked, with a deep yawn.

"I'm sure. Why don't you get some rest? I know you must be tired. Get some sleep and we'll start again in the morning when you wake up."

"I don't think so, Nick. You wanna know why?"

"Yeah, Wanda, tell me why."

"Because as soon as I went to sleep, you would leave and I'd never get the whole story. And I need to know the whole story. You do understand that, don't you?"

"I understand."

"Good for you. Which reminds me. Why didn't you tell me about killing André?"

"Black said not to. He said if you ever asked, to ask you if the words *conspiracy to commit murder* mean anything to you, counselor."

Wanda rolled her eyes. "That's the same ten-cent answer I got from him, even though it didn't turn out that way."

"What's that supposed to mean?"

"Nothing." Wanda looked away.

Whatever it was, it was something to her, but I didn't push it. "Black's always thinking ahead, ain't he? Always thinking about us."

"That's just how he is. You know that. He cares, even though he'll never admit to it. That's why this thing with you and Bobby over Camille hurts him so much."

"I'm sorry."

"Why don't you tell him yourself?"

I didn't have a reason.

Chapter Six

Saturday, July 11, 3:28 PM

The next afternoon I drove to Brooklyn to see Ben Josephs. I gave some thought to what I was doing. I was going to see a blackmailer. In Brooklyn, of all places. I hated Brooklyn. I pulled up in front of the lot. I didn't want to just walk in there and ask for him, so I decided to call and pose as a businessman who wanted to buy no less then five cars for a limo service. That would be enough to get him to meet me somewhere. "Ben Josephs, please."

"He's out on a test drive with a customer. Can one of our other salesmen help you?"

"He's not the owner?"

"No, sir. Can one of our other salesmen help you?"

"No, that's all right. Thanks."

Just a salesman, huh. Men will say anything to get some pussy. But the plan was still sound. What salesman could resist a five-car afternoon? So I parked my car, waited long enough for him to get back from his drive, and walked up on the lot. When a short, balding white man approached me, I went into my act. "Hi there." Big smile, hand extended "My name is Patrick Mitchell."

"Well, Mr. Mitchell, what can I show you?"

"Those Cadillac's there. I need five of them. I was looking for Ben Josephs. Is he around?"

"He's right over there. I'll get him for you, sir."

He practically ran to tell him, and good ole Ben did a trot over to me. "Mr. Mitchell." Big smile, breathing hard, hand extended. "I'm Ben Josephs. What can I do for you?" After what Chésará told me about his performance in bed, I had to bite my lip to keep from laughing in his face.

"Well, Ben. You don't mind if I call you Ben?"

"No, sir. Not at all."

"I run a limo service and I need to buy five of your Cadillac's there."

"I'd be happy to show them to you, sir."

I'll just bet that you would, Ben. To sell me five Cadillacs you'd probably kiss my ass from here to across the street.

I test drove one car. I liked it, and thought about actually buying it. Then reality set in and I remembered why I was there. I got out and picked another Caddy. Ben went quickly to get the keys. While he was gone I thought again about what I was doing there. It had occurred to me that this wasn't what I was hired to do. Mrs. Childers hired me to find her missing brother, plain and simple, not take some low-rent blackmailer off her neck.

Mrs. Childers.

I closed my eyes and I could see her sitting in front me. Saw her smile, heard the need in her voice, calling out to me. *Nick.* That's why I was there. As Ben approached, I closed my eyes again. This time I saw us naked and making love. Lying on my back with her on top of me. I touched her face with both hands and drew her closer. Our lips met.

Ben threw me the car keys. "You drive," I said, throwing him back the keys.

"Huh?"

"I wanna see if it's comfortable in the back seat."

"Okay. Yeah, this is for a limo, right?" Ben asked.

We got in and Ben drove away. "What do you drive, Ben?"

"Black Acura."

"Ooooh."

"Yeah, boy, the women really go for it."

"Probably the only way a can't-keep-it-up mutha-fucka like you can get a woman."

"What you say to me, nigga?" Old Ben turned around and looked into the barrel of my 9.

"I said, it's probably the only way a can't-keep-it-up muthafucka like you can get a woman."

"Yeah, man, whatever you say. You can have the car. Please, just don't kill me. I got a family."

"Calm down. I don't want the car, Ben. But there is something I want from you."

"What, man?"

"You have a picture I want."

"What picture?"

I hit him in the back of the head. Not hard. I didn't want him to wreck the car. "Don't insult my intelligence, Ben. The picture of you and Mrs. Childers. You're gonna give me that picture, now. You're gonna give me any copies you have, and if there is a negative, I want that too. And if I hear of you ever tryin' to contact Mrs. Childers again, I'll kill you. Slow. You feelin' me, Ben?"

"Yeah, man, I feel you."

"But to show you what a nice guy I am, Ben, I'm gonna let you keep the money you blackmailed outta her. All I want is that picture."

"I don't have it with me."

"Well, where is it?"

"At my house. I can get it for you and bring it to you tonight."

"I don't think so, Ben. Let's just go get it now."

"I can't go now. I don't get off work until six. I'll get fired if I leave now. Give me a break, man."

"Give you a break." I looked at my watch. It was almost four. "I guess we'll be test driving cars for the next couple of hours, huh, Ben?"

For the next two hours, Ben chauffeured me around Brooklyn and we got better acquainted. He wasn't a bad guy, for a blackmailer. He was ex-Army, so we had something to talk about. Even knew some of the same people. If it wasn't for the fact that he was blackmailing Mrs. Childers, we could have hung out.

Mrs. Childers. I couldn't get her out of my mind. I wanted to see her, talk to her, get to know her. *Here you are again, fallin' hard for another man's woman.* I tried, but still couldn't imagine her being with him.

Once 6:00 rolled around, we got in Ben's Acura and he drove to his house. He lived in a nice house in the East New York section of Brooklyn. "Wait here. I'll be right back," Ben said and started to get out of the car.

"Yeah, right." I got out too.

"Wait a minute, man. My wife and kids are in there."

"What's your point?"

"I don't want her involved in this business."

"Good, then you'll be a good boy and get that picture. I'd hate to have to kill your wife and kids, but I will. Now let's go."

Ben unlocked the door to the house and we went in. The house was immaculate and smelled of dinnertime. "Your wife a good cook, Ben?"

"Yeah, good down home cook. Met her when I was stationed at Fort Mac in Georgia."

"Ben!" His wife yelled from the kitchen. "That you?"

"Yes, Renée."

"You're home on time for a change. You must not be feelin' well." She came out of the kitchen. She was a pretty woman, naturally pretty, not done up. You know what I'm sayin'. No makeup, no fake hair or nails. None of that. "I'm sorry. I didn't know you had company." She came toward me with her hand out. "I'm Renée, Ben's wife."

"Patrick Mitchell. It's a pleasure to meet you."

"We were just about to have dinner. Have some?"

"No, I just came to get something from Ben and then I have to go, but everything smells delicious."

"We're having fried pork chops, baked macaroni and cheese, candied yams, collard greens, corn bread and freshly squeezed lemonade."

"Mmm, sounds good, but I really can't. But maybe you'll give me a rain check?"

"That's right, honey; Mr. Mitchell has to go."

"Nonsense. You know you want to. I can see it in

your eyes. You look like a man who appreciates a good meal. You married, Mr. Mitchell?"

"Please, call me Patrick. And no, I'm not married."

"When was the last time you had a home cooked meal?"

"I couldn't even tell you."

"Then it's settled. I insist."

"Well, since you put it that way, Mrs. Josephs, I accept."

"Good. You just have a seat at the table. Ben, you call the children." I looked over at Ben as his wife went back in the kitchen. The frown on his face let me know how he felt about me staying for dinner. I didn't care; I was having fun with this. And besides I was hungry, and everything did smell delicious. Ben rolled his eyes and went to call the children to dinner.

Everything was wonderful I made a complete pig of myself. She really was a good cook. Ben was pretty quiet during the meal, as one might expect for a man in his position, but his wife was a very entertaining conversationalist. I'm a sucker for a good conversation. Ben had a nice family, two very polite kids. After dinner, they excused themselves. His wife got up and cleared the table. "Ben always has a brandy after dinner. Would you like one, Mr. Mitchell? I mean Patrick."

"Thank you. That would be nice."

"What you think you doing?" Ben whispered.

"Having a brandy after dinner . . . with Ben." As soon as his wife and the children were out of eye and earshot, I took out my gun. "You go get those pictures. I'll be in the kitchen with your wife."

Ben got up and walked away while I joined her in the kitchen. "I just wanted to thank you for twisting my arm and having me to dinner, Mrs. Josephs."

"Please, call me Renée."

"Well, Renée, everything was wonderful. Where did you learn to cook like that?"

"I'm a country girl. My grandmother taught me. Didn't you know all us country girls can cook like this?"

"Where you from?"

"Flowery Branch, Georgia. I know you never heard of it."

"No, I can't say that I have." I laughed as Ben returned with an envelope. He handed it to me and I opened it and looked inside to verify the contents. I thought Ben was gonna faint. "Well, people, I really do have to go now, but, Ben, Renée, thank you very much for having me to dinner."

"It was our pleasure havin' you" Renée said, leading me by the arm to the front door. "Anytime that you're in the neighborhood, promise me that you'll stop by."

"I don't get out to Brooklyn much, but I won't hesitate to stop by if the need arises. Right, Ben?"

"Right," Ben said as he walked out of the house.

"Pleasure meetin' you, Renée." I smiled seductively. Her left eyebrow went up, and she blushed.

Once we reached the sidewalk, I stopped and turned to Ben. "That's a real nice family you have there, Ben."

"Thank you. You got what you came for, now get out of here," Ben said, looking away, trying to sound tough.

"Renée seems like a good wife. Too nice for you to be cheatin' on her and blackmailing women."

"Yeah, sure."

I took out my gun again and pointed it at his head. It was dark, and besides, I got what I came for, so I really didn't care who saw me now. "Don't act tough, Ben. You deserve to die for what you've done, and I will come back here and kill you if I hear that you've even called Mrs. Childers again. Get me?"

"You won't."

"When were you supposed to see her again?"

"Tonight."

"Where and when?"

"Ten o'clock at Halcyon."

With that information I walked to the train station.

Chapter Seven

Halcyon was on Smith Street. in Brooklyn. I got there a little before 10:00 and went inside. I looked around for Mrs. Childers, but she was nowhere to be found, so I took a seat in the back of the room where I could see the entrance. It was about 11:20 before she finally showed up. She was wearing a powder blue dress that showed off her legs.

Mrs. Childers had a seat at the bar, looking around for Ben. She ordered. For the next half-hour I sat and watched her. I wanted to be sure that Ben didn't have a change of heart and show up. During that time, I watched as she dismissed man after man who approached her. The list was long. Knowing I wouldn't fall prey to the same fate, I got up and approached and tapped her on the shoulder. "Mrs. Childers." She turned quickly and smiled when she realized who I was.

"Nick."

"What are you doing here?" Mrs. Childers asked.

"I stopped in for a drink. Mind if I join you?" I asked quickly before she asked why I was in Brooklyn.

"Well . . ." She scanned the room again. "I was supposed to be meeting somebody here, but I guess they're not going to make it."

"Then this must be my lucky night." I sat down next to her and signaled for the bartender. "Johnnie Black, straight up. Can I get you something?"

"Hennessy Martini with a twist."

"So, tell me, Mrs. Childers. What man would be foolish enough to stand up a beautiful woman like yourself?"

Mrs. Childers turned away and made one last look around the room for Ben, shrugged her shoulders, and turned to face me with a smile. "Who said I was waiting for a man? So, Nick, have you found out anything about Jake?"

"Not really. I did have a chance to look around his apartment. Do you know if he was working on something?"

"No. I really didn't get into all that stuff he was into. A little too far over my head."

I reached in my pocket and took out the picture of Jake and the mystery woman. "Do you know who this is in the picture with him?" I handed her the picture. She glanced at it for a second.

"I've never seen her before. Where did you get this?"

"That doesn't matter. Has he ever mentioned dating any woman, other than Lisa Ellison?"

"I'm not my brother's keeper. He's very private."

"So, how do you know Lisa?"

"He's been seeing Lisa for years now. He brings her around to parties, family gatherings, things like that."

"Now, let's talk about you, Mrs. Childers."

"Me? What about me?"

"You haven't exactly been honest with me."

"What do you mean? I've told you everything I know."

"About your husband, Mrs. Childers."

"Chilly? What about Chilly?"

"Well, Mrs. Childers, he's a little more than just involved with drugs. He controls most of the drug traffic uptown."

"And?"

"Don't you think that was worth mentioning?"

"Yes."

"Then why didn't you?"

"I didn't want to scare you off."

"I don't scare easily, Mrs. Childers. But that does change things."

"You want more money." She frowned and looked away, then turned back with fury in her eyes. "Is that what this is all about? Money?"

"No, Mrs. Childers, it's about you telling me what I need to know to do what you hired me to do."

"What do you want to know?"

"Well, let's start out with what I know, and you can fill in the blanks. Chilly was a fourth-level dealer for André Hammond until him and Ricky Combs were assassinated ten years ago. Vicious Black declared a dead zone where he wouldn't allow them to sell drugs." Mrs. Childers sat up straight in her chair. I had her attention now. Funny how the words "Vicious Black" had that effect on people. "Stop me if you want to add something."

"No, you're doing just fine," she said while playing with the straw in her drink.

"When Jimmy Knowles, Charlie Rock, and Vincent Martin attempted to kill Black, that started a war between him and what remained of André's and Cazzie Riley's organizations. Well, Black was successful in eliminating his enemies, and Chilly took over. He made peace with Black and agreed to respect the dead zone."

"How do you know all this?"

"I have my sources, Mrs. Childers. So, with all that history out the way, let's begin again. Why do you think that Chilly has something to do with your brother's disappearance?"

"Like I said, it's just a feeling, that's all." I could tell that I was making her uncomfortable, but she was cute when she squirmed, so I continued my line of questioning.

"That's not good enough, Mrs. Childers. There must be something else, something you're not telling me. I've heard that if Chilly had something to do with this, I should be looking for a body."

"Don't say that, please. Jake is not dead."

"How do you know that? You know how your husband works. Public execution is his style, so if he were involved, a simple kidnapping wouldn't cut it. Now, you tell me. What did Chilly want to see Jake about?"

"I don't know!" she said louder than she needed to. I finished my drink and waved the bartender over to bring me another.

"And one for the lady?" the bartender asked.

"No, I've got to go," she said, standing up to gather her things.

"No, please don't go. I didn't mean to upset you, Mrs. Childers. I just need to know what you know. Please, have another drink with me. I promise I won't push you."

She smiled at me. It made my heart beat faster.

"Okay, but just one, then I really do have to go." Mrs. Childers reclaimed her seat and ordered. "Bring me another Hennessy Martini."

"With a twist," I said and smiled. And she smiled back. "So tell me about yourself. Your sister tells me y'all are from Philly. How'd you get to New York?"

"I wanted to get out of Philly." She let out a little giggle. "Had to, really. Our parents were really tough on us. Never let us go anywhere, do anything. It was like being on lock down. One by one, they drove us all out of the house. When Jake graduated from high school, he just never came home that night. No one knew where he was or what happened to him. He was just gone. About six months later he came to my school to let me know that he was all right and that he was going to a small college in Pennsylvania. He told me where, and he made me promise that I wouldn't tell our parents. Jake said they didn't have a son anymore."

"Kinda cold."

"They deserved it. They're dead to me now. Two years later, I left too. I hated to leave Chéz, but she was too young for me to try to take care of both of us. So, I did what I had to, to get enough money to get up here."

"What did you have to do?"

"That doesn't matter. I'm not proud of what happened. That was a long time ago. It's in the past and that's where it will stay."

"How'd you get hooked up with Chilly?"

"You really want to hear this, huh . . . Okay. So I caught the first thing smokin' and came here. When I got off the bus at Port Authority, Chilly was the first person I met. I was young, barely seventeen. I'd never been anywhere, and he offered me the world. See, my father was the type of guy who was always waitin' on some big deal or another he was tryin' to put together. But it never happened. He was always this close to movin' us up out the projects and into a nice house in the suburbs. He hated livin' in the projects. Said it wasn't a safe place to raise the three of us. That's why they were so hard on us. Especially me. He didn't want me to get involved with the wrong kind of guys. Well, look at me now, Daddy," she said and raised her glass.

"Anyway, Chilly was different. If Chilly said he was gonna do something, he got up and made it happen. I liked that. He was nice at first, then . . ." Her eyes dropped into her drink. "That war started and changed everything. Power changed him. I was just his showpiece, his toy. Something to show off to his boys. But that was all show. Then the beatings started."

"Why don't you leave him? Get away, go somewhere, start a new life for yourself."

"Sure. Just like that."

"Leave New York."

"I have, a few times, but he always finds me. Brings me back," she said matter-of-factly. "Or he gives me a reason to come back."

"How does he do that?"

"He hurts the things that are important to me."

"Chésará and Jake."

"Once I thought it was over. I went to Kansas City. I didn't tell anybody where I was going. I got a job as a teller in a bank. They were even talking about promoting me to customer service. You know, sit at a desk, open accounts, that kinda stuff. I had been there for six months when he found me. I told him I was happy and I wasn't coming back. Usually he . . . yells, he grabs, shakes me, hits me. But I was ready for that. He was going to have to kill me. He said okay and left, but it wasn't over."

"I didn't think so."

"The next day, Chéz called me crying. She said Chilly brought Jake to her apartment and he had a gun to Jake's head. He told her that if I didn't say I was coming back right now, he was going to kill both of them while I listened. I said no. Then I heard the gun go off. Chéz screamed and said he'd shot Jake in the leg. I was back the next day."

I didn't know what to say.

"You want more? I got more stories just like that one. That was just one of his masterworks. That's why you have to get proof that will stand up in court. I've seen him go to jail and come right back."

"Now you're talking like you think Jake is dead."

"I don't like to think about it. I know it's possible. The longer he's gone, the more I think about it." Her smile was gone. I thought I saw a tear run down her cheek, but she wiped it away quickly. "So, you tell me your story, Nick."

"Well, there's not much to me. Ex-Army. We've been doing this for about a year now."

"We?"

"I have two partners."

"They have names, I'm sure." Her smile had returned as quickly as it left.

"Monika and Jett."

"Monika? A lady private detective, huh? That's something that you don't hear of very often." Mrs. Childers smiled and gave me a wide-eyed, innocent look. "I used to read Nancy Drew when I was a little girl."

"I used to read Mickey Spilane mysteries."

"You have any family?"

"Yeah."

"It doesn't sound like you guys are one big, happy family."

"Not them, me."

"I see." She finished her drink and signaled for the bartender. "Looks like there are some things you don't like talking about either."

"You're right. I have some things about me that I don't like talkin' about. But I think everybody does."

"That's true. Everybody has secrets. Something only they or maybe one other person know. I know I have some secrets that will die with me."

I smiled, knowing that not only did I know one of her secrets, but it was also the reason I was here. "Tell me one," I said.

"No, then it wouldn't be a secret anymore. You tell me one of your secrets."

"Okay, but just one. I didn't just happen to be here."

"What?"

"I knew you were going to be here, so here I am."

"How did you know I was gonna be here?" she leaned forward and asked.

"I can't tell you that."

"Why not?"

"You said tell me one. If I told you, that would be two."

"That's not fair. Come on, tell me. And don't give me that line about having to kill me. That line is so worn out."

"All right, I'll tell you." I leaned forward and motioned for her to move closer. Mrs. Childers leaned toward me and I whispered, "I'm a private investigator. I wanted to see you, so I found out where you were going to be."

"You're not going to start stalking me, are you, Nick?"

I love the way she says my name. "No, Mrs. Childers, nothing like that."

"I don't have to be afraid of you, do I?"

"You never have to be afraid of me. I'll never let anything happen to you."

"Oh, so you're my own personal protector, huh?"

"At your command," I replied quickly and play-fully, but I knew that at this point I would have done anything for her.

"Well, if that's the case," Mrs. Childers said and smiled at me, "I could think of a person or two that I wouldn't mind getting rid of."

I thought about Chésará. *Something we can share. I like the thought of that.* "Now see, I could say something now, but then I'd be giving away somebody else's secret."

"So," she said. "Tell me anyway. Then it will be a secret we can share."

"No. Who do want to get rid of?"

"My husband. Remember, that is why I hired you."

"To get rid of your husband."

Then Mrs. Childers got very still and looked me straight in the eye. "Yes."

We sat there staring at each other for a few seconds before she sat back and said, "And don't try to change the subject. Tell me, is this secret person somebody you're involved with?"

"No. She's just somebody I met on a case."

"A woman. Is she pretty, Nick?"

"Not as pretty as you."

"Then I know you don't look at her the way you look at me."

"How do I look at you?"

"Like you want me."

"Do I really? And what if I do?"

"If you do, then that would give us something to talk about," Mrs. Childers said softly. She was seducing me with her eyes and the sound of her voice. "But not while you work for me. Isn't there some type of ethical thing that says we shouldn't become personally involved?"

"No, that's doctor/patient ethics that you're talking about. It's almost required for you and me to become personally involved."

"Maybe, Nick, but not tonight. Besides, I'm ready to go."

"Where do you want to go?"

"It's not where I want to go, it's where I'm going. And that place is home."

I signaled for the bartender and paid the tab.

We walked slowly to her car and talked. Talked about nothing really.

"Good night, Nick."

"Good night, Mrs. Childers." What else could I say?

Chapter Eight

I went to bed that night with thoughts haunting me like a bad dream that never goes away. I knew I'd never forget that night, Bobby held his gun in my mouth, screaming that he was gonna kill both me and Camille. It should have never happened, but I was gone, too far gone. Camille had me, and I couldn't leave her alone. I knew when I met her that she was with Bobby, but it didn't seem to matter to me. It definitely didn't matter to her.

I had never met any woman like Camille. She was fascinating to be around and to talk to. And her voice, the way she spoke with that Barbados accent, *Shit!* It simply blew me away. Her dark complexion, her flawless body, and those dark eyes. The way she'd look at me when we'd make love. For too long after that, whenever I closed my eyes, I'd see hers looking up at me.

It began the first time I saw her. I was with Black in his office at The Late Night when she came in with Bobby. Camille walked right up to me. "Bobby, introduce me to this handsome specimen of a man."

Bobby's eyes narrowed when he looked at her. "That's Nick."

That look was my first warning, but I ignored it and each warning that would follow. Camille stepped closer, put her left hand on my chest and looked up at me. "That's no way to introduce somebody, Bobby. My name is Camille Augustus. It is a pleasure to make your acquaintance. And what is your name?"

"Nick Simmons," I answered, and quickly backed up off her. But she had me then, and she knew it. Each time I saw her after that, Camille made that point clear.

When she'd call me, I'd come.

What she wanted, I got for her.

What she said, I did, without so much as a kiss.

I was riding with Black the night Camille decided she would have me. She paged me at 2:45 in the morning and I quickly called her back.

"Come see me. I want to talk. We never have enough time to sit and have a chat."

"Now?"

"Of course, now. Now is when I want you." Camille hung up the phone and I turned to Black.

"Booty call," he said.

"No, just a chat."

"Yeah, right. Nobody calls at damn near three in the morning just to talk. Talk about fuckin', maybe."

I didn't know if he knew where he was dropping me off, and at the time, I didn't care. I knocked on her door, but there was no answer. Maybe I had taken too long and she had fallen asleep. I waited awhile and knocked again. She opened the door dressed in a red gown and robe, which left nothing to the imagination. "Come in, Nick. I was beginning to think that you weren't coming."

We talked and laughed until the sun was shining brightly the next morning. I admired her beauty, the way her dark skin overpowered the red of her gown. Camille commanded my attention in more ways than one. Then she touched my hand and drew me to her. I ran my hand across her shoulder. "Kiss me, Camille." She patted my hand and stood up. "Stand up, Nick." I complied.

Camille looked up at me and undressed me without breaking eye contact. I stood naked before her and she ran one hand across my chest while the other glided effortlessly along my length. She gently grabbed the back of my neck and drew our lips together, but only for a second. Camille eased me back down on the couch and ran her tongue over her lips. Then she introduced my length to her moistened lips, her eyes still locked on mine. She slid her lips across every inch of it then she smiled and opened her mouth. It was soft and wet; if she had teeth, I never knew it. She moved her head up and down in a very slow, almost methodical motion. My excitement only intensified as I watched her, watching me. It was like slow motion, prolonging each stroke.

"Nick!" Wanda yelled.

"Huh?"

"Try to stay with me here. This is a little too important for you to be daydreaming."

"I'm sorry, Wanda. I was just thinking, that's all."

"You were just telling me that you went to your office to meet Monika and Jett. And . . ."

Sunday, July 12, 8:19 AM

The next morning, I arrived at my office to find Monika waiting for me. She had followed Chilly, and I not only wanted, but needed to hear her report. On the way home the night before and on the way there that morning, I gave some serious thought to this thing I was developing for Mrs. Childers, as well as my promise to leave other men's women alone. No one really understood, and I never tried to explain it to anyone except Monika. She understood. Over the years, that promise had kept me from becoming seriously involved with many women. Seemed like the women I took an interest in were all married, living with a man, had a man back home or whatever.

When I arrived at the office, Monika was there waiting.

"It's about time you dragged your ass in here," Monika said.

"Report."

"Yes, sir." Monika smiled and rolled her eyes. "I followed Chilly and wifey to Aureole, a restaurant on East Sixty-first Street. They met a man and a woman, both of Hispanic descent. The male was approximately five feet ten inches tall, dressed in a two-piece dark blue suit, light blue shirt, and enough jewelry to make you notice. The female, approximately five-six, red dress, fuck me pumps. I got video and still pictures. They should be ready soon."

"Video?"

"Yes, video. Jett gave me these photosensitive

sunglasses with a micro-miniature camera. The images are recorded using a standard video recorder, or it can be fed into a video transmitter in a remote location."

"Have to start callin' that boy Q."

"You keep givin' him money, Mr. Bond, he keeps buying new shit. Anyway, I was able to drop a bug on the back of Chilly's chair. There's the transcript."

"Anything we want?"

"Maybe. Page five. I circled it."

Hispanic male: *"I took care of mine, Chilly. What about yours?"* Chilly: *"Not yet, should be another day, maybe two. But I don't see a problem here."*

"It's pretty thin, right?" Monika asked.

"You're right. He may be talking about Jake, maybe not. There's just not enough here."

"The rest of the conversation was just small talk."

"Okay. You stay on Chilly. See where that leads us. Anything on those files? You find out what that formula is for?"

"Nothing yet. I should hear back from my guy sometime today I hope."

"Let me know as soon as you hear from him."

"What about you? What did you do?"

"Talked to the sister, Chésará. Other than trying to flirt, I didn't get anything we didn't already know. You heard from Jett?"

"Said he'd be here early. He should be here soon."

Almost on cue, Jett came through the door.

"Morning, people."

"Report."

"I'm fine, Nick, and how about you, Monika?"

"I'm fine, Jett." Monika giggled.

"Report."

"Completed surveillance set-up of the house. I was able to pick up cell phone frequencies for Chilly and two guys that appear to be his top lieutenants. I reviewed the tapes of the house. Nada. But that wasn't the highlight of the evening. I copied and reviewed the videotapes we found in Jake's safe. Bad boy, that one."

"Figures, watching other people fuck would be the highlight of the evening for a pervert like you," Monika said.

"That ain't it. I think I found something interesting." Jett handed me two pictures.

"Damn, she got a big mouth. Is that what I think it is?" They were stills he had extracted from the videos. "What's so interesting about this?" I asked, and handed the pictures to Monika.

"Look close. I don't think that's the same mystery woman from the first picture."

"I think he might be right, Nick. I think I saw a picture of this one too, but she had clothes on, so I didn't pay her much attention. And there was a picture with the two of them. Looked like it might have been taken at the same party as the picture you been showing of Jake."

"Where is it?"

"I put it back in the safe."

"Great. I'd rather not show this picture around."

"Guess you gotta go back and get the other pictures, Nick," Monika said. "Want me to go with you?"

"No, you stay with Chilly." I got up and started for the door.

"How are you and the Mrs. doing?" Jett asked.

"There's more to this than she's tellin' me."

"How do you know?"

"Just a feeling," I said, closing the door behind me.

I drove back to Jake's apartment, let myself in, opened the safe, and got the pictures that I had come for.

"That's strange." I was on my way out the door when I thought about the fact that we never found any camera equipment in either of our searches. I went through the apartment again. Nothing. I walked out of the apartment and two white men in suits met me.

Cops.

"Shit."

"Hold it right there, pal."

"Can I help you gentlemen?"

"Yeah. Assume the position. I'm sure it ain't your first time."

I hit the wall with a little help from my new friends. One looked over my ID and the other looked at the pictures in my pocket. "You mind coming with us?"

"Am I under arrest?"

"No. We just want to ask you some questions."

"What type of questions?"

"We'll talk about that when we get there."

So there I was, sitting alone in the interrogation room, waiting. It had been more than an hour before the door opened and Detective Kirkland walked in with that shit-eating grin on his face.

"Nick Simmons. What's it been, ten years?"

"Ten years, Kirk."

"Richards, this is one of Vicious Black's old foot

soldiers. But he dropped out of sight ten years ago."

"Where you been, Simmons?" Detective Richards asked.

"Army training, sir."

"Oh. Another smart ass, huh?"

"Yeah, yeah, Kirk. What's this all about?"

"I just wanted to see you, Nick. It's been a long time, so when I heard you were in here, I just had to stick my hand in. And what do I pull out? Do you know?"

"No. But I'm sure you'll enlighten me."

"Tell me something, Nick. What were you doing when the detectives picked you up?"

"Visiting a friend."

"They tell me that you're some type of private investigator. You working on something? Maybe something having to do with your friend?"

"Just visiting, Kirk."

"What's your interest in those women in the picture the detectives took off you?"

"They were cute. I happen to like women."

"Why do you say *were?*"

"Excuse me?"

"I'm sorry. I forgot you went to Vicious Black University. I'll break it down for you. Why are you referring to those women in the picture in past tense?"

"I didn't mean anything by it. Why?"

Richards dropped the picture I took from Jake's safe on the table in front of me. "What's your interest in these two women?"

"Why?"

Richards drew back his hand to hit me, but Kirk

grabbed him. Vintage good cop bad cop. Corny, but I played along. "What's with him, Kirk? I just wanted to know why. Am I being changed with something having to do with those two women?"

"Nick, I know you know something you're not telling me. I'm thinking that since you call yourself a private investigator, that you got a case and you're trying to protect your client."

"So far you're right."

"I thought as much." Kirk pulled out a chair and sat down next to me. "But here's the problem with that. I know more about these two women than you do, so you need to know what I know."

"I'm still with you."

Kirk held out his hand and Richards handed him more pictures. He handed them to me. The same two women, but these weren't taken at some party. These were taken at the morgue. "Both of them died of an overdose of cocaine."

"You think I had something to do with it?"

"No. But one of them had your friend's card on her person at the time of her death."

"Were they found together?"

"I will only answer your questions if you answer mine," Kirk said.

"Fair enough."

"What is your interest in these women?"

"I'm trying to find a missing person and I have, or should I say *had* reason to believe that these women may be able to help me find him."

"Jake Rollins, he the one you're looking for?"

"Were the two of them found together?"

"Answer his question!" Richards yelled.

"What's with him, Kirk?"

Richards came at me again, but good cop held him back. "They were found about two weeks apart. Now, Jake Rollins, is he the one you're looking for?"

"Yes."

"Who's your client?" Richards asked.

"What's your interest in two women that died of a cocaine overdose?"

Kirk smiled. "These weren't your everyday overdoses."

"What do you mean?"

"Who's your client?" Richards asked again.

"That comes under the heading of privileged information." This time Richards swung on me, so I put him on his back.

Kirk grabbed me.

"Get out of here, Richards!" He picked himself off the floor and left the room. Once he was gone, Kirk smiled at me like a kid who knew a secret. "What makes these different is that they had all the symptoms of a cocaine overdose, but there wasn't any trace of cocaine in their systems. And there are more just like them. We just found this one last night. Now, what do you know about that?"

"I don't know anything about it, Kirk. I'm just looking for Rollins. I found that picture in his apartment, and I thought they might know where to find him. I don't know anything about any cocaine." I knew from the start that this had a cocaine flavor to it, and it wouldn't be long before Kirk connected Jake to Mrs. Childers and then to Chilly. But now wasn't the time for me to tell Kirk that. Right now, I had to get out of there and talk to Mrs. Childers.

"Okay, Nick, you're free to go. But I need an-swers."

"Can I have my picture back?"

Mrs. Childers had the answers we both needed.

Chapter Nine

I left a message on Mrs. Childers' voice mail, telling her to meet me at Jimmy's on Fordham Road, "Now!" I drove straight there and waited. She arrived two hours and forty-three minutes later. I'd had dinner, barbecue ribs with onion marmalade, autumn salad with raspberry vinaigrette and read over the transcript of lunch at Aureole with the Childers and the Hispanic couple, while I waited. The food was good, so the wait, although long, wasn't too bad. Mrs. Childers arrived dressed impeccably, as usual. Her makeup was flawless, but in good taste. Her eyes were ablaze as she came toward me. Each step she took was meant to send a message. She was mad at me.

"So, what's with this *now* business?"

"You want to start telling me the truth *now*, Mrs. Childers?"

"This again." She gave me attitude and I loved it. "Look, I already told you, I don't know anything else to tell you. My brother is missing. I want you to find him. That's it."

"Good night, Mrs. Childers." I got up from the bar.

"Where are you going?" She touched my hand. The helpless Mrs. Childers had returned. I continued the game.

"I'll have a courier deliver a check for the refund of your retainer." I even started to walk off. She held my hand tighter.

"Please don't go. Sit down, please."

I sat down, trying my best to act like I was reluctant. "Now, you have to start telling me everything you know. Now."

"Nick, I have told you everything I know."

"Okay, let's start with what was your brother's involvement with your husband?"

"I don't know. Neither of them would tell me anything about what they were doing."

"What was your brother involved in?"

"This is stupid, Nick. How many times can I say this? I just don't fuckin' know anything. Jake never told me anything about what the fuck he was doing. Do you understand me now?"

"This picture was taken at the same party as the picture you gave me. I got it out of your brother's safe." I took out the picture and handed it to her. "Who are they?"

"This one is Pamela Hendricks. And that looks like LaShawn. I don't know what her last name is. She came to the party with Pamela."

"Does your brother know them?"

"I don't keep up with all of Jake's friends."

"Does your brother know them?"

"He might have met Pamela at some party. And LaShawn runs with Rocky, so he probably knows her too."

"What were they doing at the party, Mrs. Childers? Who invited them?"

"I did."

"Who are they? How do you know them?"

"I've known Pamela for years. She was my supervisor at the bank when I was in Kansas City."

"What does she do, fly in for parties?"

"No, Pamela got a job at Manhattan Bank as an area manager and she moved here years ago."

"Banker, huh? She have any involvement with your husband?"

"Not that I know of. She knows him, naturally, but I don't involve myself at all with Chilly's business. Even if she did have some business with Chilly, I wouldn't know it.".

I was starting to believe her. She really didn't know anything or she was giving me an Academy Award-winning performance. Either way, it didn't change anything.

"What does any of this have to do with Pamela?"

"She's dead." I dropped the morgue pictures in front of her for impact. I picked them up along with mine in the interrogation room. I figured Kirk must have wanted me to have them since he left them sitting there.

"My God."

"The police think she died of a cocaine overdose."

"The police."

"Yes, the police, Mrs. Childers."

"What do the police know about Jake?"

"They know he's missing."

"So, they're looking for him?"

"In connection with these overdoses. Pamela had Jake's card on her when the police found her body. LaShawn, whoever she is, died about the same time Jake is supposed to have disappeared."

"And you think that has something to do with Jake disappearing?"

"I don't know, Mrs. Childers. I was hoping you would tell me."

"I don't know." She looked away.

"Well, tell me something you do know."

Mrs. Childers looked back at me and smiled playfully. "I know how you know so much," she said, as if nothing that I was saying had any importance.

"Excuse me."

"I know some people too, Nick."

"And what are they telling you?"

"That you used to roll with Mike Black. Not only that, y'all came up together. Lived on the same block. They tell me that you were his enforcer. You were good at it too."

"Oh, really?"

"Yes, really. André's muscle. Let me see . . ." She was having fun with this. Too much fun. But at least she had a playful side. She always seemed so distant, like there was something else she was thinking about. But she was all smiles now. "It was you, Vicious Black, Bobby Ray, Jamaica and Freeze. You and Freeze used to work together." She laughed. "So, you're no stranger to how Chilly does his business. You used to work the same way. I heard you and Freeze were bad boys back in the day." She waved a chastising finger at me. But she was right; me and Freeze had done some shit for Black.

While André focused his attention on selling drugs, Black chose to make his money on gambling, prostitution, loan sharking, and number running. More so after Vickie OD'ed in his apartment. I remember one New Year's Eve, Black closed all the gambling houses, in spite of the money he knew he'd make that night, and had a party for everybody that worked for him. That was nice, or so we all thought. The party was held at one of the houses that was run by Gary Banks. Like everybody else, Banks made a pledge to Black not to sell drugs, which to Black was rule number one.

The party was wild, with plenty of food, drink, and women, naturally. Everybody was having a good time, except Black and Bobby. They, for the most part, sat at a table in the back of the room and talked quietly amongst themselves. At one point in the evening, Black walked up to me at the bar and asked, "You havin' a good time?"

"Yeah, man, shit. Havin' a ball," I said to a very serious-looking Black. I turned my attention back to one of the women who worked at the house. I began to walk off and take her upstairs to one of the rooms, but Black grabbed me by the arm.

"Nick! Have fun, but you and Freeze don't drink too much tonight. I got something important I want y'all to do later."

"No problem. Drinkin' ain't what I got in mind right now," I replied then went on to handle my business.

At midnight, everybody got together in the main room to drink champagne and bring in the New Year. Black said a few words, then he went and reclaimed his seat next to Bobby. About 3:00 in the morning, Wanda went around and said goodbye to everyone, and Black walked her to her car. When he returned, he looked at Bobby and nodded. Bobby got up and the two of them started going around the room, handing each one an envelope. After receiving it, each man quietly left the house. I called Freeze over. "Something's about to happen," I said.

"What you talkin' 'bout, Nick?"

"Check it. Everybody's leavin'. Either Black or Bobby hands them an envelope, and then they leave."

"I know. Black just givin' everybody a little somethin', you know, breakin' them off a little change."

"Oh, okay, cool," I said to Freeze, but I had a feeling that it was more than that. He waited until Wanda was gone, which meant he planned to do something that he wanted her to have no part in. Black always had been very protective of Wanda and her involvement in the business. His waiting until she was gone only meant one thing.

After a while, almost everyone was gone—all of the women, which let *me* know the party was over, except Cynthia. Cynt was still the only woman who ran a house for Black. In fact, the only people left were the ones who ran houses and a few of the guys who ran numbers or did loan sharking.

Jamaica walked over to the band and sent them home. He said a few words to Bobby and left with them. Once Bobby locked the door, it was on. Black got up and walked to the front of the room. "I wanted to thank everybody for comin' out and spending the New Year with us."

"We gonna get a bonus too, Black?" Banks yelled out.

Black looked annoyed by the question.

"Everybody is gonna get theirs, nigga. Trust me," Bobby said.

"I've known everybody in this room for a long time," Black continued. "I even like most of you. I don't know if y'all like me or not, and to be honest, it really doesn't matter. What does matter is that you trust me, and that I can trust you. That's what makes us a family: trust, loyalty, and honor."

With that, Bobby began walking around the room and continued to pass out envelopes. He stopped in front of me and Freeze and handed us our envelopes. "You and Freeze go stand by Mike," Bobby whispered before moving on. We got up and walked over to where Black was standing. He motioned for us to sit down and he continued talking.

"In order for us to continue to earn a livin', we have all chosen to live by certain rules. Rules that were put in place to insure that we can do that. Rules that each person in this room has sworn to me that they will uphold over everything else." Black started walking around the room. "Anybody who doesn't follow these rules puts all of us in danger. I spent a lot of time thinking about this tryin' to give the betrayal of these rules a name. I even went to the library and did some research on the subject."

Even though everybody laughed, this really didn't surprise anybody. Black going to the library, I mean. Although he basically stopped going to class when he was fifteen, Black read everything he could get his hands on.

"The word I came up with is *treason*. According to the American Heritage dictionary, *treason* means the betrayal of one's country by aiding the enemy. It comes from the Latin word *traditio*, which means a handing over. But I prefer the Columbia Encyclopedia's definition. Treason is the legal term for various acts of disloyalty. English law originally distinguished high treason from petty treason. Petty treason was the murder of one's lawful superior, or the murder of his master by an apprentice. High treason was a serious threat to the stability or continuity of the state. Shit like attempts to kill the king, the queen, or to wage war against the kingdom. Especially cruel methods were used in executing traitors.

"Now, to avoid the abuses of the English law, treason was specifically defined in the U.S. Constitution. Article Three of the Constitution says that treason shall consist only in waging war against the United States or in giving aid and comfort to its enemies. And that conviction may be had only on the testimony of two witnesses to the same overt act or on confession in open court.

"The most treasonous activity in American history was the planned surrender of the fort at West Point to the British. It was to be carried out by a general, who I'm sure all of you have heard of, named Benedict Arnold. His plan was discovered when a British soldier was captured with a document detailing the surrender. I bet most of y'all didn't know that." Black smiled. "I know I didn't."

He was right, 'cause I sure didn't know that shit either.

"Nick, you and Freeze get a bottle and pour everybody a drink," Black said. Once the glasses were filled, Black raised his glass. "By the way, several men were convicted of treason in connection with the Whiskey Rebellion." Black laughed and downed his drink. "But they were pardoned by George Washington."

Everybody laughed with him.

Now Black was standing right in front of Banks, and Bobby was standing behind him. "I like the British laws on treason better than the American. I consider selling drugs to be a serious threat to the stability or continuity of this organization."

All of a sudden, Bobby grabbed Banks and held his arms. Black hit him in the face once, twice, three times, four times. "Gary Banks," Black said and hit him again. "You're being charged—" Black hit him again. "With treason!"

Bobby let Banks go and he fell to the floor. "Pick him up and tie him to a chair," Bobby commanded as Black walked away. Freeze and I followed Bobby's order.

"Wait a minute, Black. I swear to you, I quit dealin', man," Banks said in protest as we tied him up.

Black simply said, "Freeze." And Freeze went to work on Banks. Freeze had learned his craft directly from Black and Freeze was brutal. "Betray—Mike Black!" Shit, Freeze lost his mind beating Banks.

Bobby stepped up to me and handed me an eyedropper. "What's this?"

"Acid," Bobby said quietly.

The beatin' went on for a good five minutes while everyone in the room looked on. Some people started to leave, but Black stopped them. He wanted to be sure that everyone there saw what was happening. Banks was gonna die tonight, and Black wanted to be sure all of them knew why. Finally Black said, "Freeze," and Freeze stopped.

"I swear, man, I quit dealin'," said a now bloody Banks.

"I knew you were gonna say that," Black said. "And I figured that it wouldn't be fair if I were judge, jury and executioner." Bobby cleared his throat. "Okay, Bobby thought it wouldn't be fair. So, you are being judged by your peers. Once you're found guilty, Freeze and Nick will execute you."

Bobby walked over and pulled up a chair next to Banks. "What you have here is an opportunity to admit what you did and accept the consequences."

"What's the difference? Y'all gonna kill me anyway!" Banks shouted.

"No. If Black can't prove that you're sellin' drugs, you can walk out of here with my humble apology," Bobby explained.

"No," Black said. "The difference is that I'm givin' you a chance to man up and admit that you betrayed everybody in this room. Does that sound fair to you?" Black asked sarcastically.

Banks didn't answer.

"Nick."

I stepped up to Banks and tore the sleeve off his shirt. I held the eyedropper over his arm, squeezed the dropper once, and one drop hit his arm.

Banks screamed in pain.

"Does that sound fair to you?" Black asked again.

"Yes! Shit, yes!" Banks yelled.

"Nick." I hit the other arm this time. Banks screamed again. There was no other sound in the room. No one said a word, nobody moved. They all stood and watched as Freeze and I took turns beating Banks and then burning him with acid.

"Admit what you did, Banks, so we can all go home," Bobby said.

"I didn't do nothing, Bobby I swear."

"Freeze," Black said, and Freeze happily resumed his brutal beating.

After a long time, Black stepped up to Banks. "Are you ready to man up, Banks?"

"I keep telling you, Black! I didn't do shit!" Banks protested.

"Doc," Black said.

"Yes, Black," Doc said with a very scared look on his face. Doc ran the gambling in the house and was probably thinking that he would suffer the same fate as Banks.

"I want you to go behind the bar and reach your hand behind the bottle setup next to the cash box. Let me know what you find."

Doc walked very slowly to the bar and did what he was told. He reached behind the setup. "There's another cash box back here."

"Pull it out and open it," Black demanded. "Tell us all what you find."

Doc opened the box. "Drugs and money, Black."

"That shit ain't mine, Black," Banks screamed. "I swear on my mama's grave, I don't know nothing about that! You planted it there."

"Doc, has anybody other than the bartender been behind the bar tonight, or any night, for that matter?"

"No," Doc said.

"How do you know that?" Black asked, knowing the answer.

"It's a house rule," Cynt said. "Nobody goes behind the bar but the bartender. How stupid can you be, Banks? Bad enough you're dealin', but why you gotta do it in the house? It ain't gonna do nothin' but bring the cops down on all of us. Fuckin' fool. You deserve to die."

"Thank you, Cynt," Black said. "I'm glad I didn't have to be the one to say it."

"Fuck you, Cynt!" Banks yelled.

"Fuck you, Banks. Stupid muthafucka," Cynt responded as she stepped up and slapped Banks in the face.

"Black, you gotta believe me. I don't know nothin' 'bout that shit. It must be Earl's dope."

"Jamaica," Black said.

We all looked around and there stood Jamaica, who had come back in with Earl. He too had been beaten badly. "You know I was selling that shit for you, Banks! You said we could make that paper and Black would never know it," Earl said.

"Any questions?" Black asked as he looked around the room.

Again, no one said a word.

"Tie him up next to his friend," Black said to Jamaica. When he finished, Jamaica moved away and Bobby handed me and Freeze each a 9. "Gary Banks, a jury of your peers has found you guilty of treason. The sentence is death."

Bobby walked behind the chairs and placed a black hood over their heads then moved out of the way.

Black looked at me and Freeze. "Fire."

We both emptied a clip in them.

When it was over, I drove Black home. I asked him, "How'd you know Banks started dealin' again?"

Black just looked at me like I was stupid or something. "I know everything that goes on in my organization. Remember that. Never get too far removed from anything you're in charge of, Nick."

Mrs. Childers was right. I knew exactly how Chilly handled his business. But by now, she was talkin' all over herself. "The story goes that you and Bobby Ray fell out over some woman and you cut out."

"True story." It made me a little uncomfortable that she knew.

"Tell me about it, Nick."

"You seem to know the story, so there's nothing to tell."

"There's more to your dark side. That the family you don't like talking about, Nick?"

"If you really gotta know, yes, Mrs. Childers. That's the family I don't talk about. I ran out on Black when he needed me most."

"Mike Black," she said in a way that made me a little jealous.

"You know him?"

"Of course I know him. Everybody knows Mike Black. After Chilly made peace with him, we got invited to all his parties. He always threw the best parties. He used to have them at some mansion out on the Island."

"I remember those parties. Those were the days. But those days are dead and gone. You and I need to focus on the here and now. I need to know how to find Rocky."

"Rocky doesn't come around much. He just

shows up when he needs to. I really don't know how to contact him. Even though he buys from Chilly, he doesn't like him."

"I haven't found anybody who does like your husband, Mrs. Childers. But we'll pass that for now. How does Rocky do business?"

"He usually sends somebody."

"Do you know if he knows Pamela Hendricks?"

"If he knows her, they met the same way, at one of our parties."

"It's not gonna take the cops long to put all this together and tie it all back to Chilly. But that's what you wanted, isn't it?"

"Yes, but there is no evidence. Nick, I've seen Chilly walk in and out of jail too many times to be excited about this. If they pick him up now, it will just make him mad, and he'll take it out on me."

"You're right. Rocky is the one who's tailor made to step off for this."

"What do you mean?"

"Two women OD on cocaine, both of them know your brother. Rocky, his childhood friend, is a dealer, and one of the dead women works in a bank. It has money laundering written all over it. What is Jake's involvement in this? I know. You don't know, but if I do find him, he is poised to take a fall for conspiracy."

"I never thought about it that way. Nick, you just have to find him."

The longing in her voice set me off. It made my will stronger, more determined to find him. Mrs. Childers was right about one thing. As far as the evidence went, none of this had anything to do with Chilly. The more I thought about the transcript and that thing about problems being taken care of, the more I was convinced that it was Jake he was talking about.

With all that had happened, I had completely overlooked the one person who might be able to put all this together for me.

Lisa Ellison.

She would be my target for the night.

I looked at Mrs. Childers. I wanted to stay and talk to her. But I put aside that thought and focused on what I was doing. It was better that way.

"Tell me about Lisa Ellison."

Mrs. Childers rolled her eyes and called for the bartender. "Hennessy Martini with a twist."

Without answering my question, she waited for the bartender to return with her drink. I thought about asking my question again, then I decided to rephrase it. "Why don't you like her, Mrs. Childers?"

"Because she's a dizzy, airhead bitch who thinks she's the shit, but she's not. She's just a stupid, airheaded bitch who's so caught up in her own quasi-bourgeois lifestyle that she doesn't know her ass from a hole in the ground. The fake bitch."

"So, you don't like her, huh?"

"No, Nick, I hate the fake-ass bitch."

"What does she do for a living?"

"She works for Armstrong Direct."

"What's that?"

"It's some bullshit marketing firm. She's some type of bullshit director."

"Hmm."

"What's that supposed to mean?"

"It means hmm."

"You know what I mean, Nick. Don't be funny."

"I mean your brother seems to have a thing for

professional women with lofty positions. They even look alike."

"That's just how Jake is."

I picked up my pictures. "Good night, Mrs. Childers."

"You're leaving?"

She didn't want me to go.

Maybe she *wants* me?

What's more likely is that she's just lonely and wants to talk. "I'm not gonna find your brother sittin' around here."

"Where are you going now?"

"Going to see Lisa Ellison."

"I have a better idea," Mrs. Childers said and stood up.

I got up too. "What's that?"

"Come ride with me."

Chapter Ten

We rode in silence while Mrs. Childers drove us nowhere fast. She drove out of the city, across the Tappanzee Bridge to a small house in Nyack. When we went inside the house, the first thing that hit me was the smell. It didn't smell bad; it was more like the stale odor of some place that had been closed up for awhile. The living room was well furnished, and none of it looked like it had much use. Mrs. Childers turned on some music and went around the house turning on ceiling fans and opening windows.

"This is my little hideaway," she said, opening the French doors that led to the deck.

"Hideaway?"

She smiled and went out on the deck, seemingly to avoid my question. I followed her outside and asked it again. She looked irritated by my question as well as my presence on the deck. "I come out here to get away."

"Get away from what, Mrs. Childers?"

"More to get away from all the stress and pressures, you know, and be by myself. It's so peaceful out here. It gives me a chance to relax and think."

"Bullshit." I said to myself. "Yes, it is very peaceful."

She went back in the house and I followed behind her. "Can I get you a drink?"

"Thank you. Do you have Johnnie Walker Black?"

"No. Will Hennessy do?"

"Hennessy is fine."

I sat on the couch and watched her as she poured. She looked in my direction, but she dropped her eyes when she saw I was looking at her. She handed me my drink, sat down across from me and started to talk. We drank Hennessy, quite a bit of Hennessy, and laughed and talked for hours. Talked about nothing, really. Mostly a lot of reminiscing about her, Jake, and Chésará growing up dirt poor in Philly. "Dirt poor and on lockdown. That was us. Couldn't go anywhere. Except this one night I snuck out and I went over my girl Tina's house. Naturally, she was shocked to see me. She said she was gettin' ready to go ride with Beverly. I couldn't stand that bitch, but her and Tina were cool, and I didn't have nothing else to do. So, we're standin' outside, waitin', when this burgundy Dodge Daytona hatchback pulls up. I never forgot that car." She paused. "Beverly was sittin' in the back. I don't know who the two chicks in the front seat were, but I jumped in the car anyway. They said they were going to get some weed."

"You smoke weed, Mrs. Childers?"

"Every once in a while," she said and raised her glass. "This is my drug of choice. Back then, never. I had only heard other people talk about it. But I was excited about tryin' it, 'cause you know I never did anything. I was gonna be in trouble when I got home anyway. Might as well go for it all."

"You might as well have some stories to talk about when you're back on lockdown."

"You know what I'm sayin'." She smiled. "Anyway, I started chokin' the first time I hit it, and didn't want anymore." Mrs. Childers laughed and got up to fix us another drink. While she was gone, I got up, took a quick look around and quickly reclaimed me seat. When she returned with our drinks Mrs. Childers handed me mine and sat down next to me. We talked our way through that drink and then the conversation turned.

"I remember the first time I caught Chilly with another woman. I was so mad I wanted to kill him. We were at a party at one of his friends' houses. It was the usual dope-boy party—people doing drugs, listening to music, and having sex all over the place. The place was packed, and it was so hot in there, and the air wasn't doing any good. After a while I noticed that I couldn't find Chilly, so I went looking for him. I looked outside, didn't see him. Then I started going from room to room. That's when I saw him coming out of a room with some ho, both of them still putting their clothes back on."

"The least they could have done was get dressed before they came out of the room."

"I thought so too."

"What did you do?"

"I slapped the shit outta him, cursed both of them out and left."

"That was it?"

"No. Chilly ran after me and started with the, you know, 'Baby, I'm sorry. I didn't mean for you to see that. She didn't mean nothing to me', and all that shit."

"The usual."

"But I was young, stupid, and in love—a deadly combination. So, I bought it. I went back inside with him, and everything was cool. We hung out the rest of the night like two lovebirds. Until most of the people left. So, there I am standing by the kitchen, right." She lit up a cigarette and blew the smoke in my direction. "Chilly was sitting on the couch. I waved to him and smiled. He got up, walked over to me, and backhanded me down to the floor. He yelled for me to get up. I tried to crawl away from him, but I couldn't. He grabbed me and pulled me up by my hair. This time he punched me in the face. He kept on punching me. I don't know how many times he hit me. Then he stopped. He looked at me and said 'Bitch, don't you ever raise your hand higher than your waist to me,' and he walked away. Here's the funny part."

"There's a funny part?"

"So, there I am, lying on the floor, crying, face swollen and bleedin'. Blood all over my clothes. People walking by me. The only one who helped me was that same ho he came out the room with. She helped me up off the floor, took me into the same room they were in, and cleaned the blood off my face. She even gave me some clothes to put on. After a while, Chilly knocked on the door, wantin' to know if I'm ready to go home."

"I guess I don't have to ask if you went with him."

"What else could I do? I was scared to death of him. On our way home, he was just as nice to me, like nothing ever happened."

"Why do you stay with him?"

"Please, Nick. Where am I going? What am I gonna do? I tried to get away before, and he always comes after me. There's no telling what he'll do if I try it again."

"When are you gonna tell me what's really going on, Mrs. Childers?"

"I have told you everything, Nick."

"I don't think so. You're lying about something, or at best you're not tellin' me everything."

"Can't you just listen to what I say without trying to read something into it? But no, you have to analyze every word I say. Can't you stop being a detective for a while? Can't you just hold me?" She moved closer and put her head on my shoulder. I felt her heart pounding along with her hand on my chest. I wanted to say something, but nothing came to mind, so I put my arm around her. After a while she fell asleep. I sat there holding her. Suddenly, she jerked away from my embrace and grabbed a pillow from the couch. *Maybe she can't stand to be held either.*

While she was asleep, I searched the house. After I searched the bedroom, I took the sheet off the bed. When I turned around, I was startled to see her silhouette leaning against the door. The light from the hall seemed to cling to each curve of her body. "Are you lookin' for something, Nick?"

"I was just getting something to cover you with." I held up the sheet. "You were asleep," I said as she walked toward me.

"I was. But I'm awake now." She stopped in

front of me. I thought about trying to kiss her. "I don't think we'll need this." She took the sheet out of my hand and let it drop to the floor. I could feel the warmth of her body. She looked up at me and exhaled. "Besides, it's time we start back to the city."

Chapter Eleven

Monday, July 13, 1:47 PM

It wasn't easy getting to see Lisa Ellison.
Mrs. Childers only knew where she worked and
had no telephone numbers for her. First, I got the
number and tried calling, but was immediately
pushed off to voice mail. Then I tried dropping by
her office. I introduced myself as Calvin Bailey and
said I needed to see Ms. Ellison about a personal
matter, but I couldn't get past Yvette, her personal
assistant. She was able to keep me at bay for hours
with her enchanting eyes, her inviting smile, and
her engaging conversation. She also gave me a lec-
ture about dropping by unannounced. "Next time,
Mr. Bailey, please, call ahead for an appointment."
After three hours of waiting and reading the interesting articles in last month's *Essence*, Yvette informed me, "Ms. Ellison is gone for the day."

Now, what I wanted to know was, how did she
get out? She didn't come past me, and I could see
the elevator from where I was sitting. So, I asked,

"How did she get out?" I got more of a story than an answer. Yvette was good. I thought about hiring her. She'd be perfect. "Can I make an appointment to see her tomorrow?"

"What time is good for you?"

"First thing in the morning. It has to be first thing in the morning. I have an appointment I have to keep in the afternoon."

"I'm sorry." Yvette smiled and tipped head to one side. "Ms. Ellison is busy in meetings until four."

"That will be fine. I'll see you then." I smiled at her. "Good night, Yvette. It's been a pleasure spending the afternoon with you." I left the office, looking around for other ways out of the office. Sure enough, I rounded the corner and there it was—an unmarked door with easy access to the stairs.

Tuesday, July 14, 3:00 PM

The next day, I arrived at her office at 3:00, more to talk to Yvette than anything else. I knew I wasn't getting in, appointment or not. She informed Ms. Ellison that, "Mr. Bailey is an hour early for his four o'clock appointment."

Before I came in, I took the liberty of placing a small camera in position to see the outer door and the door to the stairs. I sat talking to Yvette and watching the view on my laptop. At 3:30, Lisa came out the door and went straight for the stairs. I quickly said goodbye to Yvette and followed Lisa. By the time I got to the stairwell, she was gone. She had probably gotten on the elevator on the next floor. I ran down the steps to try to catch her in the lobby.

When I reached the lobby, I was exhausted. I used to run ten miles every day, but not one step since I got out. The elevator doors opened and she came out with the crowd. I followed her outside where she caught a cab. I tried to follow her, but I was quickly reminded that black men don't catch cabs easily in New York City.

Wednesday, July 15, 3:00 PM

The next day, I simply double parked across the street and waited for Lisa, like I should have done in the first place. I would get the hang of this private eye thing sooner or later. She came out around 7:00 and I followed her across the George Washington Bridge into New Jersey. Once she cleared the bridge, she headed north on Palisades Parkway and stopped at a little store. Then she headed back into New York to Spring Valley. Lisa pulled into the driveway of a very nice house on Harriet Lane. The garage door opened and closed behind her. No chance of catching her getting out of the car, so I gave her a chance to get settled before I rang the doorbell.

"Yes," she yelled from behind the closed door.

"Ms. Ellison, my name is Nick Simmons. I'm a friend of Jake's."

"He's not here."

"I know. That's why I'm here. Can I talk to you for a minute? I assure you, I mean you no harm." Reluctantly, Lisa opened the door. "Can I come in, Ms. Ellison?"

"Like I said, Jake isn't here, so what can I do for you?"

"Well, that's just it. I can't find him."

"What did you say your name was?"

"Nick Simmons."

"I've never heard Jake mention you, Mr. Simmons."

"Actually, Ms. Ellison, I'm not a friend of Jake's. I'm a private investigator and I was hired to find him."

"Jake's missing?"

"Can I come in, Ms. Ellison? Really, I just want to ask you a few questions."

"Can I see some type of ID?"

I handed her my ID. She looked me and the ID over carefully before stepping aside to let me in. Lisa led me into the living room.

"Have a seat, Mr. Simmons. Can I get you something?"

"Water would be fine, thank you."

Lisa returned with my water and sat down on the couch. We sat on opposite sides of the coffee table. "When was the last time you saw him?"

"Is Jake in any trouble?"

"No, the person who hired me is just concerned about him, that's all. When was the last time you saw him?"

"Two weeks ago. We had dinner together."

"Did he seem upset or distracted about something?"

"No. Who hired you?"

"I'm not at liberty to say at this time. Have you heard from him lately?"

"I talked to him about a week ago."

"Do you know Alvin Childers? Calls himself Chilly?"

"Yes, I know him. He Jake's brother-in-law. What does this have to do with Chilly?"

"As far as I know, nothing," I said very quickly

and with my best fake smile to try to put her at ease. It was obvious that the mention of Chilly's name had changed her mood. It was also obvious that Lisa, like everyone else involved in this thing, was afraid of Chilly. He was just that type of guy. These people hated Chilly. He had touched each of their lives and made it a living hell. Mike Black used to always say, "Make people fear but respect you. Fear and respect last longer than love. People will love you today and hate you tomorrow." I still had another Chilly question to ask, but I decided to save it for later.

Then I changed my mind. "Do you know if Jake had any business with Chilly?"

"I wouldn't know."

"Do you know a woman named Pamela Hendricks?"

"I . . . I . . . never heard of her," Lisa said, then she turned away and began to twirl the ends of her hair with her fingers. "Why do you ask?" Then she flipped it. "Who is she?"

"Just a friend of Jake's." I thought about showing her the pictures. She was obviously shaken by the mention of her name. A picture of her on a slab in the morgue might push Lisa to tell me the truth. And the truth was definitely in short supply with this bunch. The only one who was willing to speak freely was Chésará.

"I never met many of Jake's friends."

"What type of relationship did you have with Jake, Ms. Ellison?"

"We've been dating off and on for the last five years. We're pretty close."

"But you haven't seen or heard from him in more than a week."

"Like I said, Mr. Simmons, that's just how Jake is."

"Does he like to travel?"

"Not really."

"So, when he's not around for a couple of days, where does he go?"

"I don't know. With my job, sometimes I get very busy and I don't have time to call him either. That's just how we are. Two professional people trying to juggle a career and a relationship."

"Do you know what Jake was workin' on?"

"No. Jake never involved me in what he was doing."

There goes that twirling of the hair thing again. She's lying and I'm getting tired of being lied to. "You know a guy named Rocky?"

"Yes, he and Jake are good friends."

"You know where I can find him?"

"He hangs out at The Spot. It's his club, actually. You can always find him there."

Finally, a straight answer. I decided to go for it. "You sure you don't know Pamela Hendricks?"

"No." I showed her the picture of Pamela and LaShawn from the party. "I said no!" I dropped the picture of Pamela and Jake. She obviously recognized Jake. It hurt her to see it, but I had the feeling that she already knew about it. "I think you should go, Mr. Simmons."

I stood up and gathered my pictures. "One more thing, Ms. Ellison. Did you know she was dead?" I dropped the slab shot on her. "Cocaine overdose."

"Get out, Mr. Simmons."

"Can I use your phone before I go? I promise it won't take long."

"Go ahead."

I called Jett. "Jett, can you hear me?"

Jett had found a house with a basement for rent around the corner from the Childers' house and had set up operations, complete with a satellite up-link. I knew Lisa was shaken, and as soon as I left she would call somebody. I wanted to know who.

"I'm on it. Give me two minutes and I'll have it."

"I promised I wouldn't tie up this nice young lady's line for that long, so make it quick."

"I'm going just as fast as I can. Nice young lady, huh?"

"Yes."

"What does she look like?"

"Nice piece of business."

"Can I fuck her?" Jett asked.

"I'm not sure at this point, but I'd be glad to make an inquiry as to the feasibility of your request."

"So, does she have like big, swingin' titties?"

"No. They're practically nonexistent."

"Flat-chested, huh," Jett said. "Well, flat-chested ain't bad."

"Maybe."

"Probably skinny as a rail too."

"Exactly. But there's some form there."

"Well, you know what they say about skinny girls?"

"What's that, Jett?"

"They're all pussy," he said and laughed.

"You're too much. How much longer?"

"Almost."

"Heard from Monika?"

"No, but she's on Chilly. He can't fart without us knowin' it."

"She find out what's on those papers?" I asked.

"Not yet. But I did ID the guy they had lunch with. His name is Diego Estabon. Peruvian, supplies Chilly."

"Anything else going on that I should know about?"

"She's at home in bed alone, watching TV. She called her sister and they talked for an hour. Small talk. I'll have film and tape at eleven. Got it!"

"You're the man, Jett."

I hung up the phone and looked at Lisa. She had been doing a small pace back and forth—more like a controlled two-step watching me the whole time I was on the phone.

"You made your call, now get out, Mr. Simmons," she said as she walked toward the door. I smiled my best fake smile and followed her. "And I'll thank you not to bother me anymore."

"Goodnight, Miss Ellison." I stepped outside, but I couldn't resist sticking it to her one more time. "You sure you don't know Pamela Hendricks?" She slammed the door in my face. I got in my car and headed back to the city to find Rocky. I called Jett.

"I don't know what you said to her, Nick, but whatever it was, it must have been one major mind fuck."

"She called somebody?"

"She's on the phone with Rocky as we speak."

"Can you hook me up so that I can hear it?"

"Is the Pope Catholic?"

The next voice I heard was Lisa's. She was practically hysterical. Screaming at Rocky, insisting that he tell her what was going on.

"Calm down, Lisa. I don't know what's going on!"

"You know. I know you know. He had pictures."

"Pictures. What kind of pictures?"

"He had pictures of Jake with one of your girls."

"One of my girls? Who?"

"Don't play stupid with me, Rocky! You know who I'm talking about. The one that came with Pamela Hendricks to Jake's 30th birthday party. The one he was all over."

"Ohhh, LaShawn."

"Yeah. LaShawn. He thought it was Pamela, but it was LaShawn."

"Well, what did he want?"

"He said Jake was missing and he was looking for him."

"Wait a minute, wait a minute. Slow down. What do you mean Jake's missing?"

"I don't know. He just said he was trying to find Jake."

"He! Who the fuck is he?"

"He said he was a private investigator. His name is Nick Simmons. He said they were both dead and that she died of an overdose."

Then there was long silence, like the line had gone dead.

"What is it, Rocky? You know something. Tell me what it is."

"Look, Lisa, I really don't know what's going on, but I know how to find out. I'll call you back."

"Where are you going? What are you going to do?"

"I'm going to see Chilly."

This was working out better than I thought it would. Rocky was going to use the direct approach and ask Chilly where Jake was. "Call Monika and find out where Chilly is," I told Jett.

"No need. He's at home and Monika just came through the door."

"I'm on my way." I drove as fast as I could to the Childers' house. All of a sudden, it occurred to me that Mrs. Childers was in the house, and Rocky confronting Chilly about a private investigator asking questions about Jake wouldn't go well for her. There was no telling what Rocky knew, nor was there any way of telling what Chilly would do.

I got to the Childers' house before Rocky, so I went to the house where Jett was set up.

"Didn't take you long," Jett said.

"What's going on in there?"

"The usual. Chilly talkin' shit with his boys," Monika said. "I don't know if he knows anything about Jake, but I've got pictures and tape of him doing business. Enough that the police could arrest him in the morning for conspiracy to distribute cocaine."

"Nah," Jett threw in. "Any evidence we gave the cops would be inadmissible."

"Where's Mrs. Childers?"

"You can stop worrying, Nick," Jett said. "She went out before he got there."

"Where'd she go?"

"Gee, Nick, she didn't stop by and tell me. She got a call from her sister and she left."

All I could do was wait. Wait for Rocky to drive up and the drama to unfold. I was glad Mrs. Childers wasn't there. If things went badly, I could always stop her before she went in the house.

The wait wasn't long. A convertible drove up, and

the driver got out and ran to the door. Another car pulled up behind him. Three men ran after him. I assumed the first man was Rocky, and the men that ran behind him were his crew.

"Showtime," Monika said and leaned forward in her chair.

I was anxious. If Chilly had killed Jake, he wouldn't have any problem telling Rocky he did, then kill him if he didn't like it or thought about doing something about it.

We watched as Rocky pushed his way past Chilly's top lieutenant, Derrick Washington, when he answered the door. "Rocky? What you doing here?"

"Get the fuck out my way, asshole! Where the fuck is Chilly?"

Rocky made his way into the living room where Chilly's crew had gathered. Jett scanned the room, but Chilly wasn't in there.

"Chilly, where the fuck are you? Chilly! Chilly! I know you hear me, you ugly black bastard."

"What the fuck are you hollering about, Rock? And who the fuck you callin' ugly, you punk, square-head nigga?" Chilly said calmly, walking into the living room.

"What you do to Jake?" Rocky pulled out his gun and pointed it at Chilly.

"So, you gonna shoot me now, Rock? Is that what's happening here?"

Everybody in the room pulled out a gun and pointed it at Rocky.

"Put the gun down, Rock. You don't wanna die tonight. 'Cause if you flinch, everybody in this room is gonna shoot you so they can swear to me that they were the one to hit you with the first shot.

Now, put the gun down before they shoot you and get blood all over Gee's pretty white carpet. And you know Gee won't like it if we make a mess."

It was like watching a drama on TV. Rocky stood there and Chilly stared at him, smiling, daring him to move. I knew by the look in his eyes that Rocky didn't want to die, and Chilly knew it too. Rocky slowly moved the gun away from Chilly's face.

"You're a smart man, Rock, but you always was. That's why I like you. You got heart, but you're smart enough to know when to back down. Now, let's talk about this like you got some sense."

Chilly led Rocky into another room. Jett punched it up on screen.

"Now, what the fuck you want?"

"What did you do to Jake?"

"I ain't do nothin' to Jake. What you talkin' about?"

"Lisa just called me and said that Jake's missing and somebody came to her house asking questions."

"Yeah. I'm looking for Jake."

"Why you lookin' for him?"

"I wanna ask him something."

"Like what?"

"That ain't none of your business. All you need to know is that if you see Jake, you make sure he sees me."

"It's about that shit, ain't it? Told y'all that shit wasn't gonna work."

"Yeah, well, you just find Jake and bring him to me."

"Why? So you can kill him?"

"I ain't gonna kill him."

Chilly got up and stood by the door. Rocky got

up and walked toward him. Chilly put his finger in Rocky's face. "Don't you mention anything about Jake bein' missin' or me lookin' for him to Gee. You feel me?"

Even though Rocky didn't answer him, I knew that he felt him. Rocky was scared of Chilly too. He walked out of the room quietly and headed for the door, signaling for his boys to follow him as he walked out.

"Stay with Chilly," I said to Monika as I hurried to my car to follow Rocky. I followed him on what turned out to be a slow roll down White Plains Road to Soundview.

Chapter Twelve

I looked at Wanda. Her head was back and her eyes were closed. She had stopped taking notes a while ago. "Wanda."

"I'm still awake," Wanda answered without opening her eyes. "Where did Rocky go in Soundview?"

"He stopped at a house on Bruckner Boulevard. I don't know what he went there for. He was only inside for two minutes."

"Where'd he go then?"

"Back to his spot. I followed him there and talked to him."

"Did you find out anything?" Wanda yawned.

"You know, we can stop for a while if you want to, Wanda. I can tell you're exhausted."

"I'm all right, Nick, really. I just need a quick shower and a cup of coffee and I'll be all right. Why don't you make another pot of coffee while I take a shower?"

"Okay."

"And Nick."

"Yes, Wanda."

"Please don't leave.

"Yes, Wanda."

"All right now, I'm trusting you."

While Wanda showered, I made a fresh pot of coffee. While it was brewing, I wandered around the house. It was fabulous, "I guess it ain't just drug dealers who know how to live." *A house in the old neighborhood that Wanda had restored in grand style.*

Sometimes I used to wonder what my life would have been like if I hadn't cut out. Not that I regretted the choice I made. The way things were, I didn't want to live like that, but I wondered. Would I be in jail or dead? Or would I be as fortunate as my friends and grow old and respectable in the game?

I was starting to feel a little tired, so I poured myself a cup of coffee. I went back into the living room and stared out the large picture window. Wanda returned and stood next me. She looked at me and put her arms around me. Maybe I had that '*I need a hug*' look on my face. "What are you thinking about?" she asked.

"Just thinkin' about the way things turned out."

"What do you mean?"

"You, Wanda. All this. You're a successful lawyer. You're all so respectable now. Black and Bobby married. Shit, Bobby's a father."

"He's a good father too. You should talk to him."

I chose to ignore her comment.

"Freeze walkin' around in a suit like a legitimate business man."

"That one wasn't easy."

"I can imagine."

"Cuisine is a nice place. I thought Mike was crazy when he told me that he wanted Freeze to run the restaurant, but Freeze stepped up," Wanda continued.

"I don't think he's happy about it."

"Maybe. He may not be happy, but what he is, is fiercely loyal to Black."

"Unlike me, right?"

"You tell me, Nick. You're the only one who can answer that question."

I walked away from the window and sat down. Wanda followed behind me and reclaimed her spot on the couch.

"Regrets?" Wanda asked.

"No. Not really. I mean, the way things were. Every day was the same, more violence and more murder."

"The only difference is, your life didn't change. You did your violence and murder for the government."

"Yeah, right."

"Well, it's true. The Army recognized your skills: enforcer, soldier, killer, assassin. Call it what you want to, Nick, but they programmed you with their objectives and put you right back to work. But you see, things changed here after André. We were out of the drug business and we started moving into more legitimate businesses."

"That's the part I didn't see coming. When Black said we were getting out of the drug business, I thought it would just be gambling and women and

he'd just go right on highjacking trucks and robbin' warehouses. 'Cause let's face it, Black was a
thief." I started laughing.

"Always was." Wanda joined me laughing so
hard she almost spilled her coffee.

"Damn, the nigga could steal."

Although Black made most of his money on
gambling, he was always on the lookout for something he could steal. His preference was hijacking
trucks. He knew a woman who worked as a waitress
at a truck stop. She would feed Black information.
Using her feminine charms, she would find out
from truckers what they were going to be carrying,
and what route they were going to take. This was
the most important factor in his plan. With that information, Black would set it up so the truck
would have to stop, and then we'd have them. His
favorite method was a half-naked white woman in
distress. You know, short shirt, titties hanging out
all over the place. What man could resist a white
woman in distress? Once the driver was out of the
cab, either me, Jamaica or Bobby would come up
on the driver from behind and take him.

Once the driver was secure, Bobby would drive
the truck away. This didn't go smoothly at first
though, but it got better as Bobby learned how to
handle the big rigs. Now, once Bobby was gone in
the truck, Black would always ask, "Is that your rig
or the company's?" If it was the driver's rig, Black
would tell the driver where he could find it. If not,
he would sell the truck for parts.

Even though he didn't like doing it, Black would
sometimes rob warehouses, but only if it presented

a tempting enough prize. And there definitely had to be minimal risk involved. Warehouses were usually dangerous, because, as Black said, "Time waitin' to load the truck is time waitin' to get caught." Black was never one to take chances that would put himself or his organization in jeopardy. "Remember, no risk," Black would say before we went on any job. "Bail ain't cheap." Getting caught was never on his list of things to do.

Black had gotten some information that there was a warehouse that offered just such an opportunity. His first thought was to wait and see if his informant could give us a target to hit. When that didn't happen, Black decided that it was too much money involved to pass, so it was on.

The information came from a woman who worked as a routing supervisor at the warehouse. Black got his hooks into her because of her favorite pastime, gambling. She owed Black five grand, so one Sunday afternoon around dinnertime Black and I paid her a visit.

Ayana was a great cook. After a very filling meal, she set it out for us. "Black, look. I know I owe you some money. And to be honest with you, I just ain't got it."

This caused Black to put his gun on the table. It wasn't any big deal, 'cause Black would never shoot a woman. If that became necessary, he'd get me or Freeze to do it for him. "But I do have something that may be worth something to you."

"And what might that be, Ayana?" Black asked.

"Yow know I work at a warehouse in Jersey. Well, there's a shipment full of electronic equipment comin' in. You know, flat screen televisions, DVD's, boom boxes and digital cameras, just come in from China. After the shipment passes through customs and all that shit, it's taken to this warehouse and I schedule it to be shipped out to locations around the country. My position gives me the inside track on what's in house and what's worth taking."

After making sure that he wasn't playing in anybody else's backyard, Black formed a plan. He got her to draw a map of the warehouse and to identify the good stuff from the junk by marking the target pallets with a piece of black tape. This saved us a lot of time. Black simply walked around and told me ('cause I learned to drive the forklift) which one to pick up, while Bobby took over the security shack at the gate and Jamaica stood guard at the door.

By 1:00 the truck was half full. Everything was going smoothly until the folklift died on me. Black and I looked around for another forklift. "You find one?" Black asked.

"No," I told him.

"Try to get this one working." I tried everything I knew, which wasn't much, to get it running.

"We're wasting time, Nick. Get down from there. Jamaica, come here," Black said as he took one gun out of his pocket and took off his coat. "We're gonna have to do this the hard way. I saw some hand jacks while I was looking for another forklift. We'll each get one." Black looked at his watch. "It's a little after one. I want to be out of here by three. We got about two hours to get as much as we can and get out of here."

We all got busy. We were done by 2:30. Black and Bobby left in the truck while Jamaica and I followed in the car. We'd been driving for a half hour maybe when we passed through a small town. Once we got a little ways out of town Bobby began to slow down then came to a complete stop.

"What's wrong now?" Jamaica asked.

After a while, Black came to the car. "What's going on, Black?" Jamaica asked.

"There's a road block. We passed a bar a little while ago. They're just out here harassing drunks. I don't think they'll bother us, but to be on the safe side, Nick, you wait 'til I'm gone and make your way around through those trees just across from the road block. If Bobby opens his door, fire a couple of shots in the air over the truck. Then you get away from there in case they shoot back. But I'm betting that these locals will just take cover. That should give Bobby a chance to drive off."

"What if they come after you?" I asked.

"Then we'll bail," Black said as he walked away.

Once Black was gone, I got out and headed for the trees. I took up a position across from the roadblock and waited for Bobby to get there. The cop talked to Bobby for less than a minute before letting him drive on without incident. Jamaica and I weren't that lucky. When I got back in the car it came our turn to go through the roadblock, they made us get out. The cops searched us and looked in the car, but not closely enough to find the guns under the back seat. Then they made Jamaica take the breath test and walk a straight line, even though neither of us had been drinking. After that twenty-minute ordeal, Jamaica took off and tried to catch up with Black and Bobby. What we found, we never saw coming. About twenty miles up the road, we saw Black and Bobby walking.

"What now?" Jamaica asked.

"Maybe the truck broke down," I replied as Jamaica slowed down.

"What happened to the truck?" Jamaica asked as they got in the car.

"We got jacked, that's what the fuck happened," Bobby screamed. He told us that they had to stop because a car was blocking the road. Two men were standing in the middle of the road arguing. Once they stopped, two more men, one on each side, opened the truck doors and ordered Black and Bobby out of the truck at gunpoint. They took their guns and jumped in the truck and drove off. The other two returned to their cars in the road and then they drove away too. "They ran it like clockwork, just like we would have." The whole thing was over in less than a minute.

Bobby cursed and complained the whole way back to New York. Black, on the other hand, never said a word. Still, we knew that in his mind, he was going over every minute of the robbery. And we knew he was pissed. He already had a buyer; they'd agreed on a price. Him and Bobby were supposed to meet with him in the morning and drop it off.

Once we got back to The Late Night, Black told me to drive him somewhere. I had a good idea where we were going, and sure as shit, I was right.

Black pounded on Ayana's door until she opened it. "Black?" a half-sleep Ayana said. "What you doing here? Did something go wrong?"

Black didn't say a word. He just kept walking toward her, and Ayana kept backing up, until she backed her way into the bedroom. Black closed the door behind him.

I propped up some pillows and made myself comfortable on the couch. Every once and a while I would hear Ayana yell, "I didn't tell nobody! I swear, Black. I didn't tell nobody!"

I awoke to what smelled like meatloaf cooking. "Good morning, Ayana," I said. "Where's Black?"

"It's afternoon, and Black's in the bedroom. If you want to take a shower or whatever, you can use the bathroom down the hall. Lunch should be ready soon," Ayana said.

I took a good look at her. She didn't look like Black beat her down. Ayana was in her late thirties, maybe early forties. But she was still an attractive woman. She was probably a very pretty woman when she was younger.

I made my way to the bathroom and took a quick shower. When I got out, as promised, meat-loaf, along with mashed potatoes, collard greens, fried okra and cornbread were on the table, but no sign of Ayana. Not wanting the food to get cold, I sat down to lunch. It wasn't too long before Black and Ayana came out of the bedroom. She went in the kitchen and Black sat down and began eating. "Well?"

"I don't think she crossed us," Black replied. "But we'll talk about that later."

After we finished eating, I took Black home. On the way there, I asked my question again. "Well?"

"I been thinkin' about this all night. I haven't even been to sleep."

"Well?" I asked a third time.

"You heard what Bobby said. They ran it like clockwork, just like we would have. The bandits were organized. Other than 'get out;' they never said a word. It happened so fast, I couldn't really tell if they were black or white, but the one that took my guns sounded like he might be black.

"You sure she didn't tell anybody?"

"I just spent all night making sure she didn't," Black said like I had asked a stupid question. "Now, if she didn't tell anybody, somebody had to figure it out. He's the one we're looking for." I drove a while longer thinking that Black had simply stated the obvious. But I should have known better.

"I want my truck back, Nick. And I'll have it," Black said.

That night when I got to The Late Night, the kid was there talkin' to Black. The kid—that's what we used to call Freeze back in those days. Back then, all Freeze did was run little errands for Black and hang out at the club, messing with the ladies. They were seated in the back of the club. Black was doing most if not all of the talking. Freeze just did a lot of nodding. When I walked up, they stopped talking and both looked at me like I had no business there. I spoke then walked away to do my usual, which was hanging out, messing with the ladies. They sat there for most of the night, then suddenly Freeze jumped up and rushed for the door.

It was quiet for the next couple of days. Nobody even mentioned the robbery, especially around Black. Then Black called me and told me to meet him at The Late Night before it closed. We never closed before 8:00 in the morning. I was with a girlfriend, and she wasn't too happy when I rolled out of bed, "It's 6:30, Nick. Where you going?"

"Out."

"Out?" She pulled back the covers. "Only place you need to go is in, back in this bed. I want to feel you inside me."

"I'll be back," I said and armed myself. "You'll want to feel it even more when I get back." I left there and was up in there about 7:00, wondering what was going on. I asked if Black was there, and Sammy told me that he'd been there earlier and said that he'd be back.

Right after I got there, Bobby arrived, and Jamaica wasn't far behind. They had received the same call from Black, and neither of them knew what was up, which shocked the hell out of me. Bobby was in on everything.

We all took a seat, had a drink, and waited. When everyone was gone, Black came in. He went straight to the bar and poured himself a drink, then came over to where we were and sat down.

"So, you gonna tell us what is so important to get me off some pussy at six in the morning?" I asked.

"Mind if I finish my drink first?"

"No, by all means, finish your drink," Bobby said. "This better be good; that's all I'm sayin'."

We talked while Black finished his drink and let Sammy out. Then he led us in the back to the storage room. Black knocked on the door twice and opened it. There was the kid, sitting in a chair by the door. As we got in the clear, I saw four men kneeling down on a large piece of plastic. I recognized one of them right away. He dealt blackjack, Ayana's game of choice, at Cynt's, where she likes to play it.

Bobby started smiling, "What we got here, kid?"

"These the muthafuckas that robbed us," Black answered.

"You caught them," Jamaica said and took out his gun. So did Bobby. Black already had both his guns out, so naturally I pulled mine.

"Freeze did," Black said.

We all looked at Freeze. "By yourself? All at once?" Bobby asked sarcastically.

"By myself. One by one over the last couple of days," Freeze said quietly but proudly.

After that there was no more talk. No questions of how he found them. Me, Black, Bobby, and Jamaica lined up across from them and opened fire.

I saw Freeze a few days later and I asked him how he found them. Freeze said, "Black figured it out. That night you walked up on us at The Late Night, he was layin' it all out for me. Keep your enemies close, but watch your homies. See, Black knew if Ayana didn't tell nobody, then it had to be somebody who knew she owed Black that money and knew the broke bitch had to have something else to deal with. Black told me that there ain't too many muthafuckas that would want to touch a shipment of electronics like that. Black told me who the people were that would handle that type of merchandise. That's what led me to your boy at Cynt's. He's the one that gave Ayana the idea.

"He had him a little robbin' crew, so once I had him, catchin' the rest of them was easy. I got the last one when he rolled up in the truck."

"I never heard that story," Wanda said. "That's how things were then, but they changed."

"But you can see why I thought we were out of the dope game and nothing would change."

"None of us saw it coming, Nick. But Mike had a plan. Don't get me wrong. After the shooting stopped, he went right back to work, robbin' everything he could get his hands on. But we took that money and started buying property, opening businesses in the neighborhood. We tried to make things better."

"Just like that? Clean and easy?"

"Of course not. We still had the women, still brokering loans, still into the numbers and running the gambling houses. We still had enemies, and Mike still dealt with his enemies in the same old way. But as time went on, that got to be less of an issue," Wanda continued. "Bobby met Pam, got married and opened Impressions. A few years later, Mike opened Cuisine, and they were both basically out. Freeze started running the day to day operations. And then Mike met Shy."

"Tell me about Shy."

"She's all right," Wanda said matter-of-factly and looked away.

"What?"

"What do you mean, what?"

"You know what I'm talkin' about, Wanda. I didn't just meet you. Give it up."

"I don't know what you're talkin' about, Nick."

"Your whole facial expression changed when I mentioned her name." Wanda frowned and looked away again. "You don't like her, do you, Wanda?" I said and laughed.

"I didn't say that. What I said was, she's all right. Anything else you chose to read into my answer is pure speculation on your part."

"Whatever you say, counselor."

"It's not that I don't like her, Nick, really. She's a nice person."

"But you're jealous of her."

"No, I'm not," Wanda said, but her eyes told a different story. "Me and Mike had our time, remember. And we both agreed that we were better off as friends."

"You must not remember that I was there. Forgive me if I remember it a little differently from that."

"What do you remember?"

"I remember Black saying you two would be better off as friends. I also seem to remember you nodding your head on the verge of tears when he said it."

"You noticed that?"

"Yes, Wanda, I noticed that. I noticed a lot of things about you."

"I didn't think you noticed. I know Mike didn't."

"I always thought you and Mike would make it back. The two of you are like two halves of the same mind."

"I thought so too. But if you breathe a word of that to Mike or anybody else, I'll kill you."

"You wouldn't hurt a fly."

"That's what you think," Wanda said and smiled. "But anyway, I've adjusted and gotten comfortable with the fact that he's married now and that's that."

"Mike Black married and retired to the Bahamas. Hard to believe, that's all, Wanda."

"Make no mistake about it. Mike still runs things."

"Freeze said he likes to keep his hand in. I kinda figured that's what he meant. But you, Wanda."

"What?"

"I hear you're the mad scientist that made everybody rich."

"It wasn't just me. Sure, I handled the money, made some good investments, but everybody did their part. We changed with the times, Nick, which is how we all got to be respectable, as you say. Part of what we built here belongs to you. You just need to recognize. And ask for it."

"What's that supposed to mean? What am I supposed to be asking for."

"When you recognize, you'll know what to ask for. Now, let's get back to it. You followed Rocky to Soundview to some house and then back to whatever hole in the wall he hangs at. And—"

"The whole time I was looking for Rocky, I couldn't stop thinking about what he said to Chilly.

It's about that shit, ain't it? Told y'all that shit wasn't gonna work.

What shit? Whatever it was, it was the missing piece of this puzzle. Whatever it was, it involved this Diego Estabon guy that Chilly met for lunch.

I took care of mine, Chilly. What about yours?

Jake was Chilly's, and he hadn't taken care of him. It was all starting to make sense to me. Jake wasn't missing; he was somewhere hiding. For all I knew, he could be out of the country. I called Mrs. Childers and told her to meet me later at my office. I entertained the idea that Mrs. Childers hired me to find Jake and she would turn him over to Chilly, but then, I remembered the fear in those eyes whenever she talked about him. I couldn't be sure. And that's when that programming kicked in. I wasn't there to choose who was right and who was wrong, pick out the good guys from the bad guys. This was a mission like any other. Mrs. Childers was the client and my orders were to find Jake Rollins. What the client did with him once that was done was her business.

With a newfound sense of clarity, I went inside to talk to Rocky. I could tell from the stares I got when I walked in that this was Rocky's spot and I was the only one that didn't belong there. The Spot was crowded with ballers, male and female, along with the usual array of wannabes and hangers on. Rocky was seated at a table in the back, surrounded by his crew. I stepped up to the table, and guns were drawn immediately.

"I want to talk to Rocky."

I put my hands up and allowed them to take my gun, thinking that I could take out most of them, if not all them, before they got off too many shots. Unarmed would be little tougher, but I wasn't worried, I always carried a spare.

"Who are you?" Rocky asked, smiling.

"I'm the guy Lisa Ellison called you about."

"Let him come!" He shouted, no longer smiling.

I sat down at the table across from him. "I'm looking for Jake Rollins."

"Haven't seen him."

"What was he involved in?"

"Who are you?"

"I told you, I'm the guy Lisa Ellison called you about."

"She said you were some kind of private investigator. Who you workin' for?"

I looked around the table.

With a wave of his hand, Rocky dismissed everybody.

"What was Jake doing for Chilly?"

"I don't know what you're talkin' about. You got a lot of heart to be involving yourself in this shit. Who hired you?"

"Mrs. Childers." Since Rocky and Jake were friends, I didn't see any harm in telling him that I was working for Mrs. Childers. Besides, I thought that I would get more out of him that way.

"Gee hired you, huh?" Rocky sat back in his chair and thought for a second. "Well, if I find out anything about Jake, I'll tell Gee myself."

"Fair enough." I got up from the table, unsure of whether he would he kill me as soon as I got outside. Two women were dead—*It's about that shit*—maybe another, at the hands of Diego Estabon. *I took care of mine, Chilly. What about yours?*

I walked over to the guy who had my gun. "Can I have my gun back."

It was a statement, not a question.

The guy looked at Rocky, who shook his head, so I rammed my left elbow into his face and took back my gun with my right hand. Just in case anyone in the room thought I was going to do something stupid like try to shoot my way out of there, I held my hands up quickly. My finger was still on the trigger just in case. Rocky held up his hand and laughed, so naturally everyone else in the room laughed too.

I pointed the barrel at Rocky. Once again, every

other gun in the room was pointed at me. Rocky smiled at me and walked forward. He stopped before me. "I like you." He looked around the room, then repeated the words Chilly said to him. "You got heart." His crew laughed. "Let's see if you know when to back down."

I did, but this wasn't the time. I was a player in this game now. I couldn't fold. I had to stand, but not be stupid. I lowered my gun, but just a little, and started backing out of the room slowly, watching Rocky's eyes. His eyes switched to the right. I felt somebody coming up on me. I quickly extended my arm and caught him in the neck. I was lucky, but they were impressed.

I made it outside without getting shot. I started for my car, but something told me to keep walking. I walked down to the store on the corner, went inside and looked through the window. Rocky had sent three men after me. Two arranged themselves outside the store while the third came in after me. Over the objection of the clerk, I went in the back room looking for a door. I opened the door and pushed down a trashcan before moving into the shadows inside the store. As the man ran past me, I grabbed him. With my arm firmly wrapped around his neck, I had thoughts of breaking it, but I didn't. I hit him twice in the head with the butt of my gun.

I went out the back door and moved slowly down the alley, staying in the shadows. The second man approached. I froze. He walked past me. I watched him pass and he went in the store. They both came out, firing blindly down the alley. The third man held his post outside the store m spite of the shooting. I aimed and fired a few near misses. They took cover. I continued to fire and moved very quickly out of the alley. I took the long way around the block to get back to my car. I got in the car and drove away.

Chapter Thirteen

When I got back to my office, I immediately checked my messages to see if Mrs. Childers had called, which she hadn't. It was late, and she might not be able to get out of the house to meet me. What I had to tell her would keep until morning anyway, because to be honest, it wasn't much. And on top of that, it was only speculation. I could only speculate that Jake was hiding. And if Rocky was a man of his word, which I couldn't count on, he would tell Mrs. Childers all about the events of the evening anyway. Still, I decided to wait awhile, just to see if she would show.

It still bothered me that we never found any camera equipment in Jake's apartment. The pictures and the video were quality. It was obvious that Jake took his photo sessions seriously. I got the pictures from the file cabinet, along with my bottle of Johnnie Black. As I sat there drinking and looking at the pictures, two things hit me all at once.

First, I realized the pictures were definitely taken in at least two different places. I popped in the videotape we copied from Jake's apartment. I sat watching, without really watching, fast forwarding for the most part. Comparing the video to the still pictures that I had, I tried to get a sense of where they were taken. I turned off the video. I had seen enough. I began to sort the pictures into piles based on outfit or the lack of one. The difference in location was apparent now.

The second thing that hit me was a bit more subtle. Some of the pictures appeared to be taken in rapid session, maybe taken with a high-speed shutter. That in itself wasn't all that important, but it was the angles they were shot from. The camera wasn't on a tripod or some other stationary object. Somebody was taking the pictures. Pamela taking the pictures while Jake did LaShawn and vice versa?

"But no, it isn't."

I looked closer at the pictures and thought back to what Lisa Ellison told Rocky. *He thought it was Pamela, but it was LaShawn.* It was LaShawn in every picture with Jake. What little outfit there was may have been different, but it was LaShawn. If it was LaShawn in every picture having sex with Jake, then what was Pamela's involvement in this?

Other than the one picture of her and LaShawn at the party, there wasn't anything to connect Pamela with Jake. LaShawn came courtesy of Rocky, and Mrs. Childers couldn't say definitely that Pamela knew Jake. The cause of death connected her to LaShawn, but not Jake. "Pamela Hendricks, you begin to interest me."

Now I needed to know where Pamela lived, and

I didn't want to ask Kirkland. The need for Mrs. Childers to make an appearance just became more business than personal. It was better that way. Keep it strictly business.

But my mind was on Mrs. Childers, wondering why she hadn't at least called. Maybe Rocky told Chilly that she had hired me to find Jake and Chilly did something to her.

What was going on between Chilly and Jake? What shit wouldn't work? The answer to one would lead me to the other, and that would lead me to Jake.

By 2:00 in the morning I had given up on Mrs. Childers, and had begun to nod out. "Time to get out of here." I wanted to finish up my case notes with my new observations before I left, but my chair was so comfortable . . .

Thursday, July 16, 10:05 AM

The next thing I knew, the sun was shining bright. I had fallen asleep.

I left another voice message for Mrs. Childers. Since I hadn't heard from her, I didn't have much of a choice. I either had to ask Detective Kirkland for Pamela Hendricks' address or make my third search of Jake's apartment. I chose the latter. This was starting to get old. I was on my way to search his apartment for the third time when I began to realize it took more than just the title to do this type of work.

But I liked it.

So, if I was going to continue doing it, I would have to be more thorough, more organized. I arrived at Jake's apartment, but this time I was prepared to stay a while. I brought a camera, tape recorder, and a pad. This time I went from room to room and took pictures and catalogued everything. I wrote down and recorded my observations, no matter how small or insignificant. Everything mattered.

I came across what I was looking for—Jake's address book. There under H, as it should be, I found Pamela's address. Determined not to have any need to return, I photographed the entire book. I was about to leave when I looked out the window. There they were. The police. I should have known that they would have the place under surveillance. I knew that as soon as I walked out, they would take me into custody for questioning, and my notes, pictures, and the tape would become evidence in the investigation. I turned on Jake's computer and scanner. I scanned the notes and made a .wav file of the tape. Then I downloaded the pictures from the camera and e-mailed them to myself.

"Did Kirk give you much grief?" Wanda asked.

"Nah. Threatened to lock me up for breaking and entering, but he really just wanted me to give him something. Kirk already knew, but he made me tell him that Mrs. Childers was my client."

"Kirk's good, Nick. Very good. How long did they hold you?"

"A couple of hours, more or less."

"What did you give him?"

"Nothing really, 'cause that's what I had, nothing. He had connected Pamela Hendricks to Mrs. Childers and wanted to push the money-laundering angle down my throat. But I got the feeling that he really didn't buy into it, and wanted to know if I did."

"Did you?" Wanda asked.

"I was starting to, but I needed to be sure." I was starting to get a little tired myself. I closed my eyes and leaned back.

"What else?"

"The coroner still hasn't officially assigned a cause of death in any of the cases." I was getting tired of answering questions.

"Did Kirk think that you were a suspect in the deaths of Pamela Hendricks and LaShawn?"

"No. If he did, he never said."

"Other than Pamela Hendricks and LaShawn, how many more overdoses were there?"

"Five."

"He share any of the details?"

"Just time frame." I opened my eyes and Wanda was staring at me, but she looked away quickly. "He said the first five died within a 48-hour time frame. LaShawn died two days later, and Pamela died almost two weeks after that."

"I got the impression that Rocky didn't seem surprised to hear that LaShawn and Pamela were dead."

"I got the same impression. And after looking at the pictures, I needed to know what Pamela Hendricks involvement in all this was. I thought that if I knew more about her and why she died, I would be closer to the answers that I needed. Kirk let me go with his blessings to take a look around in Pamela's apartment."

"His blessings?"

"Crime scene. That's where her body was found."

"Ooh."

*   *   *

When I got there, I was met by a uniformed officer who let me in and told me that the scene had been tampered with once already.

"By who?" I asked.

"Seems she had a roommate," the cop said. "Chick named Felicia Hardy. She got in, took her stuff, and disappeared."

"Any idea where she went?"

"Nope. She just vanished. She used to be a cop. Quit the force a few months back to go to school full time."

"Any relatives?"

"What do I look like, huh? Check with personnel."

"Well, you knew all that other stuff." He unlocked the door and I followed him in.

"Yeah, well, Kirk told me all that stuff and said to help you any way I can, so I figured he wanted you to know."

Kirk was helping himself by helping me. Nevertheless, I didn't think he'd let me have a look at an ex-cops' file. I looked around the apartment. As promised, most of the roommate's stuff was gone. The room looked like it had been hit by a very focused hurricane. Once I had my gloves on, I rambled through it, looking, but really not expecting to find anything. If she was a cop, she wouldn't leave any clues to where she was going. There wasn't so much as a piece of paper. I left the room and closed the door behind me.

Everything else in the apartment was untouched. I looked in the kitchen. There were signs of a struggle. Then I checked the spot where her body was found. "Do you know if they found any drug paraphernalia?" The officer checked the inventory sheet. "I don't see any." I went in Pamela's room and sat down on the bed. I was sure now that the pictures and the video hadn't been taken here.

Sitting on the dresser was a picture of Pamela and a woman I'd never seen before. She was pretty, very pretty. It was taken in the living room. Maybe it was Felicia Hardy, maybe not. Since I was collecting pictures, I took the picture out of its frame and put it in my shirt. I would give it back to Kirk if he let me see her file. After one last turn around the apartment, I thanked the cop and left. I figured I'd check out LaShawn's apartment.

"Nick! Nick Simmons!"

I didn't recognize the voice. I turned around. The mailman was walking quickly toward me. "Nick Simmons, how you doing, man?" He grabbed my hand and shook it. It was obvious that he knew me, but I had no idea who this man was.

"I'm okay."

"You don't remember me, do you?"

"I sure don't," I said reluctantly.

"It's me, Reggie."

"Little Reggie McCray."

"Yeah."

"I sure didn't recognize you." Little Reggie McCray was now about six-three and all muscle. "And look at you, Reggie. How you been?"

"Been doing good, Nick. What about you? You look good, prosperous, you know."

"Thanks, man. I been doing all right, Reggie." Seeing Reggie took me back to the old days coming up on the block. "You get around the way much? How's your mother?"

"She's fine, Nick. Still living in the same house. Me, my wife and my son live upstairs."

"How's that lyin-ass brother of yours?"

"Frankie's dead."

"I'm sorry, Reggie. I didn't know."

"Frankie got shot when Black took the neighborhood to war."

"I'm sorry. How'd it happen?"

"You know Frankie always wanted to be down with Black, but you know Black wasn't havin' it. He tried to get all of us to stay in school, make something of ourselves. You know what I'm sayin'? Black was the one who got me this job. But anyway, Frankie was on his way to bein' a thug nigga. Used to hang outside y'all's old spot. What was it called?"

"The Late Night. I remember. We wouldn't let him inside, so Frankie used to hang outside with the rest of the wannabes."

"Yeah, that was Frank. Well, that night I saw him take a gun from between the mattresses. I asked him what the gun was for. He said that Jimmy Knowles and Charlie Rock sent some people to kill Black outside his house, but Black killed them. Later that day, Black caught Jimmy and Charlie at some restaurant on White Plains Road and Black killed both of them. Frankie said that was gonna start a war and Black would need him. He said that he was going to prove himself to Black, that he had to be ready when his chance came. That night, Frankie stepped up.

"Black told me that he had just sent Freeze to get the car, and him and Bobby were waitin' outside. He didn't see the car coming, but Frankie did. He yelled, 'Get down, Black!' Everybody dropped except Frankie. He pulled the gat and started bustin'. He got hit with three shots.

"By that time, Freeze had rolled up with the car, and him and Black and Bobby went after the guys. They ended up killing both of them on the roof of some building. When Black got back to the club, they told him that the ambulance came and they did what they could, but Frankie was dead."

"I'm sorry," I said again. I didn't know if I was apologizing because his brother was dead or because I ran out on the war to fight someone else's. It didn't matter. It was probably both, and I felt guilty for not being there.

"Don't sweat it, Nick." Reggie said as if he were absolving me of both crimes. "It was a long time ago."

"Thanks, Reggie." It did make it a little easier. Everyone had moved past those years. Everyone but me. "Reggie, you know the girl that got killed in this building?"

"Yeah, Pamela was cool people."

"Did you know her?"

"Enough to know she was cool. I've been delivering her mail for seven years. We'd talk sometimes, you know."

"You know her roommate?"

"I seen her. She only been staying there for a few months."

I looked around to make sure the cop was gone and pulled the picture out of my shirt. "That her?"

"That's her. What's your interest in this, Nick?"

"I'm a private investigator. Somehow Pamela's

death is tied up in a missing person's case I'm workin' on."

"Oh, yeah. I heard that you started doing that after you got out the Army."

"If I could find out a little more about Pamela, it might lead me to my guy. You wouldn't know if Felicia Hardy filed a change of address card?"

"Cops asked me that already. I told them no."

"I knew it was a shot in the dark."

"I said I told the cops that. And she didn't fill one out. But what I didn't tell them was that a couple of days after that, Felicia met me outside the post office."

"What did she want?"

"She said that she was leaving town and didn't want to leave a forwarding address, but she was waiting on some important mail. She gave me a hundred dollars and an address if I'd send it to her and forget about it."

"Where'd she go?"

"LA"

"Can you give me the address?"

"I think—wait a minute." Reggie dug around in his bag and pulled out a piece of paper. He handed it to me. "That's the address."

"Thanks, Reggie."

"No problem, Nick. I gotta get movin'," Reggie said as he walked away to continue his route. "Hey, Nick!" he shouted. "Come around the way sometime."

"I'll do that. Hey, Reggie. Thanks for reminding me of what I should already know."

* * *

As I drove back to the office, I looked at the picture of Pamela Hendricks and Felicia Hardy. I didn't think her having to go to LA right away was a coincidence. I gave some thought to what was going on around me. If there was no drug paraphernalia found in the apartment, how did Pamela die? Kirk had to be thinking murder. In an ex-cop's apartment.

Once I was back in the office, I left another message for Mrs. Childers that I would be out of town for a couple of days. Then I called Chésará, but she wasn't home either. Next I called Jett to let him and Monika know what I had found out, which wasn't much, and told them I was going to LA. With that taken care of, I called to make airline reservations and got a room at the Marriott Courtyard near the airport.

Chapter Fourteen

While I was on the plane, I thought about the fact that I had been around the world a few times, but I'd never been to LA. So, in addition to the case, I decided to do a little sight seeing, play tourist. It was late when I arrived at LAX, too late to try to see Felicia Hardy, so I rented a car, blue Mustang convertible, bought a map and rolled around to get the feel of the place.

Friday, July 17, 8:59 AM

By 9:00 the next morning, I pulled up in front of the Victoria Avenue address that I had gotten from Reggie. I walked up to the door and rang the bell. It wasn't too long before the door opened, but just a crack.

"Felicia Hardy?" When she didn't respond, I continued. "Miss Hardy, my name is Nick Simmons and I'd like to talk to you about Pamela Hendricks."

"Just a minute. I gotta put something on," she said and closed the door. I stood there thinking that she didn't have to go to any trouble on my account.

"Come on in." She opened the door a little wider and I stepped inside. I heard the door close and felt the barrel of what felt like a .44-magnum stuck in my back.

Naturally, I raised my hands.

"Just keep walking toward that wall and assume the position." I complied with her request. Felicia proceeded to search me, a very thorough search at that. Not the kind of pat-down you'd get from a man. With her gun in her right hand, she ran her left hand over every inch of my body, which included a handful of groin.

"Huh," she mumbled as she continued.

When she was finished, Felicia had relieved me of my ID and all three of my guns. Most people would have missed the holster that hung midway down my back.

Felicia slowly backed away from me. "Now turn around, nice and slow."

I complied.

Without breaking eye contact, she carefully picked up a set of handcuffs. I watched her move. Her picture didn't do her justice. Even in a big T-shirt and sweats she was much prettier in person.

"Hold out your hands."

Once again I complied with her request. I was impressed as she put the handcuffs on me, still staring into my eyes, still pointing that big-ass gun in my face. "Sit down over there."

"Thank you," I said, remembering my manners.

I sat down in the closest chair, and Felicia sat across from me.

"Give me a reason not to shoot you and call the police."

"Believe me, Ms. Hardy, I mean you no harm. I'm a private investigator. I'm looking into a missing persons case and I believe there is some connection to Pamela Hendricks."

"Who are you looking for?"

"Jake Rollins. Do you know him?"

"For the time being, you let me ask the questions. How did you find me?"

"I'd rather not say." She raised the gun. "I saw your file," I lied.

"Bullshit! How'd you find me?"

"Change of address card."

"Bullshit! If you got the information from the post office, the police would be here." She pulled back the hammer.

"Somebody owed me a favor."

"Reggie."

I smiled.

"I knew I shouldn't have trusted him."

"Don't be too hard on Reggie. He didn't tell the cops. Or anybody else."

"But you, he just up and told you."

"Like I said, he owed me."

"What do you know about Pamela?" Felicia demanded.

"I was going to ask you that."

"It's early and I'm not in the mood for games."

"I know she died of what appeared to be a cocaine overdose, but the police didn't find any traces of drugs in her system. I know you and her were roommates, and that you most likely found the body and called the police. I know you used to be a cop." I raised my cuffed hands. "You quit the force to go back to school. How's that going, by the way?"

"About Pamela." She lowered the gun but just a little.

"I know her and Mrs. Childers used to work together at a bank in Kansas City. I know that she came to New York from Kansas City to work for Manhattan Bank. But what I'd like to know from you is who she was, how and why she died, and who killed her."

"What makes you think I could tell you that?"

"Well, your roommate was most likely murdered in your apartment. You called the police, but you didn't wait around to talk to them. Then you break into the crime scene, take your stuff, and come out here. If I wasn't convinced by all that, then the fact that I'm wearing handcuffs and you're pointing a gun at me pushed me over the edge."

"Is that a fact?"

"Was it you who found the body?"

"Yes."

"Why didn't you stay?"

"Who hired you?"

"Jake Rollins' sister."

"Which one? The wannabe lady or the tramp?"

"The lady. She used to work at the bank in Kansas City with Pamela."

"What makes you think Pamela knew anything about Jake's disappearing?"

"I've got pictures in my jacket pocket of her at Jake's party."

Felicia stood up and walked toward me. I was smiling, enjoying the view until she put the gun to my head. "Don't even think about doing anything stupid. I don't mind killing you."

"Believe me, that wasn't what I was thinking about." Felicia carefully removed the pictures from my pocket and returned to her spot.

She rested the gun on the table and glanced at one of the pictures. "LaShawn. I knew the girl was wild, but damn." She glanced at the rest and put them down.

I made note of the fact that even though she had only glanced at them, Felicia knew right away it was LaShawn and not Pamela. "She died two weeks ago under the same circumstances as Pamela. Pamela had Jake's card on her when the police found her body."

"How do you know that?"

"The police told me."

"You're working with the police?"

"Unofficially. I guess you can say that. My guess is they weren't getting anywhere with linking Pamela to Jake, so they threw me the bone."

"Why you?"

"Other than Mrs. Childers being my client, I know a little something about the people involved in this."

"What's that supposed to mean?"

"How long were you a cop?"

"Four years. Why?"

"You've heard of Mike Black?"

"Vicious Black."

There it is again. Why does every woman say his name like that?

"Who hasn't heard of him?"

"He's an old associate. Reggie owes him a favor too."

"So, you used to run with Vicious Black, huh?"

"Yes," I said with a newfound sense of pride. "But not for the last ten years."

"Why not?"

"Joined the Army."

"So, now you're a private investigator and the police have been feeding you information." Felicia stood up again. I was hoping she was coming to take the cuffs off. They were starting to hurt, but she picked up the gun, walked toward the window, and looked out. "I didn't think the police had anything." She turned around and came back toward me. It produced the same response as it did the first time. She stood before me and raised the gun. "How do I know I can trust you? I mean how do I know that whoever killed Pamela didn't send you?"

"Then you do think she was murdered?"

"I know she was murdered. Pamela didn't do drugs."

"But that's not why you think she was murdered. Why'd you leave before the cops came?"

"Other than that innocent look in those brown eyes, tell me why I should trust you."

"I can't think of any reason right now, but if I had to come up with something . . ." I paused to give it the desired effect. "First of all, I wouldn't have come here alone. I wouldn't have let you take me without any resistance. And if I had come here to kill you, I would have just blasted you at the door."

Felicia smiled at me for the first time. She had a pretty smile. Then she laughed a little, but I guess it wasn't enough to make her take the cuffs off. She simply returned to her spot and put the gun down. I was happy for that much.

"Mind if I ask you a question, Ms. Hardy?"

"Go ahead."

"You just glanced at those pictures."

"So."

"You can barely see her face in most of them. How did you know it was LaShawn?"

"LaShawn always wears her hair like that."

"So does Pamela."

"No, she doesn't."

"In one of those pictures. The one with two of them."

Felicia picked up the pictures and fanned through them until she found it. "This one?"

"That's the one. See, same ponytail. And the picture I got of the two of you out of Pamela's room. By the way, your picture doesn't do you justice—but she's wearing a ponytail."

"That doesn't mean that's how she always wore it. Both of those pictures were taken on the same day. I remember that day. She was going to Jake's birthday party and she didn't have time to get her hair fixed. I told her with her hair pulled back like that she looked like LaShawn."

"Why didn't you go to the party?"

"I knew the type of people that would be at any party Gee was throwin'. Pamela would always ask me if I wanted to go, but I was a cop. I wouldn't be caught dead up in there."

"Mind if I ask you another question?"

"I'll save you the trouble. No, to my knowledge Pamela wasn't laundering money. That is what you and the police want to know, isn't it? What is your name, again?"

"Nick Simmons. I'm pleased to meet you. And yes, that is what I was going to ask you."

"Cops think so?"

"I got that impression."

"That's why I don't want to talk to them. Once they figured out she was murdered and it was drug related, they'd start thinking money laundering, and then they'd start looking at me. I'm sure someone has gone through my file and my arrest records, looking to link me to this shit. And if they really want to, they'll find something, whether it's there or not."

"Do you think that your leaving the way you did helped?"

Felicia didn't answer me.

"I used to tell her all the time that it didn't look good for her to be in her position at the bank and be associating with a known drug dealer's wife, going to their parties. But she would always say that for that to be a problem, she'd have to be doing something wrong, and her record at the bank would speak for itself."

"You mind if I ask you another question?"

"You don't have to ask me that every time you want to ask me something. Go ahead."

"Have you had breakfast yet?"

"No." Felicia let out a little laugh.

"I haven't either. And I'm hungry, so can we finish this conversation over breakfast? I promise I'll behave myself even without handcuffs."

Felicia looked at me as if I had lost my mind. She picked up her gun and walked toward me again. She stood in front of me, silently, as if she was deciding right then how it was going to be between us. She looked into my eyes; I locked mine in hers. She exhaled and left the room.

"Shit," I said quietly.

For a second there, I thought we were having a moment. You know, the kind that James Bond always has when the girl kisses and then releases him. I felt the pain in my wrists. "Live in reality, Nick. This ain't no fuckin' movie." I didn't think she was going to kill me, so I didn't try to leave. I couldn't, not after coming all this way. She knew something, something major, and she was scared because she knew it.

Twenty minutes later, Felicia returned to the room. She had changed into black jeans and heels. She still had on a T-shirt, but this one fit her. She had a holster, on and had traded her .44 for a 9. "You better be real." She leaned forward and unlocked the cuffs.

"Thank you. They were starting to hurt," I said, rubbing my wrists. I stood up and started walking toward the table to collect my hardware.

"Hold up," she said as I reached. "We haven't gotten that far yet."

"No guns, huh."

"For the time being, I think it's best if I carry the gun. But I tell you what." She moved closer to me. "Pick one."

"One?"

"Yes. One. And I'll hold onto that. If you're a good boy and you don't give me any trouble, I may let you earn it back."

"Either one of the 9's will do." Felicia stuck my gun in her jacket pocket and left the other two on the table. I stood for a second, looking at my guns. I wasn't getting a good feeling about leaving them.

"You coming?"

I turned around and she was pointing my 9 at me.

"Yeah, I'm coming."

I walked out of the house feeling naked. I tried, but couldn't remember the last time I went some place unarmed.

"Which one is yours?" She stopped and put my gun back in her pocket. "No, let me guess. First time in LA?"

"Yes." I stopped and frowned.

"Blue convertible." She was playing me like a tourist. Of course I was, but she didn't have to play me. I unlocked her door and she got in. As soon as I got in she said, "Go ahead and drop the top. I know you want to."

She was right, so I dropped the top.

Once we pulled off, Felicia took my gun out of her pocket and rested it on her lap. "Where are we going?" I asked.

"Simply Wholesome on Sousean. Make a left here."

We arrived at Simply Wholesome and were promptly seated. We sat quietly as our waitress arrived to take our orders. She filled our coffee cups and left us.

"You never did answer my question," I said.

"Which one? I haven't answered several of your questions."

"I noticed. How is school going?

"It was going fine until all this came down."

"What were you taking?"

"Law school. I've been meaning to do it for years, but I got caught up in the job. Out there in the streets, doing the job."

"Do you miss it?"

"Not as much as I used to. I missed the feeling you get when you knock on a door or walk up on a car."

"What's gonna happen next. I know what you mean. You're excited and apprehensive all at the same time."

"That's right. You're ex-Army. What did you do?"

"Special operations unit."

"Trained killer. Should I be scared?"

"No. You have the guns, remember." Felicia laughed. "What turned you? What made you decide to go back to school?" I asked.

"One day I had finally seen enough. Did enough. Too much."

"Sounds like you got a story."

"You don't want to hear about that."

"Yes I do, Felicia. I love a good story."

"Well, I'm not sure I want to tell you."

"What? You think it will scare me. I don't scare easy."

"No kiddin'." Felicia took a playful swing at me. "You could probably tell me stories that make mine sound like a church social."

"Maybe."

"I'll try and stick to the highlights, so stop me if I bore you."

"I'm sure I won't need to."

"Alrighty then. I've told this story so many times, one more time ain't going hurt. Officer Morgan and I—Morgan, that was my partner—we responded to a domestic disturbance call. When we got there, Officer Morgan knocked on the door and identi-

fied himself. They opened up on us right then."
She giggled. "I mean, the suspects began firing at
us through the door."

"All right now." I kept thinking Felicia was much
too pretty to be a cop. "Try to keep it real for me."

"Anyway." Felicia cut her eyes at me.

"Why'd they just start blastin' like that?"

"Drug deal in progress." She had pretty eyes,
very expressive eyes. "I was going to call for backup,
but Morgan kicked in the door and went in. By the
time I got in there, one of them was tryin' to gather
up the drugs from the table. He fired at me. I returned fire and hit him with two shots in his chest.

I looked for Morgan. He was runnin' up the
stairs. He yelled, 'They're going out the back!' I ran
down the hallway. I could see the back door was
open. Then I saw someone run out, but they were
gone by the time I got there. I started back up the
hall when one of them came runnin' out. I shot
him, kicked his gun away, and kept moving up the
hallway. I yelled for Morgan, but he didn't answer.
Shots were still bein' fired.

I heard footsteps coming down the stairs. When
I cleared the hallway, I saw one on the steps. He
shot at me, and I ducked back in the hallway. I shot
back blindly. I hit him in the back before he got
out the door. There was still shooting upstairs. I
moved toward the stairs. I looked up and saw Morgan chasing one down the stairs. I fired at him, he
went down, and I took cover to reload.

"After a while, Morgan came and sat next to me.
It was over. I killed four people that day, Nick.
Morgan killed three more. We just sat there look-
ing at each other. Both of us knew we'd had enough.

There was an investigation and it was ruled a clean shoot, but it was ugly, very ugly, what I had to go through before they cleared me. Two days later, I quit. Morgan quit about a month after that."

The waitress returned with our meals. We ate, talked, and laughed at this and that. I liked her laugh. I was starting to like her. Picture that, me liking somebody who wasn't married.

"You know what, Nick? You don't look like the type that used to run with Vicious Black."

"I don't?"

"No, you don't." Felicia smiled at me.

"Just what does that type look like?"

"I don't know. I just know you don't look like it."

"I guess that makes us even. I think you're way too pretty to be a cop."

Felicia smiled but looked away this time. "I actually met him once a couple of years ago."

"Who, Black?"

Felicia simply nodded her head.

"Really? Where was that?"

"At the police station where else? When I was a rookie. I had just gotten off my shift and was on my way out of the building. There was this man walking in front of me. There was something about the way he walked, so confident, so regal. It was almost like he was saying, 'I command all I survey.'"

"That's Black."

"I remember thinking it was odd because most times when people leave the precinct, they walk out like they're beaten, defeated and glad to be out of there. But not him. He walked with his head held high and his shoulders back. And his stride commanded attention and respect. Then he stopped and turned around and said 'That fragrance you're wearing, is it Bora Bora?' I told him that it was, and he told me that it smelled beautiful on me. He introduced himself and asked me if I worked there. I said 'Yes, I'm a cop.' He said that was a shame, so I asked him, 'Why? Don't you like cops?' He said that as a rule, he didn't. Then he said, 'And I can't make an exception, even for very pretty cops like you.' It's a pleasure to meet you, Ms. Hardy. And then he walked away."

"That's Black," I said and smiled.

"The next day I asked my training officer, Dan Cavanaugh—now that was a piece of work." Felicia dropped and then shook her head. Having the pleasure of meeting Cavanaugh, I knew what she meant. "Anyway, I asked Cavanaugh about Black and he told me this story about how he was called to a domestic disturbance at Black's apartment. One of his neighbors called the police 'cause some woman was out in the hall beating on his door and yelling and screaming. But by the time Cavanaugh and his partner arrive on the scene, the woman is gone and Black is there in the hall with some guy. So Black tells him that he talked to the woman and he was able to convince her to go home quietly. But Cavanaugh says he didn't like Black's attitude, so he tells his partner to go on back to the car. Well, when he turns around, Cavanaugh gives Black and the other guy one in the gut. He said they took it, not because they were afraid of him or anything, but Black was just showing respect for his authority," Felicia gave me her version of a girlish giggle. "Well that's my Vicious Black story. I don't know how true it is, but that's my story."

"Well, Felicia, that's not exactly true."

Felicia sat up straight. "It's not?"

"No, its not."

"How do you know?"

"I was the other guy in the hall."

"Really?"

"Really. That night, Black called me and told me about the woman. Black told me that he came out and tried to talk to her, but it only made it worse. He had something going on and didn't have time to deal with her, so he told me and Freeze to come get her before somebody called the cops."

"What was wrong? Did he have another woman in there?"

"No. He had something going on in there but there was no woman involved. Anyway, when we got there she's still in the hall, raisin' hell. Freeze walks up on her, puts his hand over her mouth, and carries her outside. I knocked on the door and let Black know that it was taken care of. I went inside and talked to him and Bobby for a minute, then I walked out with Black. That's when your boy Cavanaugh gets there. Black did explain things just like you said. And Cavanaugh did say, 'I don't like your attitude' and sent his partner back to the car to wait, just like you said."

"At least that part is true."

"Yeah, but that's where the story changes. After Cavanaugh left, Black went in the apartment and came back with an envelope and gave it to Cavanaugh."

"Cavanaugh?"

"Cavanaugh."

"Cavanaugh, huh? I guess you just never know."

As much as I was enjoying the conversation, I worked it back to the business at hand. "How long did you know Pamela?"

"We were play pen buddies."

"Really?"

"We go back a long way. I grew up in this house and Pamela lived three doors down."

"What was her involvement with Jake?"

"As far as I know, they were just friends. She met him at one of Gee's parties. There wasn't anything physical, if that's what you're asking."

"What about LaShawn? Were her and Pamela close?"

"Yes, unfortunately. She met her at one of those parties and they became instant friends. LaShawn was nothing but poison, but Pamela seemed fascinated by that whole lifestyle. Not that she was a part of it or wanted to be, but she just liked being around them. She had never been around people like that and she just got caught up."

"Hmm. Growing up in LA I would think she met plenty of people in the game."

"Pam's mom didn't play that. She kept a pretty tight reign on her kids. They weren't on lock down or nothing, they did stuff, but they did it as a family and her moms was always around."

"What about Mrs. Childers?"

"Her and Gee were close. Pamela looked out for Gee when they worked at the bank in Kansas City together. She said Gee was pretty helpless when she first got there. She'd never had a job before and she was a nervous wreck."

"By the way, you said those pictures were taken the same day."

"And?" Felicia leaned forward and smiled.

"Who took the pictures?"

"I was wondering if you had picked up on that. I would have been disappointed if you hadn't."

"Well?"

"Pamela did. Taking pictures was sort of her hobby."

"You think she took those pictures of Jake and LaShawn?"

"Maybe."

"You wanna tell me now?"

"Tell you what?"

"Why you left?"

"How long are you going to be here?"

"I'd like to say until you tell me why you left. But it'll probably be more like a couple of days."

"I don't know if I can trust you."

"Well, Felicia, you can tell me about it and I can go back to New York and do something about it. Or you can stay on the run until whoever it is you're running from catches up with you."

"Therein lies my problem, Nick. Even if I tell you, they still may come. I ain't trying to testify against nobody and live my life in witness protection. No, no, not a life for me."

I looked at my watch.

"What are you gonna do now?"

"That depends on you, Ms Hardy. What are you doing the rest of the day?"

"Since you're out here, and it's your first time and all, I was gonna show you around. Maybe you'll like it enough to come back. Look in on me every now and then. Make sure I'm still alive."

"I'd like that."

She caught me a little off guard with that one.

Maybe we did have a moment.

We talked about a little bit of everything while Felicia drove me around to all the tourist spots in LA. I felt comfortable talking to her, so for once, I let my guard down and opened up to her. "Listen, I know a quiet little spot on the beach."

"I'm not dressed for the beach."

"That's why they made malls."

Felicia and I spent the rest of the afternoon and the early evening at the beach, laughing and talking like neither of us had a care in the world. She sat with her head on my shoulder and watched the sun set. We drove to a Chinese restaurant in Torrance called Szechwan. I had Kung Pao. She ordered the sweet and spicy shrimp. The food was excellent. After dinner, Felicia drove quietly back to her house. "I had a nice day, Nick," she said and got out of the car.

"I did too," I said as I walked her to her door. "But it's early. I was hoping you'd show me some of that famous LA nightlife."

"Not tonight. I'm tired. I got a lot on my mind, and I wouldn't be good company. Will you come see me tomorrow?" she asked as she got to the door and unlocked it.

"Sure." I was disappointed for more than the obvious reason.

"Then I'll see you in the morning." Felicia kissed

me on the cheek and went inside. I had just turned
to walk away when I heard the door open.

"Nick."

"Yes," I said excitedly.

"Here are your guns." She handed them to me,
one at a time. "Good night, Nick." And once again,
the door closed. I walked away thinking of my bad
luck. I had just spent the day, a great day, with a
woman I was really interested in, who seemed to
be interested in me. The problem was she might be
involved in a murder, not to mention that I lived
six thousand miles away.

Chapter Fifteen

Saturday, July 18, 10:59 AM

The following morning, I picked up Felicia around 11:00. A bright red sundress and pumps were her attire for the day. "Not that I'm complaining or anything, but its kind of hard to hide your gun, isn't it?" Felicia rolled her eyes at me, and without hesitation, pulled up her dress, just enough to show me that she had a .25 strapped to each thigh.

"So, Ms Hardy, tell me what's going on."

"Well, since you're leaving in the morning, I was hoping we could spend the rest of the day together."

"That wasn't what I was asking and you know this."

"I know that, Nick, but trust me."

"Okay."

I didn't really want to leave her, and I didn't want to leave without hearing her story. What else could I do? I put on my seatbelt and relaxed. We

did a long lunch at a place called Killer Shrimp, on
Colfax Avenue and Ventura Boulevard. After lunch,
Felicia drove around for a while before driving out
of LA on the 101. A little over an hour later, we got
to the Town Center Drive exit. "Where are we
going?"

"Back to LA," she said, and got on California
State Route 1. "I wanted to share one of my favorite places with you."

"Where is that?"

"Shhh. You just trust me. I trusted you. You're
not afraid, are you?"

"No," I said louder than I needed to. "I just like
to know where I'm going that's all." My sixth sense
was kicking in. For all I knew, she could be taking
me someplace secluded so she could kill me. Was-
n't like she couldn't do it. After all, she was an ex-
cop on the run. But on the run from what?

"I've never taken anybody here before." She
smiled a very soft and satisfied smile. It caused my
apprehension to subside, but just a little. Apprehension. The rush. Something else we shared.

We had driven a short while when Felicia said,
"This is part of what I wanted to show you."

I looked and saw what was probably one of the
most beautiful sights I'd ever seen—The Pacific
Ocean on one side of the highway, and the mountains on the other. Felicia tapped me on my thigh.
"How do you like it?" she asked, as she drove down
the curvy stretch of highway.

"It's breathtaking," I replied, thinking that she
either needed to slow down or drive with two
hands.

"No, breathtaking comes a little later."

"Well, are we in a hurry to get there?"

"Kinda. Well, yeah we are in a hurry. Why, you a nervous passenger? I mean you're not scared or anything are you?"

"No. I just want to enjoy the view. You did want me to see this, didn't you?"

"Yes, but there's more. You just gotta trust me."

"That's funny coming from the woman who had me in handcuffs first thing yesterday morning."

"Stop being such a punk. I gave you back your guns. You'll be all right."

Felicia slowed down a little. We drove for a while longer until she got into Malibu. She made a left off the highway and started to drive up into the hills.

"Excuse me. That sign says private property."

"And?"

"Where you takin' me?"

"Trust me, Nick. If it makes you more comfortable—" Felicia let go of the wheel, reached between her legs and handed me her guns. "There, that should help."

It did.

"Thank you. But I still want to know where we're going?"

"Someplace breathtaking."

I decided to relax and roll with it. If I couldn't take her and whatever she had waiting, I deserved whatever I got. Before too much longer, we passed a sign that read, *SERRA, A Franciscan Retreat.*

I was more curious now. She parked the car and led me by the hand toward the building. As we walked past it, I followed her up a small hill. Felicia said, "Now, this is breathtaking."

And she was breathtaking.

She walked ahead of me and sat down on a

bench at the edge of the mountain. "I used to come here all the time. Get away from it all. Gives me a chance to think."

From where we were, high in the mountains, the view was spectacular, surrounded on three sides by mountains. The ocean was dead ahead. It was stunning. The only sound was of her voice. And to top it off, the sun was just starting to set. "I've been out here every night since I've been back."

"Guess you got a lot to think about."

Felicia smiled that smile I was getting fond of seeing.

I lost track of time as we sat there in silence until the summer sun dropped out of sight. I don't know what she was thinking about, but I couldn't stop thinking about what she knew. I played out several scenarios while I took turns admiring Felicia's profile, painted with a backdrop of sunset. Then she got up abruptly. "You ready to go, Nick?"

"No." I stood up and faced her. "I could stay out here and look at you all night."

She turned and walked away, and I followed her back to the car. Once we were back on the highway, I thanked her for bringing me. She didn't answer. She turned onto Sunset Boulevard and took the scenic route back to her house. She invited me in this time and offered me a drink. "Johnnie Black, if you got it."

"A glass of white wine will have to hold you."

Felicia returned with two glasses. She handed me one and took a sip of hers.

"When are you going to tell me what you know?"

Felicia put her drink down then put her arms around my neck and kissed me. There was real passion in her kiss, more passion than I'd felt coming from any woman I'd kissed in a long time.

"I will tell you everything you want to know," Felicia said then kissed me again. "In the morning."

She kissed my lips and then down to my neck. I unzipped her dress and allowed it to fall to the floor. I paused to admire her body. Felicia was beautiful. I ran my tongue along the edge of her bra while unhooking it at the same time. Her breasts were firm and her nipples grew harder when I ran my tongue across them. Felicia moaned quietly, wiggling her way out of her panties.

We kissed our way into the bedroom and fell on the bed. I kissed her calves. The closer I got, the more Felicia squirmed. I started working my way up to her thighs. I slid my tongue around the edges of her pubic hair, then spread her lips. Her back arched as I stuck my tongue inside of her. Her stomach muscles tightened, her thighs pressed together as her back arched, and she screamed in ecstasy.

I stood up, took off my pants, and lay down next to her bed. I rolled on top of her and put the weight of my body on my arms. I entered her slowly. She arched her back slightly and began to rotate her hips. We moved slowly, then faster and then slow again. Her body began to quiver again. I placed my hands gently on her face and kissed her. We continued to make love until we both passed out.

Chapter Sixteen

Sunday, July 19, 5:27 PM

I was tired when I got off the plane. I was up all night with Felicia and I got up early again in the morning, but it was worth it, in more ways than just the obvious. I wanted to go home and get some rest, but I went to the stake house first. Things were quiet when I arrived. Monika was sitting in front of the console, but not really looking. Jett was sitting on the floor, going through the paper. It didn't matter where in the world we were or what language it was in, Jett always went through the paper, page by page. "You never know what's going on unless you read the paper," he'd always say.

"Evening, people," I said and made myself comfortable.

"Where you been?" Monika asked excitedly.

"California."

"California?"

"Yeah. Jett didn't tell you?"

"Oops," Jett said, and buried his head back in the *Times*.

"What were you doing in Cali?"

"I went to follow up on a lead I got on Pamela Hendricks. Why? Did something happen?" My first thought was for Mrs. Childers' safety. "Is Mrs. Childers all right?"

"Nick, take your head out that woman's ass for a minute and take a look at this," Monika said then handed me a piece of paper.

I looked at it and shrugged my shoulders. "Is this supposed to mean something to me?"

"I'll say," Jett said. "That paper is the missing link. It puts it all together. It's the answer we've been looking for."

"Are you gonna let me in on it or do I have to guess?"

True to her word, Felicia had told me everything she knew once she got me up that morning, so I was sure I already knew the information Jett and Monika wanted to share. But they seemed so excited, why blow it for them.

Monika smiled. "That is the formula for what appears to be some type of synthetic cocaine."

"Synthetic crack to be exact," I said. "Jake developed it for Chilly."

"How did you know?" Monika asked.

"That's what I was doing in California. Chilly got the formula from a chemist named Rodrigez who used to work for the Peruvians."

"Used to? I didn't know that was possible."

"He was on the run. There was a bounty out for him. He had started a new life, quiet and low profile. But Chilly spots him at some mall Upstate. Rodrigez gave Chilly the formula so he wouldn't give him up, but it didn't work."

"Damn right, it didn't work," Jett said. "It was killin' people, and dead customers are bad for business."

"After the first five died from smokin' it, Chilly gives him up to the Peruvians. That's what Diego Estabon was talking about when he said I took care of mine. Apparently, they agreed that everyone involved had to die."

"So, what do we do now?" Jett asked.

I looked at Jett and Monika. Jett dropped his head. Monika shook hers in semi-disgust. "I told you that this wasn't something we needed to be fuckin' around in. I say we back all the way up off this. Shut all this down and go back to doing what we do. Jett hacks our way in, you kill them, and I blow it up so there's no trace."

"Jett?"

"I think she's right, Nick. The shit didn't work, so if Jake ain't dead, he's gonna be."

"How 'bout it, Nick?" Monika asked.

I didn't want to admit it, but they were right. If Jake was still alive and he had any sense, he'd be so far away that Chilly would never find him and neither would we. "I'll call Mrs. Childers and give her back her money."

"Why?" Monika asked.

"We earned our money," Jett said. "Her brother took off before her husband could kill him. Case closed."

"You're right, Jett. All this set-up does cost money."

"And our time," Monika added as she started helping Jett pack it up.

"All right, case closed," I said then got up and started to help.

"No, no, Nick, you just go on and tell Mrs. Childers whatever you need to tell her. We'll take care of this. You give me a call when Felix has something for us."

"So, like, what are you sayin'? I can't call you until then?"

"That's not what I'm sayin'," Monika said, shaking her head. She walked over and put her arm around me. "Don't stand there lookin' like we're runnin' out on you, 'cause we're not. You can call me any time, boo. But this private eye stuff ain't for me."

"She's right, Nick. This is too much like work," Jett said. "But if you're diggin' it, hey, that's cool too."

"Okay. I'll get with y'all later."

What else could I do? I was diggin' this. But I had to keep my perspective clearly in focus. Jake was gone, long gone, and if he had any sense, he would stay that way. The only thing left to do was to break it down for Mrs. Childers and move on. But there were still some things about all this that I couldn't shake—something about Pamela Hendricks, or maybe it was just the personal feelings I had developed for Felicia Hardy that was clouding my judgment. Either way, I knew it wasn't over. At least not for me.

I drove to Rocky's hangout. I wasn't exactly sure why I was going there much less what I would say when I got there. I walked in and got the same reception as the last time. It seemed like every eye in

the house was on me. That's when I saw him—
Chilly, the man himself.

He was standing at the bar enjoying the company of two very attractive young ladies. Rocky was
seated in the back at what I assumed was his regular spot. As soon as he was alerted to my presence,
he made a bee-line straight to Chilly.

I went and sat down at a table as far away from
them as I could and still keep them in sight. A waitress came to take my order. "Johnnie Walker Black,
straight up." I started to ask her if she would tell
Rocky that I wanted to see him, but I kinda figured
that he'd get around to it sooner or later. Chilly
looked over his shoulder as Rocky pointed me out
to him. I didn't think he'd do that, but fuck it. It
was time I got this over with. Chilly dismissed
Rocky with one hand and patted one of the ladies
he was with on the ass, then started for me.

"Mind if I sit down?" Chilly asked.

"Be my guest," I replied as the waitress returned
with my drink.

"No check for this table. His money's no good
here," Chilly said as he took a seat. "Nick Simmons.
I haven't seen you since the old days. I thought
Bobby killed you and that Army shit was just a
cover."

"No, Chilly, I'm still alive."

"Rocky's snitchin' ass told me you're a private
investigator now. That's a long way from where you
came from. What's the matter? Freeze and them
ain't got no spot for you, or is Bobby still tryin' to
kill you?" Chilly laughed. "Let me quit fuckin' with
you. Shit, if Bobby really wanted you dead, you'd
be dead."

"Good point."

"So, what brings you here?"

"Stopped in to have a drink." I raised my glass and downed it. Chilly smiled and motioned for the waitress.

"Ain't too many of us old heads left in this game. Muthafuckas now ain't got no honor. No respect for the game. Niggas like you and me got to keep it real, you know what I'm sayin'?"

"Yeah."

"What's up with you? Like you mad at me 'bout something. That shit between me and Black is over with. I got nothing but respect for him," Chilly said as the waitress arrived. "What you drinkin', Nick?"

"Johnnie Black, straight."

"Johnnie Black, straight up, and bring me a Crown on the rocks. You know I was the one who made peace with Black?"

"So I heard. Why don't you tell me about it?"

Chilly looked at me for a while. "That's right. You were gone when all that went down, so I guess you don't know. After Black killed Jimmy Knowles and Charlie Rock, Vincent Martin kept it going for a long time. I kept tellin' Vince's dumb ass that all this war shit was bad for business, but he wasn't hearin' me. Him and Charlie was like brothers, so Vince was takin' the shit too personal."

"So, you gave him up to Black?" I said coldly.

"Shit no! I ain't that type of muthafucka. But after a while, it didn't matter anyway. One night Black caught Vince and his whole set laid back. They was all at Vince's house chillin'. Black busted up in there and killed them all."

The waitress returned with our drinks, served them, and departed quickly. She glanced over her shoulder and smiled at me. I winked in response.

"Black, Bobby and Freeze walked in blastin', like they was playin' a video game and shit." Chilly began making shooting motions with his hands. "Boom, boom, boom. I hear nobody even got off a shot. Musta been eight, ten muthafuckas in there. They killed everybody quick, except one guy. He said he was layin' on the floor, shakin' with his gun in his hand. Said Black walked up to him and sat on the floor next to him. Black said to him, 'Bet you wanna know why you're still alive.'

"But the boy is so petrified that he can't even talk. He just shakes his head. He said all Black said was, 'Tell Chilly to come see me.'" Chilly motioned for the waitress. He finished his drink. "Bring us another round," he told her and handed her a twenty dollar bill. "That's for you, baby." We both watched her as she walked away. "I might just have to fuck her tonight. Anyway, me and Black always been cool. We wasn't never close like y'all or nothin' like that, but Black gave me my respect. And you know how he carried his. I ain't ashamed to say that the only reason I ain't dead is because Mike Black didn't want to kill me. He did right by me."

Damn right, Black let you live to make all that money. "There ain't too many like Black."

"That's what I'm sayin'. These young bucks like that bitch-made nigga there," he pointed at Rocky, "ain't loyal to shit but money."

"It's a new day. With new players."

The waitress served us another round of drinks. Chilly raised his glass. "To the old days."

"I'll drink to that." All that talk about honor and loyalty was starting to wear on me for personal reasons.

"Let's cut the bullshit. I know why you're here.

Same reason I'm here. Jake. I know Gee hired you to find him."

"Rocky tell you that?"

"Nah. But that's exactly what I'm sayin'. He got no idea who you are or where you come from. That bitch ain't have no business tellin' me that you was a private eye. Him and Gee go back some years. He should be loyal to her over me, but as soon as you came through the door, he comes runnin' to me like a little bitch and told me everything. But you see, Nick, I already knew all about that."

"Did you?"

"Shit yeah! What, you think I just let Gee run wild, doing whatever she wants? Hell no! I keeps her on a long chain. I knew she wrote you a check for ten thousand dollars, so I did some checkin'. That's when I found out you was a private investigator. I figured she hired you to look for Jake. I got me a little honey at the bank. She keeps tabs on Gee's account for me. Gee will fuck up some money if you let her. But that's my fault. She was a young girl when I met her. She didn't know shit. I should have taught her the value of money instead of just throwin' it at her. But that's my problem."

"It's probably too late now."

"You got that right. You have any luck findin' Jake?"

"Not a clue," I lied. I started to lay it all out for him, cut the bullshit, but I thought better of it. "I figure he's someplace hidin' out. What I don't know, is why. What was he into, Chilly? Was he doing something for you? The way I get it, you were the last person to see him before he dropped out of sight." I was pushing my luck and I knew it, but I had that *I don't give a fuck* attitude in full effect.

"You take chances, Nick. But I know what kind of nigga you are, so fuck it. I respect a muthafucka that gets right to it."

"I'm glad to hear that. So, what was he doing for you?"

Chilly laughed. "He wasn't doing nothin' for me. I just wanted to talk to him about some shit I been hearin', that's all. I want you to find Jake, and I want you to let Gee know where he is. After you tell Gee, then I want you to tell me."

"Why? so you can kill him." It was a statement, not a question.

"No, I'm not going to kill him. You have my word on that. I just want to talk to him. He was into something. I just want to know what."

He reached in his pocket.

I put my hand on my gun.

He dropped a stack of money on the table in front of me. "That's five thousand dollars there. Take it."

I complied.

"I'll give you five more when you tell me where he is. And there's something else I want you to do for me."

"What's that?"

"In the last three weeks, Gee's been takin' a lotta money out her account. Cash money, twenty thousand dollars. You tell me where that money went, and that twenty is yours."

I thought about making a quick twenty grand right there by telling him about how Ben Josephs

was blackmailing his wife. But what honor I had
left—and my loyalty to his wife—stopped me. "I'll
look into it."

"You know me, Nick. I'm a man of my word and
I pay."

"Thanks for the drink." I got up and walked out
with the five grand in my pocket. I got in my car
thinking how things had just taken a weird turn.
At this point, I was sure that Jake had just taken
off, so I drove by Cuisine to see if maybe Freeze
had anything for me.

Cuisine was crowded and I couldn't find a place
to park. I drove around, finally finding a spot about
two blocks away. I had walked about a half block
when I heard somebody say, "Got a light, man?"

I turned around and was met immediately by a
fist in my face. There were three of them. One
grabbed me from behind and held me while the
other two hit me repeatedly. I recognized one of
them from Rocky's joint. I fell to the ground and
they started kicking me. Once that was over, one
said, "Chilly sends his regards."

They left me lying there and walked away laughing. I struggled to my feet and breathed deeply. I
would have to repay their kindness. I started walking the rest of the way to Cuisine. I made it as far as
the lobby before I passed out.

When I came to, I was lying on a couch, a woman
was tending my wounds, and Freeze was standing
over me. "What happened to you?"

"Some of Rocky's boys tried to warn me off and
blame it on Chilly," I said and stood up slowly.

"How you know it wasn't Chilly?"

"'Cause Chilly just—," I got up and reached in my pocket. I still had the money. "Chilly gave me five thousand dollars to find Jake."

"I thought you was workin' for Gee."

"I am. He still wants me to tell her where he is, as long as I tell him too." My head was still spinning, so I sat back down.

"I told you not to fuck with this. Now look at you." Freeze laughed. He walked over to the desk, put the phone on speaker and dialed a number. "Fucked around and got your ass kicked."

"I think my ass was the only thing they didn't kick."

Freeze just shook his head. "This is Freeze. Let me speak to Rock."

"This, Rock. What's up, Freeze? I ain't—"

"Shut the fuck up, nigga, and understand what I'm tellin' you. You sent your boys after Nick Simmons tonight."

"I didn't have nothing to do with that, Freeze. I—"

"Shut the fuck up, bitch! Nick Simmons is family to me. You feel me, Rock? So, I'm tellin' you now, if that shit happens again, fuck peace. I'll kill you and your whole set. Got that?" Freeze hung up the phone and started laughing. I laughed too, but it hurt.

Freeze took me out to Perry's house so he could check me out and give me something for the pain. It was damn good seeing Perry again after all these years. Like everybody else, Perry treated me as if I never missed a day.

"I brought somebody by to see you, Perry," Freeze said.

"Yeah, who's that?" Freeze stepped aside. "Nick! Damn, it's good to see you. Y'all come on in. Hold up. Neither one of y'all shot or bleeding?"

"No, man. We just came to visit," Freeze said as we went inside Perry's house.

"Okay, 'cause I still remember the last time you two came to my house this late."

"So do I. How could I forget?" I said to Perry. I looked at the smile on Freeze's face and I could tell he hadn't forgotten either.

"Couldn't forget what, Nick?" Wanda asked. "Y'all were just full of stuff I didn't know about. I'm starting to feel like an outsider."

"Don't feel like that, Wanda. We never even told Black. But you know Black; he found out anyway."

"Found out what, Nick?"

"Back in the day, me and Freeze did a little free-lancing."

"What kind of freelancing?"

Even though we still sorta worked for André, who was one of the biggest drug dealers around those days, Black absolutely forbid any of us to have any direct involvement with drugs. Black made his money highjacking trucks, robbing warehouses and payrolls. We all made crazy money, but me and Freeze wanted to, needed to, make some money on our own.

"So, what we gonna do, Nick? We can't roll, so how we gonna get paid?" Freeze asked.

We kicked around a bunch of stuff, but everything we thought of either wasn't worth the risk or wasn't enough paper to make it worth the effort. It all came back around to the fact that fast, easy money was spelled D-R-U-G-S. Then it came to me. "Look, who's making the money?"

"Dope boyz," Freeze replied.

"Right, so why can't we get that money?"

"'Cause Black will kill us if we started rollin', that's why. And don't you say that he'll never find out. That muthafucka is psychic about that shit. You ain't forget what we did to Banks when Black found out he was dealin'?"

"No, I ain't forgot. But who said anything about us dealin'?"

"You did."

"No, I didn't. I said why can't we get that money. There's a difference. You interested?"

"I'm listening."

"Dope boyz rollin' around every day with stupid cash on them. I'm talkin' about rollin' up on them and robbin' them niggas while they laid back."

"You talkin' about rollin' up on a bunch of heavily armed muthafuckas while they do business? That ain't no plan, that's suicide."

"You ain't scared, are you, Freeze?"

"Hell no!"

"I didn't think so. But I ain't talkin' about hittin' them while they doing business. That would be suicide. I'm talkin' about catchin' them comin' out their cars. They get out the car, bam! We hit them quick and bam, we out."

"That could work. I mean we know who they are. I don't like most of them niggas anyway. And as long as we don't take their dope, Black won't have shit to say."

So it was set.

Me and Freeze became stick-up kids. We'd hit two or three a night sometimes. And the money was good—three, four, five grand a pop for a minute's work. Most times we never had to fire a shot. But after a while, word got around and things started to dry up. The money was less and the security was more. But we were addicted to that cash, so the plan changed.

We started robbin' them while they were selling quantity. Things were going good. It was easier than we thought, except this one time. We overheard a guy, used to call himself Forty-eight, who had a real high, squeaky kinda voice, talkin' about he had some white guys on the hook and he was gonna retire on the money he was gonna make.

"You mean we gonna take," Freeze said to me, making fun of the way Forty-eight talked.

We sat and watched as the players went into a motel room on Boston Road. Once the deal was in progress, we busted in.

"Nobody moves, nobody gets hurt!" Freeze shouted.

I looked at the guy carrying the briefcase with the money. Forty-eight and his boy raised their hands and backed away from the dope, but the two white guys with the money started beefin'. "If you know what's good for you, you'll walk out that door quietly." The white boy made a play for his gun.

Freeze wheeled around, "Shut up, white bread!" and caught him in the mouth with the pump. "You're speaking out of turn."

I covered with the semi while Freeze grabbed

the case and we backed out of the room. It wasn't long after we got out before somebody started blastin'. I fired back while Freeze headed for the car. The firefight continued until we were in the car and away.

We both looked at each other and started laughin'. "That was gettin' kinda hectic," Freeze said as he drove away. "Must be a lotta money in that case for them to have backup outside."

"I think this is the biggest score we ever had," I said as I opened the case. "Maybe we can retire."

We were both laughing so hard that neither of us noticed the black Ford that pulled up alongside of us, until they started blastin'. With the first shot, they busted out the back window on the passenger side.

"Where the fuck did they come from?"

"I don't know!" Freeze yelled as he floored it. He sped away down Boston Road with the Ford on our tail.

"Get us out of here, Freeze!"

"What you think I'm doing, writin' a love song?" Freeze turned sharply against traffic, but they stayed right with us. He turned on 222nd and then back onto Boston Road. "You see them?" Freeze demanded to know.

"No, I think you lost them."

"Damn right, I did! I told you I'd lose them!" That was when the back window got shot out.

"Shit!"

Freeze turned on Eastchester Road and kept going until he hit Laconia Avenue "I thought we lost them."

"You did. These are different guys."

"What do you mean, different guys?"

"That it's not the same guys. It's a different car. Blue Chevy, coming up on your right." I began firing through the shattered window, trying to get them off us, but they kept coming. "Turn here! Try to lose them in the projects!"

Freeze turned on 229th Street and drove through Edenwald Projects. "Damn! These guys are good." He couldn't shake them. We came out of the projects and back onto Laconia, up 219th and onto Bronxwood Avenue.

"Who the fuck are they?" I asked.

"I don't know. How the fuck should I know?"

"You just lose them." A car pulled out in front of us and we crashed into a parked car. I grabbed the case and we got out blastin'. "This way!"

"I ain't going down there. There's dogs down there!"

"Shoot them! Let's go!" I yelled as I started running down the alley.

"Look out!" Freeze yelled. I turned quickly, in time to see that two more guys were shooting at us. I caught a bullet in the shoulder. "Ahhh! Shit!" If I hadn't turned when Freeze yelled, it would have hit me in the chest.

"You hit?"

"Yeah, in the shoulder! I'm all right. Keep going!"

I could hear the dogs barking in front of us and the guys firing behind us. I started firing in both directions. The barking stopped and the dogs ran in the opposite direction, but the guys kept coming. Freeze ran toward the building and shot the lock off. We ran through the building and out the front door. A car came down the street. Freeze

stood in the middle of the street with his gun drawn.
The car stopped in front of him.

"Get out!"

Both doors swung open and the people ran
away from the car.

The guys came out the door and opened fire on
us again. This time it was Freeze who got hit. He
went down.

"Freeze!" I ran toward him, shooting that semi-
auto wildly in their direction. They took cover. I
kept shootin'. I pulled Freeze up and pushed him
in the car, got in and drove away.

I looked over at Freeze. "Where you hit?"

"In the gut! Shit, that hurts. They got me in the
leg too."

"Who the fuck are they?"

"How many times you gonna ask me that shit? I
told you I don't know."

"They still on us?"

Freeze struggled to turn around. He was bleeding pretty bad. "I don't see anybody."

I drove around for a while to make sure we'd really lost them, whoever they were. Then I drove as
fast as I could to Perry's house. Freeze had passed
out at some point, so I had to carry him. He was in
pretty bad shape. Perry said if it had been any
longer, he'd be dead. He took care of our wounds
and I made him promise not to tell Black, but he
found out anyway.

"You saved his life, and he saved yours," commented Wanda.

"That's just one more reason why we're so tight."

"You ever find out who those guys were?" Wanda asked.

"Yeah. They were cops. They had a sting set up on Forty eight. We just picked the wrong guy to rob that time."

Chapter Seventeen

Monday, July 20, 4:42 PM

I slept late the next day. It was well into the afternoon before I finally rolled out of bed. It was almost 5:00 and I was still feeling a little groggy from the pain pills I had gotten from Perry. I thought about going back to bed, but I picked up the phone and checked my messages.

Felicia had called and left me a message;

The least you could have done was call me and let me know that you made it back safely. Anyways, I didn't call to fuss. I just wanted to say that I miss being with you. Bye, honey.

I was really starting to like Felicia Hardy and I missed being with her too. I started to call her back, but then I remembered the last time I started feeling this way about a woman. I hung up the phone and called Mrs. Childers instead. It had been more than a week since the last time I saw or talked to her.

I left a message on her voice mail and asked her to meet me at Sparks Steak House on 46th Street around 9:00. I was a little late getting there and much to my surprise, she was there, looking impeccable as usual.

"Hello, Nick."

"Hello, Mrs. Childers. I hope I didn't keep you waiting very long?"

"I've been here about a half hour. But that's okay, I wanted to get out of the house anyway. Have a seat."

"Thank you." Once I was seated, her smile turned to a frown. I guess she noticed the cuts and bruises on my face.

"What happened to you?"

"I ran into some people who had something to prove."

"It looks like they did a good job. Are you all right?"

"I'll be fine."

"What have you found out for me, Nick?"

"Well, Mrs. Childers, I don't think your brother is missing, or that anything happened to him. I think Jake is somewhere hiding."

"What makes you say that?"

"He was involved with Chilly in some type of scheme to develop synthetic crack."

"Synthetic crack?" She looked at me strangely. "I've got a good idea, but just what exactly is synthetic crack?"

"Basically, it's crack without the cocaine."

"How is that possible?"

"I really don't understand how the formula works. Your brother's the chemist. But the long and short of it is that it didn't work. At least seven people have died from it."

"Pamela?"

"Yes."

"That's not possible. Pamela didn't use drugs."

"I know that, but I believe that anybody who knew anything about it had to die. Pamela was just runnin' with the wrong people."

"I'll try not to take that personally." She rolled her eyes at me and turned away, but she turned back quickly. "If that's the case, then what makes you think that Jake isn't dead too?"

"Because Chilly is still looking for him."

"How do you know that?"

"Trust me." I thought about telling her that he gave me five grand to find Jake, but she didn't need to know that, or the fact that he had somebody keeping tabs on her account and wanted to know about the money she gave Ben Josephs. "Anyway, as far as I could tell, Chilly hasn't killed him. But he is nowhere to be found. So, I guess that concludes our business."

"I guess it does," Mrs. Childers said and gave me a strange look. "Did you talk to Rocky?"

"That's something else I wanted to ask you."

"What's that?"

"What type of relationship do you have with Rocky?"

"He's a friend of Jake's. Why?"

"Your friend?"

"Well—"

"Well?"

"Well, not really. Me and Rocky don't speak to

each other anymore. We haven't spoken since before I left Philly."

"Why?"

"I don't think that's any of your business."

"Mrs. Childers, you made all this my business. What happened between you two?" She frowned and looked away. The waiter finally came to take my order. "Hennessy Martini for the lady, and I'll have Johnnie Black, straight up." Once the waiter departed to get our drinks, I went back to the question. "What happened, Mrs. Childers?"

She rolled her eyes and looked away. "Do you remember me telling you that I did some things that I'm not proud of to get away from Philly?"

"And?"

"I asked Rocky for the money so I could get away from there. He told me he would give me the money and that I should come by his apartment to pick it up. When I got there, he tells me to come in the bedroom. When we get in there, he tells me that I could have the money, but I had to fuck him first."

"Pathetic."

"I was a virgin, Nick, so I told him that I couldn't do that. I started to leave, but I wanted to get away from there and I knew that nobody else was gonna give me the money. So I did it. After he was done with me, Rocky said he was sorry and gave me the money. I took it and left."

"I'm sorry. I shouldn't have pushed it." What else could I say?

"No, you shouldn't have." When the waiter returned with our drinks, Mrs. Childers drank hers down like water. "Can we get out of here?"

"Sure. Where do you want to go?"

"I don't care. Anywhere." She threw some money on the table. "Just come ride with me." She got up without waiting for an answer. I shot my drink and headed out the door behind her.

We drove around for a while and ended up at her house in Nyack. After she opened up the house, she went to make us a drink. I sat on the couch and watched her as she poured. I had noticed that she wasn't making eye contact with me when she talked. There was fear and uncertainty in her eyes. She handed me my drink then sat down across from me and started to talk.

We drank, and like I said, she talked for over an hour and then she stopped. She got up and walked over to the French doors. I approached her and touched her arm. It seemed to startle her.

"Is something wrong?"

"No, just wondering what you must think of me."

"What do you mean?"

"I mean what do you think of me, Nick?"

"I don't know. I think you're nice. Very pretty."

"Is that all you see in me, Nick? A pretty face . . . nice. Nice to look at, but not much more, right?"

"I didn't say that."

"You don't have to, because it's the truth. That's all I've ever been, pretty. Oh, look at Gabrielle, she's so pretty. All my life I've gotten by on my looks."

"You ain't all that now." I knew I had touched a nerve, so I tried to make light of it. "I was just being nice when I said you were pretty."

"Very pretty, that's what you said, Nick." She laughed. "You said I was very pretty."

"I was lying, 'cause you look like you been hit in the face with a bag of quarters. I bet little children scream and run to their mothers when they see your ugly ass."

"Stop it, Nick. I'm not that bad. And besides, it wasn't a bag of quarters, it was a fist."

"I know. I was trying to be nice about it. But I can see, and I see that makeup doesn't hide everything."

She looked away from me and stared into her drink. "I've never been in control of my life. I went from my father's house to Chilly's. The first day I met him, he told me that I was the prettiest woman he'd ever seen. From that day on, I never wanted for anything. After a lifetime of being told 'No, you can't. That's not for you, Gabrielle,' everything was yes. All because I was pretty. But that's all I was. All I've ever been. I was just something for him to show off to his peeps, to look good on his arm. I don't have a life of my own. I'm Chilly's wife, Mrs. Childers, even to you, Nick. Well I'm not, my name is Gabrielle. My friends call me Gee. Since I'm not your client anymore, it's time you started calling me Gee too."

"Okay, Gee. Why don't you get me another drink?"

"I didn't say you could start ordering me around," she said, snatching the glass out of my hand. "Want any ice?"

"No, just Hennessy will be fine."

She handed me my drink and sat down next to me. "You've never told Chilly that story about you and Rocky, have you?" I asked.

"He'd kill Rocky if I told him. I never told anybody. Not Jake, not even Chéz. You're the first."

"What makes me so special?"

"I don't know. I've told you a lot of things about

me. Shame that none of it is good, but that's the way it is."

"There must be some happiness in your life."

"You tell me what there is to be happy about. I live in fear, Nick. I never know when Chilly's gonna snap. Sometimes he can be so sweet to me, and other times he's like a nightmare."

"Maybe it's time you wake up."

"Maybe. Maybe it is time to get my life back."

She began to cry.

"I never meant for things to turn out the way they did. You have to believe that, Nick. It was never supposed to happen."

"What are you talking about?"

"Huh?"

"What are you talking about?"

"Nothing." She got up and poured herself another drink. "I've been babbling on like a fool. I am a fool."

"When are you gonna tell me the truth, Mrs. Childers? I mean Gee."

"I have told you the truth, Nick." The tears were gone.

"I don't think so. I can't help you if you don't tell me the truth."

"There's nothing else to tell. Jake is gone. You said it yourself, it was all about this synthetic crack."

"Okay, if that's the way you want to play it." I finished my drink and stood up. I was ready to go. I wanted to call Felicia, but Gee got up too and took the glass from my hand. I looked at her. I mean really looked at her for maybe the first time. She was miserable. The more she talked about her life, the more I wanted to, needed to talk to Felicia, hear her voice, hear something positive. Mrs. Childers returned my glass to me full. I thanked her and took a sip of my liquor.

"Maybe now that you don't work for me, you'll start paying me some attention."

"Just what makes you think I haven't been payin' attention to you?"

"I see the way you look at me."

"I—" She put hand over my lips.

"I'm hot." She stepped closer, resting her chest against me. "And I'm sticky. I'm going to take a shower." I took a moment to contemplate the way her moods took dramatic swings. Not five minutes ago she was crying. Now she was almost predatory. She stepped away and turned around. "Unzip me." I unzipped her dress and she walked away as I lost sight of her in the darkness. The light came on in the bathroom. I stood motionless, watching as she turned on the shower. Then she looked back at me. I took that as my invitation to join her.

She kissed me, then put her arms around me and kissed me again. "Undress me, Nick."

I took my time undressing her slowly. Once I was done, she stepped into the shower. "Aren't you coming?"

I undressed myself very quickly and followed her. My presence was met immediately by her arms around my neck and her tongue in my mouth. I picked her up by the waist, and she wrapped her legs around me. I angled her back against the wall and entered her. Despite the lack of foreplay, she was dripping wet. I like it like that.

"Harder, Nick! Fuck me harder!" I pounded her furiously against the wall. "Yes, Nick! Yes!" She screamed her delight.

We went at it in the shower for a while before we got out. Without bothering to dry ourselves, she hopped up on the bathroom vanity and spread her legs. "Come here," she said, motioning with her finger. I quickly complied. I placed my hands on the mirror to steady myself as well as get some added leverage. She lifted her legs and grabbed her ankles.

For reasons which I can't explain, Ben Josephs crossed my mind. I thought about what Chésará said. *'Cause he can't fuck. Gee said that he couldn't keep it up long enough to do anything for her. Gee said she rocked the house two times and he came.*

Well, she was rockin' that house with a vengeance, but I was hanging right in there with her. Then her eyes bucked open, her body began to quiver, and her mouth opened as if she wanted to scream, but no sound came out.

Mrs. Childers picked up a towel and walked out of the bathroom without a word. I grabbed a towel and followed her out, drying myself as I walked. She wrapped the towel around her body and headed for the bar. She poured a drink for each of us and handed me one. I drank mine, and watched as she came from behind the bar. She poured her drink across my chest then proceeded to lick it off. Once she was satisfied that she had gotten every drop, she led me into one of the bedrooms, and we went for it again. "Your turn now."

I lay down on the bed and she climbed on top of me. I felt her ease herself down on me, grinding her hips into mine, pinning my shoulders against the bed and staring in my eyes. I felt paralyzed. I couldn't move and I didn't have to. She rode me furiously until I felt myself expand and explode inside her. I had to laugh because when I came, she screamed louder than I did.

Chapter Eighteen

Mrs. Childers dropped me off at my apartment about two in the morning. She was nervous during the ride about what Chilly might do if he were home when she got there.

I had drunk my share of Hennessy and could feel the makings of a serious hangover coming. I popped a couple of aspirins, took a shower, and crawled into bed. I went to sleep thinking, not only about what I just did with Mrs. Childers in the shower and in just about every room in the house. I thought about Felicia mostly. Although I found Gee—*now it felt funny saying it*—very attractive, I missed Felicia. I just had sex with Gee and it was great, but in some strange kind of way, Gee's sex made me long for Felicia's touch even more. I wanted to see her face, hear her voice, to see her smile and be excited by her touch. I rolled over. I didn't understand it, and I was too buzzed to try.

Tuesday, July 21, 8:03 AM

The sound of somebody's fist making contact with my door—or maybe it was a foot, I'm not sure which—woke me from my sleep around 8:00 the next morning. "Stop fuckin' bangin'! I'm coming!"

I dragged myself out of bed and made my way toward the door. What I found were two uniformed cops informing me that Detective Kirkland wanted to see me at the station right away. Once I got through cursing them out for making all that noise so early in the morning, I told them to wait, that I would be right out. I gave some thought to getting back in the bed, but that would only make them bang on the door some more. Still, I took my time getting ready.

An hour later, I found myself sitting alone in an interrogation room, waiting for Kirk to show up. As luck would have it, Richards walked through the door.

"What happened to you, Simmons?" Detective Richards asked.

"I walked into a door?"

"Yeah, right. Looks to me like that door worked you over pretty fuckin' good."

I didn't see any point in commenting, so I didn't. Richards was an idiot anyway. Finally Kirk came in and slammed the door behind him. "Sorry to keep you waiting." He stopped in his tracks when he saw me. "Shit, what happened to your face? No, wait. Let me guess. You cut yourself shaving."

"No, he walked into a door." Richards laughed.

"Had to be one or the other," Kirk said and took a seat next to me. "Anyway, Nick, I had you brought down here to see if you found out anything more about Jake Rollins."

"Why do you want to know, Kirk? What do you care about my missing persons case?"

"Because your missing persons case may be tied to several drug cases and a murder."

"I know about the drugs. What murder are you talking about?"

"Pamela Hendricks," Kirk said.

"Wasn't that one of the people who you told me died of this mysterious drug overdose?"

"That was our first impression," Richards chimed in.

"Why are you calling it murder now?"

"Nick, in case you haven't noticed, we're the police. That means we investigate." I guess Kirk was trying to be funny, but he wasn't successful. "That investigation has led us to come to a different conclusion."

"What brought you to that conclusion?"

"As near as we can tell, this Hendricks woman didn't use drugs," Kirk asserted. "There were signs of a struggle in the general area where the body was found. So, I'll ask you again. What have you found out about Rollins?"

"Nothing, really. I've been working on another case. The more I talk to you guys, the more I'm convinced that I don't want any parts of this. As a matter of fact, just last night. I told my client that I don't think Jake wants to be found."

"You can say that." Richards laughed, and Kirk shot him a look. The more he talked, the more the sound of his voice annoyed the shit out of me. Maybe Kirk felt the same way. "Your client thinks her husband, Chilly, is involved, doesn't she?"

"I'm not at liberty to say."

Richards jumped out of his seat. "You're startin' to piss me off with that privilege shit, Simmons."

"So?"

Kirk looked at him and shook his head. "Sit down, Richards."

"Like I said, Kirk, that's all I know."

"What about Felicia Hardy?" Kirk asked.

"That's the roommate, ain't it? Wasn't she a cop?"

"Yeah, you talk to her?"

"No."

"What were you doing in California?"

"I told you, I have another case. Why, is she in Cali?"

"We think so," Kirk said. "Her and the Hendricks woman grew up there. I think maybe she went back there."

"Hmm. Sorry I can't be any more help to you, Kirk. But like I said, I backed off of this."

"Then you wouldn't be interested to know that Jake Rollins' body was found last night. He was shot once in the head with a heavy caliber weapon at fairly close range."

"Has anyone informed my client?"

"Somebody is taking care of that as we speak."

At least I didn't have to be the one to tell Mrs. Childers that I was a fool. Or at the very least, I was a lousy detective. Just one day ago I told her that her brother was alive and hiding somewhere from her husband. Now the cops were there to tell her he was dead. She was probably screaming that Chilly did it right now.

Maybe I was just kidding myself into thinking I could be a detective. I had to start facing the reality that I'm not a detective. I was a trained killer, that's what I was.

If it wasn't for Reggie, I would have never even found Felicia, and I wouldn't know anything about this whole synthetic crack thing.

"Where was the body found?"

"Behind a dumpster at a restaurant on Third Ave. The body had been there awhile."

"You know how long?"

"Not yet. Few days at least. People at the restaurant said they'd smelled it for days before they finally checked it out. Here's what makes this whole thing a little more interesting. It seems that Rollins worked for the same company as another body we found three days ago with his throat slit from ear to ear."

"Coincidence?" I asked nonchalantly. As far as I was concerned, I was out of it.

"I don't think so. They were both chemists, working for the same company. They didn't work together, but still, I'd say that was a bit more than just a coincidence. Wouldn't you say so, Nick?"

"Maybe." The shit was starting to get deep now. The other guy was probably this Rodrigez guy that Chilly's Peruvian friend, Diego Estabon, was supposed to have taken care of. If that was the case, maybe Chilly did take care of his, as promised, in a couple of days. I began to consider the possibility that maybe Chilly had found and killed Jake days ago, and he was just setting me up to be part of his alibi.

"You ever seen this guy before, Simmons?" Richards asked. He walked up to the table and handed me a picture of the dead man. "His name is Norman Vogel."

My heart stopped.

"We fished him out of the East River near Pier 17."

The shit just went from deep to fucked up. If Rodrigez and Norman Vogel were the same person, then Felix had me, Jett and Monika deliver him gift wrapped to the Peruvians. And if that was the case, we were in this up to our necks. I picked up the picture as causally as I could. "No, never seen him before." I dropped the picture. "You finished with me?"

"No, Nick, we're just getting started," Kirk said.

"You think I killed them?"

"Not necessarily, but I'm not ruling you out. I'll tell you what I do think, though. I think you know exactly what's going on here."

"What makes you say that?" I tried to laugh it off, but he was right. I knew exactly what was going on here. I just wasn't about to tell him.

"These are your people, Nick. Scumbags and drug dealers, all of them. So, let's start with what happened to your face."

For the next hour, Kirkland and Richards asked me questions that I knew the answers to, but refused to tell them. Anything I said at this point would lead right back to my front door, so my answer to every question was the same. "I don't know anything about it." I knew they had nothing to hold me on, not yet anyway. The only thing that was on my mind at that point was Felix.

As soon as the police released me, I called Monika. "Monika, this is Nick."

"No need to be so formal, Nick. How you doing?"

"Not good. I'm on my way over there now. Call Jett and tell him to meet us there as fast as he can."

"My house? What's going on, Nick?"

"We have a problem. Jake is dead. Police just found the body."

"Good for them. How is that a problem for us?"

"I'll explain everything when I get there. Just call Jett. I'll be there in about twenty-five minutes." I must have been driving faster than I thought, 'cause I was there in fifteen minutes. Jett was there when I got there, which would save me the trouble of telling the story twice.

"Are you sure it's the same guy?" Jett asked pacing back and forth around the living room.

"Yeah, I'm sure. It's too much of a coincidence not to be."

"Something ain't right about this. It's too messy, too public. The police can tie this back to us. Felix should never have put us in this position," Monika said.

"Have you tried to call Felix?" Jett inquired. "Find out what the fuck is going on?"

"Not yet. And if I did, what's he gonna say? 'I don't know anything about it; this shouldn't have happened.' Best he doesn't know that we even suspect he had any part of this."

"If the cops connect us to Vogel, the shit is over. Fuck Felix. He set us up to take this fall," Monika said.

"We don't know that," Jett said.

"The hell we don't. Who else could it be? I never did trust Felix," Monika said as she got up and looked out the window. "I mean, what do we know about him anyway?"

"It all goes back to that last mission."

"What are you talking about, Nick?" she asked.

"The way the whole thing went down. I mean, what were we really doing down there?"

There was silence.

"We've all thought about it. I know I have. There we were in South America killing drug dealers, blowing up drug plants and seizing their financial records. We were small teams, each working independently. But all of a sudden, the entire unit is needed to take out one plant. Then boom, everybody dies."

"Except us," Monika asserted.

"And we'd be dead too if you didn't fall on approach and break your ankle."

"I never will forget searching the area for survivors," Jett said. I looked over at him. He looked like he was in another world, sitting there in the middle of the floor. "Knowing that there wouldn't be any," Jett continued. "But the whole time I'm thinkin', Nick. I'm thinkin' something ain't right. Something in the milk ain't clean."

"I hate it when you say shit like that, Jett. Like white milk is so pure, so clean that—"

"Give it a rest for now, Monika. Okay? We pick up the whole black, white thing at 0700 tomorrow," Jett said and bounced up from the floor. I had to agree. This wasn't the time.

Jett resumed his pacing routine. "Then the way they got us out of there. Quick and quiet, like we were down there doing somethin' we didn't have no business doing. But shit went wrong and everyone died but us. Well shit, we don't know what we know, so what could we tell anybody? And who's gonna ask? You have to know what was going on to even ask the damn questions."

What he said was confusing at first, then I realized just how right he was.

"Then we get processed out, and the very next day there's Uncle Felix. But the money's been good, so I ain't sayin' nothin'."

"Imagine if we had told Felix no," Monika said.

"Like I said, it's not like all of us haven't thought about it. But that's the case with any of the shit we've done, in or out. If we become expendable, we die. More so now."

"We don't know who the fuck Felix is. He never identified himself as a representative of—shit, anything!" Monika exclaimed. "We all just went along with it for the money. The fact of the matter is that we're mercenaries."

"She's right, Nick."

"Don't you think I know that? We aren't some kinda high-powered secret government agents. They didn't recruit us into the CIA or any shit like that. They pushed us out and threw some bones our way to keep us happy and quiet."

"I need a drink." Monika picked up a bottle of gin. "What do we do now?"

"Make it two." Jett got up and followed Monika to the kitchen. She poured herself and Jett a glass. "You want one, Nick?"

"Hell no. I don't know how y'all drink that shit anyway."

"Like this!" they said almost at the same time then drained their glasses. "I got some Johnnie Black for you, Nick."

"Thanks."

Monika handed me a glass. "So, what are we gonna do?" she asked.

"For the time being, I need to stay as far away from this as possible."

"You a suspect?" Jett asked.

"And I quote, 'I'm not ruling you out.'"

"That's not good, Nick," Monika said.

"Jett, start diggin' into Felix. Find out everything you can about him—bank records, property he owns, the whole nine."

"I'll crawl up his ass with a microscope."

"That's disgusting, gray boy," Monika said.

"We got to start covering our tracks, but first we need to be sure that Vogel is the one that Estabon was talking about."

"How we gonna do that?"

"Monika, I want you to talk to Chilly, see if you can't get him to confirm that Rodrigez and Vogel are the same person."

"Why me? What makes you think Chilly will tell me anything? Why can't Jett go?"

"We can't send Jett."

"That's right, Monika. He won't tell this gray boy nothing." Jett laughed. "But you, on the other hand, with all them lips and tits and hips you got . . . Shit, he might confess to murdering 2Pac and Biggie Smalls."

"So, what are you trying to say?"

"Just that he's more likely to talk to you because you're a woman. Just tell him that you're my associate," I said, and they both looked at me.

"Excuse me," Monika said.

"Oh, I forgot to tell you. Chilly gave me five thousand dollars to tell him where Jake was after I told his wife."

Monika poured herself another shot of gin and shook her head. "This shit gets weirder and weirder as we go along."

"Tell me about it."

Chapter Nineteen

With nothing else to do, I went by Freeze's apartment and beat on the door. For fifteen minutes. It was early, but I knew he was there. He opened the door and put a gun in my face.

"Why all the tension and animosity? Show me love, nigga."

"Fuck you, Nick. What you doing here? You know what fuckin' time it is?" He walked away from the door and flopped down on the couch.

"Which question do you want me to answer first? What am I doing here, or what time is it?"

"Start with what time it is."

"It's almost seven-thirty."

"Now, what the fuck are you doing here so fuckin' early in the morning?"

"I came to visit you, man."

"You know, Nick, it ain't that I'm not glad to see you, shit, most people don't beat on the door for fifteen minutes. After a minute or two they just go away."

"I knew you were here."

"How you know I was here?"

"The rug. You still turn the rug over when you're home."

Freeze looked at me and frowned. Slowly, the frown became a smile and turned into a laugh. "Glad you back, Nick."

"You hungry?"

"Why, you gonna cook?"

"Hell no. But I'm buyin'."

"Good, 'cause there ain't no food here anyway."

"Well, get dressed then."

About a half-hour later, Freeze came out of the back, escorted by a very attractive young woman. I stood up to meet her. "Nick, this is Pauleen. Pauleen, that's Nick."

"Nice to meet you, Pauleen."

Judging only by the way she rolled her eyes and sucked her teeth, I could tell that Pauleen wasn't glad to meet me.

"I'll be right back, Nick. I just need to roll her home."

"How long?"

"Fifteen minutes."

Once Freeze got back from droppin' off Pauleen, we set out to eat breakfast. While we ate, Freeze told me about his night. Before Pauleen, I mean. She was the closer. There was a problem at Cuisine. A customer had a complaint with his meal and the manager had gone home sick. The only one left to talk to him was Freeze.

"So, the guy starts yellin' at my ass, talkin' 'bout how the service was fucked up and the food was cold. Nick, I'm talkin' about right up in my face."

"I know you can't stand that. What did you say?"

"I was cool. So I back up off him and I go through the whole nine, apologizing for the food and the service and shit. I tell the waitress no check for this table. Then I tell him, get this, to call ahead for a reservation the next time he wishes to dine with us, and he would be my personal guest for the evening."

"You said that shit?"

"Shit yeah! I'm fuckin' tired of hearin' Wanda's mouth 'bout this customer service shit. But I ain't feelin' that shit, Nick."

"Why you do it then?"

"That's where Black wants me."

"End of story. So, what happened with you and old boy?"

"Okay, after I told him all that shit, he jumps up in my face again. Only this time, he got his finger in my face. Now it's all about how I better be glad I did that, because he's some fuckin' body and what a word from him would do to my business. Then the muthafucka poked me in the chest. Nick . . ." Freeze started laughing.

I laughed too. "What?"

"Nick, I reached for my four-five."

"No you didn't."

"I was about to pull and blast, but the waitress said 'Freeze', and I chilled. But I was about to drop his ass. You know I hate that shit, all up in my face and shit."

"At least you didn't do it. Maybe you should take one of them sensitivity classes or something."

"Fuck you, Nick."

"Just tryin' to help."

"So, what's up wit' you? You find Jake yet?"

"No, not exactly."

"What's that supposed to mean?"

"I mean Kirk found his body."

"So that's it, right? You through wit' that shit, right?"

"No, not exactly. There's a whole lotta other shit going on with this."

"Like what?"

I leaned forward. "It's all about this pipe dream Chilly had about synthetic crack."

"Pipe dream is right. Muthafucka been talkin' about that shit for years."

"Jake developed it, but everyone who smoked it died."

"Chilly kill Jake?"

"I don't know."

"What all that got to do with you bein' through with that shit?"

"Cops found a guy we snatched with his throat slit. He might be the one who created it and gave it to Chilly's stupid ass."

"Cops know you killed him?"

"We didn't kill him. We just dropped him off on Pier 17. But that ain't gonna matter now 'cause we all up in this."

"Yeah, I can see where it could all turn on you," Freeze said. "Maybe you should talk to Wanda about this."

"Maybe I should."

"So what are you gonna do?"

"I'm keepin' a low profile today."

"Fuck that, Nick. Hang out with me."

"Where we going?"

"I don't care. You drivin'. Check!"

We hung out the rest of the day. It's funny; me and Freeze are so different from who we were back then, but it still felt like I never left. Freeze dropped me off at my apartment, before going back to the club. I tried to call Felicia, but I got voice mail. I left a message then I called Jett. He had been trying to get information about Uncle Felix.

"I'm not gettin' anywhere with this, Nick. At this point, I can't even tell you if Felix is really his name. But I'm on it. I'll get him."

"I know you will. You heard from Monika?"

"Not since this afternoon. She said she was going to meet Chilly. What's going on with you?"

There was a knock at the door.

"Hold on, Jett. Someone's at the door."

"Hope it's some pussy!"

"Let's hope." I thought about Felicia, but that wasn't about to happen. Still, fantasy is a good thing.

"See if she got a friend." I heard Jett holler through the phone. I went to the door, and looked through the peephole. The hallway was filled with cops. I went back to the phone.

"Jett, a whole group of cops are at the door."

"What do they want?"

"Whatever it is, it ain't good." The knocking began again. "I'll call you back."

The banging got louder as I walked back to the door.

"Police!"

I opened the door and was met by Kirk.

"Nick Simmons?" A uniformed officer spoke while Kirk smiled at me.

"What's going on, Kirk?"

"We have a warrant to search these premises," the officer said.

"You gotta be kiddin' me."

He handed me the warrant. I looked at it. Maybe I shoulda called Wanda. Thinking that I had nothing to hide, I let them in. Cops seemed to swarm all over the place. Kirk was still standing in the hallway by the door, smiling.

"What's going on here, Kirk?"

"We found Lisa Ellison, Jake Rollins' girlfriend, dead in her living room. Shot at close range with the same caliber weapon that Rollins was killed with."

"What does that have to do with me?"

"Your fingerprints were found on—" Kirk broke out his notepad. "On a glass, the coffee table, the phone, and the inside doorknob."

"Am I under arrest?"

"No. And that's only because I don't think you'd be stupid enough to shoot her and leave prints everywhere."

"So, what's going on here?"

"Well, Nick, you searched Rollins' apartment on more than one occasion, and your prints put you at the Ellison murder scene. That makes you a suspect in both murders, as far as I can see. We're just looking for what you found and aren't telling us about, that's all, Nick. After we're finished here, you're going to ride with me down to your office, where we'll execute this warrant to search your office."

"This is fucked up, Kirk."

"Maybe, but just for laughs, why don't you explain to me when you were there and what you talked to her about?"

"I was there last Wednesday night about eight. I asked her a couple of questions about where I might find Jake. I had a glass of water. I used the phone and I left."

"This may sound like a stupid question, but you never know. Was she alive when you left her?"

"Of course she was."

Once they finished terrorizing my apartment, we went to my office and they did the same. Since I didn't kill Jake or Lisa, and there was nothing in either place to connect me to Vogel or Rodrigez or whoever he was, I wasn't sweatin' the search. Until . . .

"Detective Kirkland, I think we got something here." Kirk looked at me, smiled, and walked away. I had no idea what they had, but I was going to see. I fell right in behind Kirk.

"Take a look at this."

The officer had Jake's file in his hand and gave Kirk a piece of paper. At least it wasn't the murder weapon. Kirk looked over the paper carefully then handed it to me. It was the formula for synthetic crack. What a time for Monika to start filing.

"What is this?" Kirk asked me.

The officer gave Kirk another piece of paper. It had to be the analysis that Monika's friend had done.

I waited for Kirk to finish reading before I answered. Kirk handed me the paper. "Does the phrase 'withholding evidence' or 'obstruction of justice' mean anything to you."

"They do now."

"Book him."

Chapter Twenty

The more I thought about it, the surer I was that Monika, and Jett were right. This private investigating stuff sucked. I hated cops, and I had been spending too much time with them fuckas. Now I had to help them. It just went against everything.

Me and Kirk had a long conversation, during which he threatened to charge me with murder if I didn't start cooperating. I knew he couldn't make a case there. However, withholding and obstruction they had me on. But I still stuck to my story. "I don't know anything about that." I still felt like a snitch sittin' there. This shit sucked. He wanted to know how I'd gotten the formula. No biggie there, since he already figured I got it from Jake's safe. I gave him that and told him that I had only gotten the analysis back yesterday. "Jake was already dead. Case closed, so we filed it."

We danced around the same points for hours, then he had some uniforms take me to the holding cell. The benches were cold and hard. Naturally, it was crowded with just us.

Thursday, July 23, 12:45 PM

Jett arranged my bail, and I was out by lunchtime. When we got back to my apartment, Monika was there waiting for us. Not only had she cleaned up after the cops, but she had cooked. Monika never cooked. She hated it, so even though I was skeptical about eating it, I knew it was made with love.

For the rest of the afternoon, we sat around and talked about our situation until the sun went down. Monika got up to leave. "Where you going?" Jett asked.

"I'm going to meet Chilly," she replied, heading for the door.

"I thought you got with him last night?" I asked, getting up to see her out. "You ain't fallin' in love with him, are you?" Me and Jett laughed, but Monika, on the other hand, saw no humor in it at all. She stopped dead in her tracks.

"You two-silly ass muthafuckas done lost y'all's *gotdamn* minds! This is strictly business, understand?" She said with her finger on my nose. I still was laughing. "Business that you're sending me on, so remember that." And with that, she left.

"She's kinda touchy. Must be that time of the month," Jett said as he got up. "I'm outta here too, Nick. I'll catch up with you tomorrow."

"I'll git wit' ya, Jett."

With the house now empty, I gave some thought to sleep, which I hadn't done since the day before. I put on some music. Freeze had been bumpin' some bootlegged 2Pac, and he let me borrow it.

Jake's funeral was the next day, so I thought about whether I would make a cameo appearance. I took a shower and fell asleep to the sound of Pac tellin' me how I was *Fuckin' Wit The Wrong Nigga.*

I didn't know how long I had been asleep; it was quiet, but somebody banging on my door soon replaced that quiet. My first thought was that it was Freeze exacting a measure of payback for pounding on his door the day before. I picked up my gun and opened the door, prepared to shove the gun in his face.

"Remember me?"

"Felicia."

"Surprise!" She threw her arms around my waist and gave me the kiss I'd been dreaming about since the last time she kissed me. I responded in kind.

"What are you doing here?"

"I missed you." Felicia kissed me on the cheek. "Did I come at a bad time?"

"No, not at all."

"Can I come in?"

"I'm sorry. Of course you can come in." I stepped aside and closed the door behind her. "I'm just surprised, that's all. Have a seat. Can I offer you something?"

"No, I'm fine. Nice place. Mind if I look around?"

"Be my guest."

Felicia wandered around the apartment with her hands on her hips, looking over her shoulder to see if I was watching. Which I was. She swung her hips harder and I smiled. "What you smiling about?" she asked as she walked past me.

"Just happy to see you, Felicia. What made you come back here anyway?"

"You did."

"I did?"

"Yes, you, Nick."

"How did I do that?"

"Two ways. First, I missed you and I wanted to be with you." She went into the kitchen. She looked impressed. It was clean for a change, thanks to Monika. She came out. "Seems you got me a little dick-whipped."

Felicia wandered into the bedroom.

"Nice bed," she said and came back out, carefully closing the door and tapping the doorknob. Felicia turned around and came toward me. "And second, you gave me a shot of your courage, so I decided to come back and face things head on, you know, take a more proactive approach to this thing."

"Well, it's pretty much over."

"You solved the case?" Felicia's face lit up. She was excited for me. I thought that was sweet of her.

"Nope."

Man, I was diggin' her, look at her eyes, her smile. I took a step closer to Felicia.

"Cops found Jake dead a couple days ago."

"Oh, really?"

"Yes, really. Cops searched here and my office last night. They found the formula and the analysis of that synthetic crack, so I'm done with it."

"That means you'll have some time to spend with me." She reached for my hand and squeezed it. Then she touched my face with the other hand and kissed my cheek.

She started to walk away, but I pulled her back toward me.

I touched her face and pressed my lips against hers. I started to walk away, but she pulled me back toward her and kissed me. Believe me, it was more fun this time. I liked it and I wanted more.

She kissed me again.

We stood awkwardly, looking at each other for a long time. And then, almost at the same time, we started taking off our clothes. I felt the vibration of my pager, but I didn't care.

Friday, July 24, 1:17 AM

When I woke up, it was past 1:00 in the morning. I looked at Felicia. She was out for the count. I got up and put on my pants, and once again, I felt the vibration of my pager. I checked the number. "Monika." It was late, but I called anyway.

"This is Detective Richards."

"I'm sorry, wrong number." I hung up quickly. What was Richards doing there? I called again.

"Hello," Detective Richards answered.

"Richards, this is Nick Simmons. Where's Monika?"

"You're her partner, right?"

"Yeah. Where is she?"

"She's been shot, Nick. Shot five times. Doesn't look good for her."

"When was this?"

"Around ten, we figure." While I was busy laying down mack. I cursed myself for not answering.

"They took her to the hospital."

"What hospital?"

"Lebanon."

"What happened?"

"I'm not at liberty to say. Was she working on the same case?"

"I'm not at liberty to say."

"Come on, Nick, give me a break. Anything you can give us would help."

"Come on, Richards, give me something, that's my partner. My friend. My family."

"You know I can't do that," Richards said. I could hear Kirkland's big mouth in the background. I couldn't make out everything he said, but I did hear him say, "There was no sign of forced entry. Nothing appears to be missing, so we can assume it was someone she knew," which answered all my questions. When I heard him say, "Pick up her partner, Nick Simmons. See what he knows," I knew it was time to hang up.

"I'm going to the hospital, Richards. You can catch me there."

I went to Monika's room in the intensive care unit. The nurse stopped me from going in the room. "I'm sorry, sir. Family members only."

"I am her family." I pushed by her.

Jett and I were the only family she had, or at least that she communicated with. Monika and her mother fell out long before she joined the Army. When she was fifteen, her mother's boyfriend grabbed her ass when she walked by him. She told her mother what happened, but her mother didn't believe her. She accused Monika of flirting with him and told her that's what she got for dressing like a tramp. They hadn't spoken since.

A doctor came in to check on her. To be honest, she didn't look old enough to be a doctor. She told me that Monika had been shot five times—two shots in the chest, two to the head. One hit her above the left ear. She caught the other one in her eye. They were not able to save her eye. The fifth bullet was in her hand. Knowing Monika, she was probably trying to catch it. I felt my eyes begin to water.

I sat there with her, holding her hand and talking. I didn't know if she could hear me or not, but I didn't care. I wanted her to know that she wasn't alone, that I was there with her and that she was going to be all right. If 2Pac could take five shots and live, she could too.

"Nick, 2Pac is dead," Wanda asserted.
"Freeze says he ain't," I replied.

Monika was strong, in both mind and body. Next to Mike Black, she was probably the strongest person I'd ever met. I sat there wondering how it happened. Was her attacker there when she paged me? Was there something I could have done to prevent this from happening? Even if I left right then, the best I could have done was get there in time to talk to the police. *I still should have answered.* There was nothing I could have done, but still, I felt like shit. I should have been there. I should have been there watching her back.

But no, fuckin' Felicia seemed a little more important. The chair began to feel harder than it had all night, so I walked to the window and watched the sunrise. I don't know how long I stood there, but when I turned around, Jett was sitting there.

"How long you been here?"

He didn't answer. He just sat there, kinda stone faced. He was pale, paler than he usually was. He just sat there staring at Monika, he didn't even blink. Since he wasn't talking I went and sat down.

Finally, after about an hour, Jett spoke. "I love Monika."

"I do too," I replied.

"I don't think you understand, Nick. I really love her. I love both of you. You and Monika are closer to me than my own family, man . . . I was there, Nick. I was right fuckin' there, Nick. Right there."

"What happened, Jett?"

He went back to staring at Monika. Since he wasn't talking again, I told him what the doctor said. I couldn't tell if he was listening or not. I'd never seen Jett like this and it worried me. Jett was always live. This wasn't good. They had been my two closest friends, my only family for years. Now one might die, and Jett, I couldn't tell where he was. I had a pocket full of questions and no one to ask.

"She called me, Nick. She said things didn't go well with Chilly. She said to meet her at her house. When I got there, I heard the shots. I ran to the door, yellin' for Monika. I went inside and saw her. Lying there. I picked up the phone and called the cops. She tried to talk, but I couldn't hear what she was sayin'. I did what I could to stop the bleeding and make her comfortable." Then he stopped

talking again. He still hadn't taken his eyes off
Monika. He still hadn't blinked. Another ten minutes or so went by before Jett started talking again.

"I heard a noise in the back. I got to the back
door in time to see someone drive away. I got to
my heap and I followed him. He didn't pick me
up. He stopped at a house on 229th Street. I put on
my gloves and went in after him. He didn't hear
me come in. Caught him in the bathroom pissin'."

"Who was he, Jett? Was he black, white? What did
he look like?" No answer. Just that pale, glassy-eyed
look, like my questions annoyed him. I decided I
would save my questions until he was finished. He
looked back at Monika. I watched the tears roll
down his cheeks. My eyes began to water again. I
got up and walked back to the window.

"I popped him in the back of the neck and
dragged him into the living room. I put him in a
chair and tied him up then I slapped him around
until he came out of it. I took out my knife. He
tried to get free." Jett shook his head. "That wasn't
happening. The more he moved, the tighter they
got. I asked him who he was and why he shot
Monika, but he didn't answer, so I cut him. Just a
little cut on the arm to get him bleedin'. But he
didn't say shit. Didn't even flinch. I told him I
would cut him every time he didn't answer me. He
just looked at me, so I cut him again. But he wasn't
talkin'. I worked him over pretty good, but the bastard wasn't sayin' shit. So I went back to cuttin'
him."

"How many times did you cut him, Jett?"

"I don't know."

I forgot my promise not to ask any more questions. At least he answered me. But he stopped

talking again. Just staring at Monika. It took almost a half-hour before Jett spoke again. "We had been there for hours, Nick. Blood was all over the floor. He was shakin' and shit. I was really fuckin' pissed when I saw the sun coming up. I walked up to him and cut his throat."

"You killed him?"

"That's what I just fuckin' said. I cut his fuckin' throat."

I sat down in that hard-ass chair and buried my head in my hands. "Jett, you killed the only person who could tell us who tried to kill her and why."

"He wasn't gonna talk, Nick, so he had to fuckin' die."

"You're probably right."

"We don't need him to tell us shit, Nick." Jett finally faced me. The expression on his face didn't change. "That fuckin' Chilly knows why."

"What did you do with the body?"

"I left him there."

"Come on." I got up and walked out the door. Jett was right behind me. He drove me to the house and we went inside. There he was. The sunlight was shining brightly through the window on him. A pool of blood surrounded the chair. Jett stood there and looked at him while I searched the house. It was empty. No clothes in the closets, no food in the refrigerator. Nothing to go on. "Let's go."

Chapter Twenty-one

I drove Jett's car back to the hospital and left him there to be with Monika. In the condition he was in, that was the best place for him. He would be of no use to me, and maybe just a little out of place where I was going. My destination was Woodlawn Cemetery, for Jake's funeral. I drove back to my apartment to pick up my rifle. Felicia was gone when I got there.

I stood quietly off to the side and saw Mrs. Childers and Chésará holding one another and crying. But my eyes were on Chilly. There he was, standing there with that smug look on his face, not consoling his wife in her time of loss. That's because the ugly fuck did it. He probably had Lisa killed, figuring that Jake must have told her what was up. And Monika. I was gonna kill him.

I looked around the crowd. There was an older couple watching from the other side as Jake's casket was lowered into the ground. The woman was crying and the man just held her close to his chest. I figured that they were Jake's parents. I wondered who called them. Chéz, most likely. Mrs. Childers—I mean Gee—wouldn't call them. She said they were dead to her. Maybe she felt they should know their son was dead.

I thought about losing my parents when I was eleven. No one really knew what happened to them. One day they just didn't come home. My brother and sister went Mississippi to live with my father's brother and his wife. They didn't want me. My uncle said they were just babies. They would raise them in the church. They would be all right. But I was into too much trouble and he wasn't havin' it. Not in his house. Said I was probably the reason my parents didn't come home.

He didn't know I was listening.

I never saw my brother and sister again. I didn't think about them much. Now I was feelin' kinda family, maybe I would go to Mississippi and try to find them. What would I say to them? They probably wouldn't even remember me.

It was decided that I would go live with my grandmother, and after a while, it didn't matter as much. My grandmother was good to me. She showed me much love. She died five years later, but I had a new family by then. And after Black kicked my ass on my first day on the block, they showed me much love too.

While I was daydreaming, the funeral party had broken up and Chilly was safe inside the limo. I followed the limo to their house. I had no idea what I was going to do. Would I simply ask him what happened with Monika the night before? Or would I just drop him because he deserved to die? When the limo arrived at the house, it was crawling with cops. I parked the car down the street. As soon as the limo stopped, the cops opened the door and took Chilly into custody.

"Shit!"

I watched as the police car drove past me. I looked at Chilly, he looked at me. The feelings were mutual. I drove away thinking about Monika, and before I knew it, I was back at the hospital. When I got to intensive care, Jett was gone and Detective Richards was there.

"What happened, Richards?"

"Simmons, I'm sorry about your partner. I know how it feels to have a—"

"Fuck all that! What happened to her?" I yelled and pounded my fist against the glass. It frightened the nurses, so I tried to calm down. "Just tell me what happened." I expected Richards to be his usual arrogant, white boy cop self, but he was cool.

"She was shot in the living room. There wasn't any sign of a struggle. Her gun was still in her shoulder holster. We figure she either knew the guy or he caught her off guard. He came in, she turned, and he shot her. Your other partner," Richards checked his notes, "James Bronson, says the door was opened when he got there. Paramedics told me he probably saved her life, stoppin' the bleedin', before he left the scene. He wasn't real clear about why he left the scene. Says he went after the guy who did it. He was pretty shook up, so I didn't press him about it, but we're gonna need to talk to him."

"Where is he?"

"He left about fifteen minutes ago."

I started to ask if he said where he was going, but I knew better. I knew Jett. The only thing on his mind was finding the people involved, and killing them. And he wouldn't be inviting the cops along. "Thanks."

"Like I was sayin', I know what it feels like when your partner gets shot." Richards walked away. Maybe he wasn't such an asshole.

I talked to the doctor before I left the hospital. She told me Monika's condition hadn't changed. "It's all up to her now." She promised that she would do all she could. I thanked the doctor for everything she had done. My mind was on finding Jett.

Where would he go? I drove by the house he followed Monika's assailant to, looking for anything that might lead me to who was responsible. No cop cars, no yellow crime scene tape. Just in case somebody was watching the house, I parked a couple of blocks away and walked back. When I went inside, the body was gone. All the blood was cleaned off the floor. There was no trace that Jett had tortured and executed a man there. I went through the house anyway. Nothing.

"What now?"

I didn't feel like sitting around the hospital, so I drove by Rocky's spot. I didn't think he was involved in Monika's shooting, but I was mad. I had a little payback I wanted to deal out.

When I got there, a crowd had formed. The police were standing around a convertible Impala stopped at the light. I parked and approached the crowd. I watched as they took two bodies out of the front seat. "What's going on?" I asked an old man in the crowd.

"Somebody shot those three men in that car." The third body was removed from the car. It was Rocky. My first thought was Jett.

"You know if they saw who did it? Was he white?"

"I don't know."

I thanked the man and returned to my car. With nowhere else to go, I went back to my apartment, hoping that Felicia had come back. I needed to see her, but that wasn't happening. The place was in darkness.

The phone rang.

"Listen, Nick," Jett said. He still didn't sound good.

"Where are you?"

"I'm at the stake house by Chilly's. I know who did it."

"Who?"

"I can't talk now. Meet me here."

"Jett, wait!" I yelled, but he was gone. I drove as fast as I could to the house. When I got there, Jett was gone. I was about to leave when I noticed some papers next to the phone. It was the research Jett was doing on Felix. I picked up the papers, walked outside and got back in my car. I drove down the street slowly, noticing Jett's car parked on my right. I parked up ahead of him and walked back to his car, coming around to the driver's side. "What's going on, Jett?"

I looked in the car. His eyes were wide open. "Jett!" I shook him. That's when I saw the trail of blood coming from his ear. I opened the car door and Jett fell into my arms.

He was dead.

I asked a lady walking by to call the police. I sat there in the street holding Jett until the paramedics came. I talked to the police, doing an excellent job of telling them as little as possible until Richards showed up.

"What's going on, Simmons? First one of your partners, then the other. What are you involved in?"

"I don't know. My case was closed when you found Rollins dead body with a bullet in his brain."

"I didn't tell you this, but Rollins was already dead when he was shot. His neck was broken. That's what killed him.

"How he died don't matter. He's dead. You found that formula and arrested Chilly."

"You think he's involved in this?"

I looked at Richards like he was stupid. *Of course I think he's involved. Monika met him last night. Whatever happened, happened, and she wanted me and Jett to meet her. Now Jett gets popped a block from the fucka's house.*

"What happened here?" Richards asked, taking the hint that I wasn't going to answer his question.

"I don't know."

"Were you with him?"

"No. He called me and said to meet him here."

"Did he say why?"

"No. He hung up before I could ask him."

"Look, Simmons, I'm really sorry for you. I know you think Chilly is involved in this. It's pretty fuckin' obvious that your partner here did too.

We're a block from his house, for Christ's sake. But please, let us handle it."

"Yeah, right." I turned and started back for my car.

"Where are you going?"

"I need a drink."

Chapter Twenty-two

There was no doubt about it, I was drunk. Tripping over the rug by the door was a real indicator of that. Staggering the way I was, the couch was as far as my drunk legs would carry me. I disarmed myself and sat down. Fell down, actually. Fortunately for me, I had left a bottle of Johnnie Black on the coffee table. I picked up a glass and started to pour. I decided that was too much trouble, so I raised the bottle to my mouth. I could actually feel the liquor flowing through my body. The only problem was that it wasn't helping.

I had just returned from the hospital. Monika hadn't regained consciousness and was still in intensive care. It didn't matter. I still had to tell her that Jett was dead.

For the second time, I faced myself with the same question. "If I had only gotten there sooner, could I have saved him?"

I didn't know.

The only difference was that this time I wasn't fuckin' Felicia or some dumb shit like that. I was on my way. His body was still warm when I got there. "If I had only—"

No point torturing myself about it now. Jett was dead and Monika was fighting for her life. I slammed the bottle down on the table. This game had gone on long enough. Somebody was going to have to answer for both of them.

I wanted to hurt somebody, make somebody feel my pain. But who? I was sure that Chilly ordered up both hits, but he was in jail. I gave serious thought to getting myself arrested so I could kill him, but the thought faded quickly. I could get Freeze to arrange it, but I wouldn't get any satisfaction from just knowing he was dead. I had to do it. I wanted him to feel all my pain. I wanted to look in his eyes before I pulled the trigger. "Say good-bye." I wanted him to know why he had to die. Not just for me, but for everyone he terrorized over the years. Johnnie Black called out to me, as if he wanted to drink to these thoughts. I gladly obliged him. "A drunk never argues with his bottle." It was almost a rule. A good soldier always follows rules. No, a good soldier always follows orders. "What do drunks do?" They drink, stupid!

Saturday, July 25, 11:19 AM

When I woke up, the bottle was empty and I was on the floor. I stood up slowly and looked around the apartment. I took a moment to think about how I got that far away from the couch and who made this mess. I needed someone to blame. I looked at the empty bottle. "Had to be you."

I was hungry, but I didn't feel like cooking, so I grabbed my keys and looked around for my guns. I didn't see them and I didn't care. I would find them when I got back. The liquor store was my first stop. My first drink of the day convinced me that it wouldn't be my last. I walked to the bar on the next corner. "Might as well kill two birds with one stone." Since it wasn't quite time for lunch and a little too late for breakfast, I had steak and eggs. Johnnie Black replaced the orange juice. While I sat there getting my eat and my drunk on, I gave some thought to, you know, calling a halt to feeling sorry for myself and doing something about it. All this drinking wasn't gonna bring Jett back from the dead or make Monika open her eyes. And on top of that, it wasn't making me feel any better, just drunker.

With that thought in mind, I was able to keep the drinking to two shots. On my way out of the restaurant, a man asked me for some spare change. I made his day with a picture of Alexander Hamilton.

When I got back to the apartment, I put my bottle down on the coffee table, headed for the shower, and tried to pull it together. I love long, hot showers. It is, to me, the greatest joy next to gettin' pussy. With my head clearing, I began to think about how I was going to exact my revenge. I might not be able to get Chilly, but I would tear through his whole set. I would be the nightmare now, but they wouldn't be waking up.

All at once, I became very conscious of the fact that I was just one guy and he had an Army. But I knew in my heart that I wouldn't be alone. Freeze had my back, just like the old days. And for that, I felt like shit. I would be dragging Black's organization into a war. Maybe even Black himself. How could I do that after what I did?

I turned off the shower and came back to reality. If it was gonna get done, it would be me doing it. I would have to have a plan. Pick them off, one by one, in methods that were more creative. I put my pants back on and resumed the search for my guns. It wasn't like I didn't have an arsenal here. But it was the principle of the thing.

There was a knock at the door. I looked out the peephole and didn't see anybody. "Who is it?"

"It's Gee, Nick. Please let me in." I looked again and still didn't see her. I opened the door, stepped aside, and prepared to receive her. She took a step inside. I looked at her face. Her jaw was swollen and—

"Get in there!" The door swung open and there was Chilly. Gee stumbled to the floor. Chilly pointed the gun at me and grabbed her, jerking her back to her feet.

"I'm sorry, Nick," Gee whimpered.

"You stay right where the fuck you are! You move and I'll kill you."

"You're gonna try to kill me anyway. What's the difference?"

"Right."

Chilly fired at me.

I didn't move. It came close to hitting my arm. I don't think he meant to hit me with that shot. It was meant to get my attention.

It did.

I wasn't afraid to die. I just didn't want to die like this, half-naked and unarmed.

Chilly looked at me then at his wife. "Get over

there with him. You two belong together." He pushed her in my direction. "Ain't neither one of you worth a shit."

"You all right?"

"I'm okay," Gee said softly without taking her eyes off Chilly.

"How'd he get out?"

"Bail," Gee whispered.

"Don't ask her nothin', muthafucka! You wanna know how I got out, you ask me!" Chilly screamed. "Cops can't hold a muthafucka like me on some bullshit tip like this! You two dirty muthafuckas set me up!"

"Set you up?" I had to laugh. It might have been foolish to laugh at a man who was pointing a gun at me, but that shit was funny.

"You two think you're slick. Had this shit all worked out. Neither one of you muthafuckas can be trusted. Your ho ass, out there fuckin' everybody. And you, nigga, everything they said about you is true. I thought that was all bullshit. I thought you was old school. I came to you on the real, straight up business. Showed you more respect than you deserved. You took my money!"

"You took money from him?" Gee looked puzzled.

"Oh, he didn't tell you? That wasn't part of y'alls little plan? Stupid bitch! You always was a stupid bitch, Gee. This nigga been playin' you! I gave him five grand to tell me where Jake was. But the difference between me and this nigga is that I have honor. I still wanted him to tell you where your brother was, just as long as he told me too. You ain't loyal to shit, are you, muthafucka? Fuckin' my wife. You a dirty muthafucka. Bobby shoulda killed your ass." He spit in my face and moved the barrel of his gun against my forehead, in case I wanted to do something about it. "Yeah, y'all got a nigga set up."

"So, I guess Jake didn't develop that shit for you? All those people dyin' ain't your fault?"

Now it was Chilly who was laughing. "I didn't kill nobody. That's on Jake. Who knew he was a sorry ass chemist?"

"You practicin' for your day in court?"

"I ain't going; you are."

"Who killed Pamela Hendricks?"

"Let's see—didn't she die from that bullshit *her* punk-ass brother cooked up?" He cut his eyes at Gee.

"What about Lisa?"

"You killed her. Your fingerprints were at the murder scene."

"Rocky?"

"You killed him too, 'cause he sent his boys after you."

"What about Jett and Monika?"

"I don't know no damn Jett. And Monika," he licked his lips and smiled a smile that annoyed the fuck out of me. "Shit! I had other plans for her fine ass. So you see, my nigga, you the one gonna die for this."

Although I hated to admit it, he had a point. He could still walk away from all this, leaving me to step off for it.

"Get me a drink, Gee."

"What?"

Chilly slapped her to the floor and quickly returned his gun to my forehead. "I said get me a fuckin' drink."

Figuring it was best to stay low, she crawled over to the coffee table and poured him a drink. Gee got to her feet and walked slowly toward him, reaching out to hand him the glass. He took his eyes off me to reach for the glass. "Don't even think about it."

Gee threw the glass in his eye. Chilly's hands flew to his face.

I went for the gun and knocked it out of his hand. It fell to the floor. He punched me in the face; I fell to the floor. Chilly backhanded Gee and she went down too. He was strong as hell. I got to one knee, but before I could get up, he was on me. He rammed his knee into my face and I fell back against the coffee table and rolled over. Chilly came at me, kicking me in the back. Gee got up, Chilly kicked her away. She jumped on his back and scratched his face. Chilly shook her off of his back quickly. She hit the floor hard. Chilly turned to look at her. It gave me enough time to get to my feet.

I rushed at him. Clenching both of my fists, I hit Chilly in the face. He fell back and stumbled over Gee. I went straight at him, hitting him again and again. Chilly swung at me and missed. I got one arm around his throat and the other around his head. I squeezed with everything I had. When he struggled, I squeezed harder. He tried to get my arm from around his neck. I squeezed harder. I could feel him gasping for air. I jerked his head as hard as I could to the side. Chilly stopped struggling.

I looked at Gee. She hadn't moved.

I let his body drop to the floor. My back was killing me.

I looked around for his gun. Conveniently, it had fallen by the couch. I picked it up, sat down, and looked at their bodies on the floor.

Gee began to move and I got up slowly. I helped her to her feet and over to the couch. "Are you all right?" I sat down next to her.

"I think so." Her hands were shaking, so I held them.

"You were all right back there."

"Huh?" She looked at me like I was stupid.

"I mean you didn't just stand back screamin'. You came through for me. Thank you. You saved my life."

"It wasn't all that." She smiled. "My back is killin' me."

"Mine too."

She looked at Chilly. "Is he dead?"

"I don't know. And I'm not all that interested in going over there to find out. If he moves, I'll shoot him."

Chapter Twenty-three

"Was he dead?" Wanda asked.

"Yeah, Wanda, he was dead."

"What did you do then?"

"I called Freeze and told him where I was and what happened. He said he was gonna call you. Then I called the cops. They came and arrested me for murder."

"What happened to Mrs. Childers? Was she taken in too?"

"No. The cops talked to her, took her statement, then they had an officer take her home."

"Do you know what she told them?"

"We went over our story before the cops came. It was pretty much the truth."

"Did you talk to anyone before I got there?"

"You asked me that already, Wanda. No, I didn't talk to anybody."

"Good."

"How did Black find out I was in jail?"

"Freeze told him. Freeze has been keeping Mike up—all of us, really—keepin' us up on what you've been doing."

"Bet you've all been havin' a good laugh."

"Why do you say that?" Wanda asked and laughed. "We all care about you and what you do, Nick." Turning serious, Wanda continued. "I don't know how I can get you to see that. Whether you accept it or not, whether you accept us or not, Nick, we *are* your family."

I didn't say anything. What could I say? I'd been fighting that war within myself for years.

"Chilly was right about one thing."

"What do you mean?" she asked.

"When he said Bobby shoulda killed me over Camille."

"Camille. Not Camille again. You need to let that go, Nick. She wasn't worth it then, and she damn sure ain't worth it now."

"You've never met Camille, have you, Wanda?"

"Yes, I have. Twice actually." Wanda smiled and I wondered why.

"When?"

"Before you or Bobby met her."

"Where?"

Wanda took a deep breath. "I met her in Mike's bedroom."

I guess Wanda could tell by the look on my face that I wanted to hear the story. Needed to hear it. "Mike was supposed to be going with me to a fundraiser."

"Black? Back then, at a fund raiser?"

"You know Glynnis Presley?"

"Ain't she an aide to some congressman?"

"Senator now. But yeah, that night began our long association. Anyway, I went there to pick him up. He wasn't ready when I got there, so he got in the shower and told me to pick him out something to wear. I walked in the room, and Camille was in the bed. I apologized for walking in on her, but she didn't seem to care." Wanda let out a little laugh. "She invited me to join her in bed."

"That was Camille."

"She was poison, Nick."

"You couldn't possibly understand."

"Yes I can, Nick. More than you know."

"I was sick when I left there that night, Wanda. Can't you see that?"

"I know. I don't think I'll ever forget that night. Bobby with his gun in your mouth, screamin' he was gonna kill you. Mike with his gun to Bobby's head. He just kept sayin', 'Bobby, put the gun down.' I remember lookin' at his face, his eyes. I could see the pain he was in."

"My two best friends. Bobby was ready to kill me. And Black, shit! I can't even imagine where his head was, with a gun to Bobby's head. Him and Bobby are like brothers. And the reason was Camille. I called her when I left there. Told her what happened. She didn't care. She laughed at how she had us. And she had us. She told me to come fuck her. I was on my way, but I needed a drink first. Three, really. Camille was dead when I got there. Two shots to the head."

"Camille," Wanda said as she got up from the couch. She walked slowly, thoughtfully, toward the window. "Oh, Nick. There is so much you don't know about that night."

"Why don't you tell me about that night? I've been talking all night. You talk for a while."

"Do you remember passing Freeze on your way out?"

"Yeah."

"I mean really remember. Do you remember him carrying a large envelope?"

"I remember."

I remembered it all.

"Bobby, put the gun down!" Black yelled.

I felt Bobby's hand tighten around my throat.

"I'll kill you!" Bobby screamed.

Black put his gun to Bobby's head. "Bobby, please," he said quietly. "Take the gun out of his mouth and put it down."

Black moved his gun away from Bobby's head. Bobby let go of my throat and slowly eased his gun out of my mouth.

I reached for my throat and took a step away from Bobby.

Bobby stared at me. "Don't think this is over."

I started to walk away, trying to catch my breath.

"I'ma kill you!" Bobby shouted. "And that bitch!"

I left Black's office at The Late Night and walked across the dance floor on my way out of the club. You ran after me. "Nick, wait."

I saw Freeze coming. "Yo, Nick, you're gonna wanna see this." I just kept walking.

"I remember."

Wanda walked toward me and held her hand out. "There's something I want you to see." I accepted Wanda's hand, and she led me into the bedroom. "Don't even think about it."

"Furthest thing from my mind." I looked Wanda up and down and smiled. "Until you brought it up."

Wanda led me to her dresser and let go of my hand. She removed the picture from the wall and opened her safe then took out an envelope and handed it to me. "This is what he wanted you to see."

I sat down on the bed and Wanda left me alone. The envelope had a notebook in it. I sat quietly and began to read. It was a journal, a very detailed account of all contact Camille had with any of us. All about our operation—where our gambling houses were, and who ran them. Everything. From the first time she met Freeze at the Knicks game. *She fucked him too.* She wrote at length and in great detail about Black. It troubled her that she never could get Black to talk to her, much less tell her anything important. She wrote, *Black would say just enough to get me out my dress.*

That was how I should have played her.

Camille wrote about her and Bobby. About how she was so turned on when she met me. She wrote everything, every conversation she'd heard, everything she saw. Everything I ever told her. She even described her desire to seduce Wanda.

I sat there reading for hours. Was she five-O? Couldn't be. No cop would keep this type of journal and leave it around to be found.

Wanda was back in her spot on the couch and I joined her there. "Where did Freeze find this?"

"Freeze searched her apartment."

"What was he doing there?"

"Mike sent him."

"Why?"

"Why do you think Mike would? She was a cancer growing in his organization."

"What happened that night?"

"After we read the journal, Mike made Freeze take Bobby home. Then me and Mike went to see Camille."

"To kill her."

"No, Mike offered her twenty thousand dollars to go back to Barbados. She refused. He asked her to explain herself. She said it was just to protect herself, and that she had another copy of that book. She said she would use it when she needed to, and for more than twenty thousand dollars."

"So Black shot her."

"No. You know Mike would never shoot a woman."

I looked at Wanda.

"I shot her, Nick."

"You."

"Yes, Nick, I shot her. It had to be done. She was poison, and she was eating her way through our entire organization. There's enough evidence in that journal she was keeping to put all of us in jail for long time. I know how you felt about her, and I hope you can forgive me, but I did what had to be done."

"All these years I thought Bobby killed her."

"No, Nick, he didn't. I killed her. Bobby said he felt stupid to be so fooled by her. Camille had you all fooled."

"That's all well and good, but it doesn't change the facts. I betrayed Bobby."

"Whatever, Nick. I'm going to bed. You're welcome to stay here if you want. I have plenty of room."

"I might take you up on that." I yawned.

"I hope you do. We still have things to talk about, so I hope you're still here when I wake up. Good night, Nick."

"Good night, Wanda. And thanks."

"For what?"

"For being there." I stood up and hugged her.

"I wouldn't miss it for anything in the world. Just don't run away from us this time. We love you." She kissed me on the cheek. "Good night, Nick."

I watched her walk into her room and close the door behind her. I wanted a drink, but I really didn't need one. I went to the bedroom next to Wanda's, kicked off my shoes and lay down on the bed. I had talked out the whole story and I still didn't get it. I thought about what Wanda told me. I tossed and turned, trying to get comfortable, but I couldn't. Everything kept rolling around in my mind. I just kept thinking about Chilly. And Camille. And Bobby. And Gee. Nothing is as it seems.

And then it all came together.

I put my shoes on and left.

Chapter Twenty-four

"Hello, Gee."

"Nick!"

"Surprised to see me?"

"Yes."

"I just bet you are. Mind if I come in?"

"I'm sorry, Nick. Come in, please."

"Thank you." I stepped inside the house. Mrs. Childers was dressed to kill, as usual. "You look very nice today. Were you on your way somewhere?"

"No, I just got back. Have a seat. Can I get you a drink?"

"Thank you."

"Johnnie Walker Black, straight up, right?"

"You remembered. I cannot help but be touched."

"When did you get out?"

"Yesterday."

"Well, what happened?"

"I'm out on bail." She returned with my drink. "What about you? How are you doing?"

"I'm okay."

"You should be happy. The nightmare is over. Chilly's dead. That's what you wanted, isn't it?" When she didn't answer, I finished my liquor and said, "Now that it's over, don't you want to tell me what really happened?"

"What do you mean?"

"I didn't stutter. What the fuck really happened?" She just sat there and looked at me with those eyes. Those eyes that got me into this mess in the first place. "Look, Mrs. Childers—I mean, Gee—I killed Chilly. He's dead. It's over, so why don't you tell me the truth?"

"Nick, I don't know what to say. I—"

"You knew where Jake was all along, didn't you? You knew all about this synthetic crack shit."

"Yes."

"That seems like a good enough place to start."

Gee fumbled around for a second or two, and then she got up and poured herself a drink. "Chilly wasn't there the night Jake came looking for him," she said as she poured. "I asked him what he wanted to see Chilly about."

Wednesday, June 30, 9:15 PM

"Come ride with me, Gee. We need to talk," Jake said.

"What's the matter with you?"

"I'm in trouble, Gee. Maybe we all are."

"That's nothing new. What's wrong now?"

"Three months ago, Chilly came to me with this formula. Says it's gonna make all of us rich. He wanted me to develop it for him."

"What kind of formula?"

"For synthetic crack."

"What do you mean, synthetic crack?"

"It's a chemical compound that has the same effect as crack, only there's no cocaine in it. All the ingredients are legal, and it's twenty times cheaper to produce. Only problem is people died from using it."

"You did it? You made it for him?"

"That's what I'm trying to tell you, Gee. LaShawn sold some to some people she gets high with, and they all died."

"My God, Jake, why did you do it?"

"Why do you think? He said he would kill Chéz if I didn't do it. What else could I do? Now he says he's gotta start covering his tracks. He said there can't be any trace of this that will tie it back to him. That includes me. He's gonna kill me, Gee. He's got to. I would be the only one who can connect him with all of it."

"You've got to get away from here, Jake. Far away, where he'll never find you."

"Live in reality, Gee. Didn't you try that? Didn't he find you? Didn't he shoot me in my fuckin' leg until you said you would come back? You remember that, don't you?"

"All right! All right, Jake. What are you gonna do?"

"I don't know."

"Jake, you got to disappear."

"No."

"Yes. Listen to me. What if the cops could tie all this back to Chilly? They'd have him for murder, and we'd be free, Jake."

"You want me to go to the cops?"

"No, but the cops need the evidence, and it has to be solid enough so he doesn't get off."

"How we gonna do that without going to the cops? And I'm not going into witness protection. He'll find me and kill me. He'll kill all of us."

I looked at Mrs. Childers, thinking that this was the story I'd been waiting to hear since this whole thing began. "What happened then?" I asked.

"I told Jake that we weren't going to tell the cops a thing. That he had to disappear, go to the little hideaway he had in the Hamptons. Chilly didn't know about the place. Then I told him that I'd hire a private detective to find him. That you would get the evidence we needed and turn it over to the cops."

"So you hired me, and led me into all this."

"I didn't mean for anybody to get hurt."

"Except me."

"This is your business, Nick. You were getting paid to take the risk."

"Who hit me that first night in Jake's apartment?"

"Jake. He went there to put the formula in the safe so you would find it, but you got there first. He thought Chilly sent you, so he took off your glove to get your fingerprints on something, so the police would connect you to Chilly."

"How did Jake break his neck?"

"The night that you went to see Lisa Ellison."

"Yeah, what about it?"

"After you left her house, she went to see Chéz

to find out what was going on. They argued, but Chéz didn't tell her anything."

"Chésará was in on it too."

"Of course she was. Lisa told Chéz that she thought she knew where Jake might be, and she was going out there in the morning. Chéz called me and I went out there to warn him."

"Why?"

"She didn't need to know. Lisa is weak. If anybody put pressure on her, she'd give the whole thing up and that would ruin everything. I went out there to tell Jake she was coming and not to let her know he was there."

"What happened?"

"When I got there, I told Jake that Lisa was coming out there and that he shouldn't talk to her."

Wednesday, July 15, 11:45 PM

"Why not, Gee?"

"Don't you see how that will ruin everything? If she knows where you are, she'll give you up the first time somebody asks her anything. You know how she is, Jake. If Chilly steps to her and says boo, you know she'll drop the whole thing."

"Okay, okay. Anything else I need to know about?"

"Yes."

"What now?"

"There is something else I have to tell you." Mrs. Childers stood up and walked to the window. She didn't want to be the one to have to tell him, but he needed to know. She took a deep breath and turned to face Jake. "I don't know how to say this any other way, so I'm just gonna drop it. LaShawn is dead."

Jake jumped up from the couch. "What?"

"She's dead, Jake. And so is Pamela."

"What? How?"

"They both OD'd on that stuff you created."

"That's not possible!"

"I'm sorry, Jake."

Jake ran up the stairs and she went after him. He stopped at the top of the steps and he started to cry. "Why?"

"You said it yourself. Everyone who knew about it had to die."

"But Pamela didn't have anything to do with this. Why'd Chilly have to kill her?"

"I don't know."

"You didn't say anything about that. They weren't supposed die." He was getting hysterical. "That wasn't part of your great plan, Gee!" He grabbed her shoulders and started to shake her. "Why, Gee? Why? Why did they have to die?" Jake screamed.

"Stop it! You're hurting me."

"Why?" Jake screamed.

"He just kept shaking me. He was hurting me! So I pushed him off. I didn't think I pushed him that hard, but he lost his balance and fell down the steps. I tried to grab him, Nick, but I couldn't hold him. As long as I live, I never will forget how he looked. His head was tipped to the side, lying there like he was staring at me. I ran down the steps. I shook him. I screamed his name, but he was dead."

She started crying.

I didn't sweat her about it. She killed her brother. I couldn't even imagine the burden she must be carrying around with her. "I didn't mean to kill him. Really, I didn't push him that hard. I didn't! He just lost his balance."

I put my arms around her and held her, trying to give her a chance to compose herself. I still had a lot more questions to ask. I didn't want to, but I had to. "What did you do then?"

She tried to pull herself together enough to answer me. "I panicked. I ran out of there."

"Where'd you go?"

"I went to Chéz's apartment and told her what happened. I was practically hysterical, but Chéz was calm. Calmer than I was, anyway. She cried a little and said that we would deal with it in the morning. Then she gave me some of her sleeping pills and made me go to bed. We went back out there early the next morning. We both cried when we first saw him laying there, staring at us. Chéz rushed over and closed his eyes, then she turned to me.

"She told me, 'We got to move the body, Gee.' I told her no, we should call the police, but she practically slapped me. Things had gone too far. If we called the police, I would be the one going to jail."

I didn't respond, but waited silently for her to finally give me the rest of the truth. She continued uneasily.

"Chéz went and got a blanket, and we wrapped him up in it. It wasn't easy, but we dragged him out to the car and into the trunk. Chéz told me we would make it look like Chilly killed Jake."

"How?"

"She pulled out a gun and shot Jake in the head."

I raised my eyebrows, waiting for further explanation.

"Remember I told you Chilly shot Jake in the leg once when I tried to run away?"

I nodded.

"Well, he left his nine with Chéz that night. Said it was to remind her that if she went to the police, he'd come back and use it to kill her. Chéz still had that gun, and she brought it to Jake's that night. When she pulled it out of her purse, I didn't even have time to react before she shot Jake in the head. Once she calmed me down, she explained that the cops would trace the bullet to Chilly when they found Jake's body."

She paused for a minute, wringing her hands before continuing. "We heard a car pull up in the driveway. We turned around and Lisa was getting out of her car. She ran toward us screaming. She saw Chéz shoot him. We tried to explain, but she wouldn't listen. She just kept screaming 'You killed him!' Then she ran back to her car and drove away. We went after her. She drove to her house and went inside. She had calmed down a little by that time, and she let us in. I told her what happened and why we did what we did.

"She told us we were crazy if we thought she was going to believe that story, then she picked up the phone. She said, 'All I know is that I saw you kill Jake.' She was calling the police.

"Chéz said, 'I can't let you do that, Lisa.' She

told Lisa to put the phone down. Said this was our chance to finally be free from that animal Chilly."

Mrs. Childers dropped her head and stared at the floor as she continued.

"Chéz pulled out the gun and pointed it at Lisa. She told her again to put the phone down. When Lisa saw the gun, she freaked out and ran at Chéz. They fought for the gun. I started screaming at them to stop, but they just kept going.

"The gun went off. I looked at Lisa. I could see it in her eyes. Chéz dropped the gun and backed away from her. I watched Lisa fall to the floor."

"Don't tell me. It was an accident."

"Nick, you have to believe me. I'm telling you the truth. That's exactly how it happened. We never meant to kill anybody. We never meant for any of this to happen."

"That's a pretty fantastic story." I got up and looked around, then picked up my glass and walked slowly into the other room. I needed a drink. I poured a glass of Johnnie Black and drank it down. I poured another one. I could hear her crying. I didn't know what I was going to do. I thought about calling the police, but I didn't want to. She was in enough pain. She had killed her brother, and she was just as responsible for Lisa's death as Chésará. Maybe it was an accident. Her story fit the facts. I couldn't be sure. She had been lying to me from the start. Everything she had told me was a lie. She was good at it. I poured her a shot of Henessey and took it to her. "Here, drink this. You look like you could use it."

Her hands were shaking. "Thank you." She drank hers straight down and let the empty glass fall out of her hand. She looked up at me with those eyes. They didn't look so pretty now. Her tears left a trail of black mascara. "What are you gonna do now? Are you gonna call the police?"

"No. Well, that depends."

"On what, Nick?"

"You have anything else you want to tell me about?"

"Like what?"

"Did you kill Pamela or LaShawn?"

"No."

"What about Rocky? You and Chésará kill him too?"

"No!"

"You sure?"

"No! I mean yes! I'm sure."

"Who shot Monika?"

"I don't know."

"What about Jett? Who killed Jett?"

"I don't know anything about either of them, Nick. Please, you've got to believe me."

"Why should I believe you now?" I had to ask. "You've told me nothing but lies since page one. Why should I believe anything you tell me now, Mrs. Childers? I'm sorry, *Gee*. Tell me, why should I?"

"I have no reason to lie to you now."

I finished my drink and stood up. "Okay." I picked up the phone and dialed.

"Who are you calling?"

"I'm not calling the police."

Freeze answered on the first ring. "Yo."

"I need you to back me up."

"When and where?"

"Now. I'll be there to pick you up in about an hour."

"I'll be here."

I hung up the phone and started for the door. Mrs. Childers got up and ran behind me. "Where are you going?"

"To a family reunion."

Chapter Twenty-five

I was tired.
I hadn't slept in two days.
And I needed a shower.
But I didn't care.

I drove as fast as I could to Cuisine to pick up Freeze. As I drove, I couldn't help but think about the story I'd just heard.

"Wow." That was about all I could say about it. "Wow."

I had to reconcile within myself the fact that Chilly hadn't killed Jake or Lisa. He probably didn't have anything to do with Rocky, Pamela, or LaShawn either. I pretty much figured that LaShawn's death was, like everything else, an accident. She more likely than not just got a hold of the wrong package.

It was Gee who dominated my thoughts. I couldn't turn her over to the police. She had been through enough in her lifetime. Her life to this point had been filled with nothing but betrayal and violence.

For the rest of her life, she would have to deal with
the sight of Jake's dead body staring at her. She
would hear his last words, "Why, Gee?" over and
over again. She would have to live knowing that
Chésará killed Lisa so she could be free. And all
this was the result of her association with Chilly.

That to me was punishment enough.

But now Chilly was dead.

I killed him.

He had caused so many people so much pain.
In a way, he was responsible for all the deaths.
Maybe he deserved to die, maybe not. It wasn't for
me to judge. I understood now why it was so important for Mike to get out of the drug business
and go legit. He had too much of a conscience,
too much love for life to continue with the legacy
that André set out for us, the path Chilly followed.
I respected and appreciated Black more now than
I had at any time in the last ten years. When all this
was over, I had to call and thank him, not only for
bailing me out, but for giving me so much to remind me of who I am and where I came from.
Maybe I would even swallow my pride and make
peace with Bobby. It was long overdue.

When I got to Cuisine and went inside, I found
Freeze sitting by the door, ready to go. "What took
you so long?"

"Traffic."

"Well, let's go," he said, practically jumping to
his feet.

"You drive." We started out the door. "Wait! I
need three clean weapons."

"Three nines?"

"No, forty-fives."

"You? Packin' a forty-five? Why the change?" he asked as we got in his truck.

"Kirk knows that a nine is my weapon of choice. And I'm tired of talkin' to him."

"Oh, by the way," Freeze said. "Wanda came here looking for you."

"Did she really?"

"Yeah, she did. She said if I saw you I should tell you not to do anything stupid."

"Okay, you told me. And I'm not going to do anything stupid. I'm going to kill somebody, and you're going to make sure that I don't do anything stupid."

"You startin' to sound like the Nick I used to know."

"I'm startin' to feel like him too."

"It's good to have you back, Nick. I don't want to sound soft or nothin' like that, but I missed you, man."

"I missed all of you."

We stopped at Cynt's, one of the gambling houses we'd run for years. *We*. I felt a part of all this again. Maybe this was what Wanda meant when she said I needed to recognize.

"Hey, Freeze. And who is this fine-ass man you got with you?" Cynt said as she twisted her hips in our direction.

"How's it going Cynt?"

She threw her arms around my neck and gave me a kiss that raised an eyebrow on Freeze, like there was some past thing between us that I never knew about.

"How are you, Nick? I heard you were back in the city. I was wondering, like everybody else, why you hadn't come around. But I see you picked back up with your old thug buddy here."

"Let's go to your office, Cynt. I need to get something out of your safe," Freeze said.

"You two, rollin' together, just like old times." Cynt said and turned toward the steps to her office.

I looked at Freeze. He looked at me. We both watched Cynt walk her big, pretty ass up the steps. We both smiled. "Just like old times."

Once we were in her office, Cynt opened the safe and stepped aside. She had a small arsenal in that safe. "Help yourself. They're all clean, acid on the serial numbers. Damn near impossible to trace."

I stepped up and picked out three .45's and two silencers. Freeze grabbed one too and an AK-47. "Just in case things get thick out there."

"That should thin things out nicely," Cynt threw in.

"Got any gloves, Cynt?" I asked.

"What do I look like, Macy's?"

"Come on, Nick. I got some for you in the truck. Let's go."

"Good to see you again, Cynt," I said as I followed Freeze out of the office.

Cynt grabbed my arm.

"You make sure you come back and see me soon, Nick," she said and kissed me on the cheek.

"I'll do that."

* * *

As soon as we got in the truck, Freeze turned to me and shook his head. "What's up with you and Cynt?"

"I swear, man, I don't know what was up with that."

"Nigga, when you gonna get enough of fuckin' with Bobby's women?" Freeze laughed. "I'm just fuckin' with you, kid."

"Bobby still fuckin' Cynt?"

"Nah, Pam got that nigga pussy-whipped and on lockdown since the day she met him."

"Pam, that his wife?"

"Yeah, she's a good girl. Real solid, you know. She's been good for Bobby. Mellowed him the fuck out."

"Maybe after this is over with we can roll by there."

"Time you and Bobby made peace and put that Camille shit behind y'all. Bitch been dead for ten fuckin' years and shit."

"I feel you."

"Where the fuck we going, anyway?"

"Greenwich."

"Connecticut?"

"Yeah. Wake me up when we get there."

When we got to the house, there was a gated entry and a guard posted. I told Freeze to roll by so we could get a look at the place. I sure missed Jett. He would have tapped into some satellite and had a birdseye view of the setup. But that wasn't the only reason I missed him. He was a good friend. I thought about Monika lying in that hospital bed, fighting for her life. I was here for them.

I didn't see any camera surveillance, but I knew there had to be some. Once I had satisfied myself with the layout of the grounds, I told Freeze to give me five minutes and then drive to the gate and I would join him there.

I made my way around to the gate and put the silencers on the guns and waited in the brush for Freeze to pull up. As he approached the gate, the guard came out and stopped him.

"Good evening, sir. Can I help you?"

"No, but he can." Freeze pointed at me.

"What?"

He turned around and I put two shots in his head. I dragged him into the guard shack and opened the gate. Freeze drove through the gate. I got back in the truck, and we headed for the house. He stopped the truck around the side of the house. "Well, what's the plan?"

"Give me five minutes, then come in after me."

"You got it."

I moved toward the house, staying in the shadows. The lock was no problem. I moved quickly through the house, guns drawn, looking for my objective, checking each room before moving on to the next. The thought did occur to me that the bastard might not be there. If he wasn't, I'd burn the bitch down.

"Monika would like that," I said to myself.

I heard footsteps coming toward me. I got out of sight. Once he passed me, I put two in the back of his head. I dragged his body into the first room I came to. I recognized him. He was Lieutenant Commander Snow. He was in command of a different special ops unit, but he was a part of our little community. At that point, I knew I was in the right place.

I had been through all the downstairs rooms and was making my way up the steps when I heard more footsteps coming. I put my guns in their holsters and went over the rail. I would hold on until they passed.

I watched as they stopped at the top of the steps and talked. I hoped it wouldn't be a long conversation. My arms were starting to hurt. They started down the steps. I was in a bad spot if they saw my hands. I gave some thought to letting go if they did. I looked down. "Bad idea."

Fortunately, they passed me by. Once they were out of sight, I came back over the rail and continued up the stairs. I could have shot them too, but I figured it would give Freeze something to do. He always did like to compare body counts.

I walked down a long hallway until I saw a light coming from an open door. As I got closer, I heard voices. I heard his voice. My heart began racing and I moved faster. I came through the door and there he was, Uncle Felix, seated behind a marble desk. I should have blasted him on sight, but first I had to know why.

"Come on in, Nick. We've been expecting you," Felix said with a smile. "Have a seat."

I took a step closer.

"Why don't you just put those guns down, nice and slow, while you at it, Nick?" I recognized that southern accent. I turned to see General Peterson seated on the couch with an M16 pointed at me. He was my commanding officer for our last tour of duty. It was all starting to come together. I took a deep breath and complied with his orders.

"That's a good soldier, Nick, but you always were," the general said, laughing. "Shit, I got half a dozen men in this house and one at the gate, but you walked right by them like it wasn't shit, didn't you, Nick?"

"Sit down, Nick. Take a load off," Felix said.

"I told you he was the best soldier I ever commanded, Felix. Made you a damn good operative, didn't he?"

"Yeah, he was good."

"Tell me about it, Felix. Why'd you do it?"

"Do what, Nick? Oh, you mean Jett and Monika, don't you?"

"Yeah. Monika was too good to be taken by any of Chilly's boys without gettin' off a shot. It had to be you."

"No, Nick, it was me," the general said. "Monika let me in, no problem. Perkins—that was the boy that Jett cut up—well, she made him while she was out on her little date with Chilly. Once he was compromised, it wouldn't take her long to put it all together just like you did. So we had to kill her. Then Jett showed up. Perkins covered while I left. His orders were to kill Jett, but you see how that turned out."

"Then you brought in a cleaner to clean up after Jett. Who killed Jett?"

"Lieutenant Commander Snow had that honor," the general said. "Jett saw us when we were coming out of the house where he killed Perkins, so we let him follow us to Chilly's house. Your boy was careless, Nick. He let Snow walk right up on him and shoot him with a twenty-two in the ear. Very effective."

"I just want to know why."

"Well, for that I got to take you back a ways," Felix said as he got up and poured himself a drink.

"You see, Nick, the whole time you were in South America, you may have been under the general here's command, but you were working for me."

"Just what were we doing down there, Felix?"

"You were conducting the war on drugs as an agent of the United States Government, sort of," Felix said. He and the general laughed, but I wasn't amused. Maybe they would let me in on the joke.

"Well, not exactly," the general said.

"You and your unit were there, not to stop the flow of drugs into this country, but to streamline it. You see, Nick, I have a friend down there. He came to me and asked for my help in eliminating some of his competition. In return, we would be partners in his rather lucrative enterprise."

"Cocaine."

"Right. So, I went to my friend the general here, and he was kind enough to donate the services of your unit. But he said to me that instead of just eliminating some of his competition, hell, let's get rid of all the bastards or at least do damage to their operations."

"So you sent us down there to assassinate key people and destroy drug labs. The whole time we're thinking it's for good old Uncle Sam, we were doing it all for good old *Uncle* Felix. Good plan. What went wrong?"

"Who said anything went wrong? You and your unit were doing an excellent job," Felix said smugly. "Especially your team, Nick. The entire campaign was a success."

"That's right. Your team was especially destructive. That Monika sure can blow some shit up," the general added. "How is she doing anyway, Nick? I understand it doesn't look good for her."

"She's a fighter. She's gonna make it."

"No, she's not, Nick. If she makes it out of intensive care, she'll be dead before she gets to her room," Felix said.

"We'll see about that. But we'll pass that for now. So, you brought us all back together to eliminate the eliminators, but we fucked it up when Monika broke her ankle. We were all supposed to die that day."

"I knew you were smart enough to figure that much out," the general said. "I was just gonna line you all up and shoot you, but Felix said that he could use your team for some other jobs he had going. Said you three had a skill set that he would make excellent use of. So, I got y'all out from down there. Handled the debriefing myself, and turned you over to Felix."

"I figured that part out too. As long as Felix had his hand around our throats and we didn't know what was really going on down there anyway, we were non-threatening. What happened to change that?"

"My friend wasn't the only one with influential friends. There were stories in some circles of American servicemen participating in a drug eradication effort. If those stories ever made their way to Capitol Hill, there would be hell to pay," Felix said. "And all that hell would fall on me, Nick."

"You three were the only ones who lived, and like I said, you were smart enough to figure it out," the general said.

"And I wasn't gonna take the chance of you bein' subpoenaed to testify before some fuckin' Senate subcommittee," Felix said.

"So, you killed Jett and you tried to kill Monika."

"I didn't want to, Nick, but you can surely see where I didn't have a choice in the matter. You three were the best operatives I had. It's gonna be hard to replace you," Felix said.

"What about me? Why didn't you try to kill me?"

"You're a killer, Nick. You would be hard to kill. I thought about asking you to join us, but as your presence here proves, you're too damn loyal to your friends. Even if you said you would go along with it, there would always exist the possibility that you would flip and try to kill us all. Anyway, since you were making a fool of yourself playing private detective, I just figured that either that animal Chilly would kill you, or the cops would have you for murder. But if neither one of those options panned out, don't think I wouldn't send a team to kill you. And they would have to be good to get the job done."

"Thanks for the compliment."

"No problem."

"Well, gentlemen, I've heard enough." I started to reach for my third weapon.

"Good, so have I."

I turned around as Freeze came through the door and fired two shots to the general's head. Then he turned to Felix and fired two shots at him.

"What'd you do that for?" I screamed.

"What are you talkin' about? You said you had heard enough. I figured that meant it was time for them to die."

"Yeah, but I wanted to kill Felix."

"I tell you what, I'll let you kill the next one."

"It's not the same. Fuck it, never mind. Let's just get the fuck outta here."

Freeze walked over and looked at Felix. "Why didn't you tell me he was the one you were lookin' for?"

"You know him?"

"Shit, yeah. Didn't you hear him? He's partners with Estabon, who supplies Chilly."

"Why didn't you tell me?"

"You didn't ask me about him or Estabon. You just asked me about Chilly."

"Damn."

"Sorry, Nick. How was I supposed to know?"

"Forget it, man. Thanks for havin' my back."

"Anyway, what were you gonna do with your guns on the floor?"

"I had three guns, remember."

"That's right. Yo, I was listening to them talk about you. You that bad a muthafucka?"

"Yeah."

"Well, come on, Shaft, and I'll buy you a drink."

"Okay, but just a quick one. I got one more body to account for."

"You ain't thinking 'bout going to Peru to kill Estabon, are you?"

"No. Something a little closer to home."

Chapter Twenty-six

"Who is it?"

"It's Nick."

Felicia opened the door and let me in. She threw her arms around my neck and kissed me. "I'm so glad to see you." She kissed me again and again. I was glad to see her too.

"Surprised to see me?"

"Yes. I heard about Chilly. I thought you were in jail."

"Wanda got me out."

"Who is Wanda? Should I be jealous?"

"No. Wanda is not only family to me, but she's my lawyer."

"All right now. I just want to know who the players are in this game before I get in."

"Baby, this ain't no game."

"Oh, so you the real thing, huh?"

"Is there anything to drink?"

"Sure. I have a bottle of Zinfandel. You want some?"

"Is that a trick question?"

"What do you—" She looked confused. "Oooohh! You want some?" Felicia got up to get the wine. "Nick, you can have all you want of this. As much as you want of this."

She returned with two glasses and sat down next to me. "Here you go, baby. You look tired."

"I really haven't slept in a couple of days." Felicia looked sad. "Smile, Felicia. I ain't ever that tired." She smiled and sipped her wine.

"What happened with the police?"

"I'm out on bond, but Wanda thinks they'll be willing to accept that my killin' Chilly was self defense."

"That's good. What about the rest of them?"

"I think they'll probably drop the whole thing on Chilly and call it a day. He was responsible for all of it anyway." I finished my wine. "Felicia, do you mind if I take a shower?"

"Not at all." She popped up from the couch and held out her hand. "Come with me. Let me get you some towels."

"Thank you. A nice hot shower is what I need," I said as Felicia turned on the light in the bathroom. "It will help me relax."

She turned on the shower and started to undress me. "Not too relaxed that you pass out on me."

I shook my head.

"I could use a shower too. You want some company in there?" she asked as she removed the last of my clothes.

"Is that a trick question?" I got in the shower.

*   *   *

Felicia bathed me, then we made love in the shower, and again once we made our way to the bed. I enjoyed making love to her. In spite of her tough cop exterior, Felicia was an extremely sensual and highly sexual woman. While we made love, I had to ask myself a question. Was I in love with her? And would it make things any different?

As advertised, I waited until after we made love to pass out. When I woke up, Felicia was gone. "Felicia!"

"I'm in the kitchen. Don't get up. I'm fixing you breakfast." She stuck her head in the room. "How does breakfast in bed sound to you?"

"Great. You're all right, you know that?"

"I'm more than all right, but I'm breakin' it on you slowly. I wouldn't want you to feel overwhelmed. I know how you men are."

Felicia went back to the kitchen while I got up and went to the bathroom. I took care of matters in the bathroom, got back in the bed, and waited for Felicia. She came in carrying a tray with a flower in a vase. She made Spanish omelets, hash browns with link sausages. "Toast, coffee, and a Mimosa."

"All this for me?" I said, trying my best to look surprised and honored all at once. "Will you be joining me?"

"Of course. I'll be right back." She came back with her food and got in bed next to me. She was a good breakfast cook. I'd be interested to see if that translated to being a good cook period. We ate and talked. Sausages inspired sexual innuendo, mostly. I told her about Monika and Jett; she cried a few tears for me.

Man, I was diggin' her.

When we finished eating, Felicia took the trays back to the kitchen. She came in the room, got back in bed and snuggled up close to me. Felicia told me she had an appointment with her professor the next day, to talk about getting back into law school. "Now that it's over, I want to try to get my life back."

"That's good that you're gettin' your life back. But there's something that has always bothered me."

"What's that?"

"Why did you leave?"

"I told you, I was afraid."

"You know I don't believe that. If Chilly had Pamela killed because she knew what was going on, what did you have to be afraid of?"

"He might have thought that she told me." Felicia looked away.

I touched her shoulder. "Look at me, Felicia. Why'd you come back?"

"I told you, I missed you."

"It's over, Felicia. Chilly's dead. Jett's dead. Monika may die." I put my arm around her. "Please tell me the truth."

"Nick." She kissed me on the cheek. "I told you the truth, I came back because I missed you, and you gave me the courage to face things. To finish what I started."

"What was that?"

"I told you why I left the force. Well, I didn't tell you the whole story . . . Once the shooting stopped, Morgan and I searched the house. I told you about the cocaine. Well, there was a hundred and fifty thousand dollars in cash. Morgan said we could split it. He said he had an old friend who could get rid of the drugs for us, but I told him no, I didn't want anything to do with the drugs. Morgan said fine, I could keep all the money. He could make twice that from selling the drugs."

"That's why you were so worried about the cops investigating you. You were afraid they would find out."

"Yes." Felicia looked away, but she turned back quickly. "So we robbed a bunch of dead drug dealers. Nobody would care about that, right?"

"You would think. What happened?"

"It was Rocky we robbed."

"When did you find that out?"

"I was looking at some of Pamela's pictures. I recognized two of them from pictures she took at Jake's party. Then Morgan called me and said that Rocky knew. He said he would kill both of us if we didn't give back the drugs and the money."

"How did he find out it was you two?"

"Morgan's source. He tried to sell the dope to one of Rocky's people, who then told Rocky he got it from Morgan. Before they killed him, Morgan called and said he wanted to see me. He had bought into his uncle's bar in Queens. He said to meet him there and we would figure out what to do. But he was dead when I got there. Police called it a robbery."

"What happened then?"

"Nothing."

"Nothing?"

"For the next couple of months, nothing happened. Then about a month ago, Rocky called me. He told me he wanted the money back, or what happened to Morgan would happen to me. I was supposed to meet Rocky here the night Pamela

died. I tried to call Pamela, to tell her to stay away
from here, but I never did catch her. Pamela was
dead when I got here."

"Is that why you killed Rocky?"

"Pamela died for something me and Morgan
did. When I woke up and you were gone that
morning, I called Rocky and told him I only had
half of the money. He said to meet him at his club
that night. I had the money, but I knew he would
kill me anyway, whether I gave it to him or not."

"That much was obvious."

"I waited outside the club until I saw him pull
up in the convertible. Two of his boys were up
front; Rocky was in the back seat. I walked up to
the car and shot the three of them in the head.
Then I swung around and put one each in their
chests. I threw the gun on Rocky's lap and got
away from there."

"Nobody would care if three piece of shit drug
dealers whacked in the street, right?"

"That was my plan, Nick. I made it look like it
was just another drug-related murder."

So, there it is. I had actually solved the case. The
big question now was, what was I going to do about
it? I didn't know what I was gonna do. I knew one
thing for sure. I knew then that I was finished trying to play private detective. Too much like being
a cop for me. I looked over at Felicia. I put my
arms around her, and she rested her head against
my chest. Whether I was in love with her or not, I
couldn't turn her over to the police for what she'd
done. She didn't do anything that I hadn't done.
Felicia got revenge for her friend. I couldn't roll

her over for that. Just like I couldn't turn in
Mrs. Childers, or Chésará for that matter. I just
couldn't see myself helping the police. If they figured it out on their own, that would be different.
But I knew they would make Chilly the fall guy.

   Case closed.

Chapter Twenty-seven

"Oh, Nick! That feels so good," Vivian moaned. I looked down at the dance floor at Impressions. From above the stage, I could see the entire club. I came here with Freeze. He didn't tell me where we were going, he just said, "We need to ride." Next thing I knew, we're gettin' valet parked at the club. "What we doing here?"

"Time you and Bobby made peace and put that Camille shit behind y'all. Bitch been dead for ten fuckin' years."

Now, why he wanna go and do that?

Freeze knew I'd had a rough week. I wanted to relax, clear my mind, and have a little fun. I needed to think about where I was going from where I was. But I got lucky; Bobby had already left for the night. "Good. I wasn't up for that tonight anyway." That's when I saw an old girl friend of mine named Vivian Merrick, who was more than willing to take a trip down memory lane with me. Her company was just what I needed to take my mind off of everything I had been through.

I had just come back from Jett's funeral in Iowa. Explaining to Jett's parents how and why he died was hard, but it was harder to tell Monika. The afternoon she came out of her coma, I ran frantically down the hall, screaming for a doctor or a nurse or anybody. Once the doctor checked her out, she left us alone. I told Monika that Jett was dead and how things played out with Chilly. She cried softly when I told her about Jett. "I'm going to take his body home to his parents in Iowa tomorrow," I said. "I talked to them yesterday. The funeral's gonna be on Saturday."

"I'm going with you," Monika said softly as the tears poured from her eyes.

"Monika, I don't think you'll be strong enough to leave the hospital in time for the funeral."

"Don't argue with me, Nick. He saved my life and yours, too. He died going after the bastard that shot me. I have to go," Monika mumbled as she began to drift off to sleep.

"You get some rest and we'll talk about it in the morning." I knew better than to argue with her. Even in her condition, Monika was still as strong-willed as ever.

As promised, Monika went to Jett's funeral, albeit in a wheelchair and in the company of a private nurse. After the funeral, I took Monika back to the hospital and sat with her a while until she went to sleep. I left there and went to check on Gee. I walked up to the house and saw the FOR SALE sign in the yard. I drove downtown to Chésará's apartment building. The doorman told me that Ms. Rollins had moved out and he was not at liberty to say any more on the matter. I was happy for them. They were finally free.

"Nick, that feels so good," Vivian moaned. "You're gonna make me cum!"

"Nick! You up here?" Freeze yelled, seeming to appear from nowhere.

"Yeah!"

"Well come on. I'm ready to go."

"Alright . . . alright . . ." My voice trembled. "I'm coming."

"Well hurry up then," Freeze said shaking his head as he turned away. "You ain't changed a bit."

Once I finished doing my thing with Vivian, I met Freeze at the bar and got myself a drink. Freeze looked at me and shook his head. "You ain't changed a bit, nigga."

"Give me a break. I'm tryin' to relax."

"You looked pretty intense from where I was standing."

"Whatever."

"I gotta go by the office, then we outta here. Come on."

"What you gotta go to the office for? Bobby ain't up there is he?"

"No, Wanda's up there. She got something for me, so stop actin' like a bitch and come on."

I followed Freeze upstairs to the office. I didn't appreciate him calling me a bitch, but if I wanted to be honest with myself, he was right. After reading Camille's journal and talking to Wanda about it, it made the whole situation easier to deal with. In fact, it was like a tremendous weight that I'd dragged around with me for years had been lifted from my shoulders. I needed to put this shit behind us and move on. So, what was my problem? The fact remained that I was fuckin' Camille behind his back. I didn't think that Bobby would pull out his gun and shoot me on sight, but I wouldn't put it past him. I did some foul shit, and now I had to step up and face it.

Freeze burst into the office. "What's up, Wanda! What you got for me?"

I followed him in. There was a woman standing by the window, wearing a tight black mini-skirt and black heels. She turned around, and to my surprise, it was Wanda.

"I got a message for you. It wasn't anything that couldn't have waited," Wanda said as she walked toward Bobby's desk. "How you doing tonight, Nick?"

"I'm good. How are you?"

"I'm tired and I'm ready to go home. But Bobby wants me to see tonight's act. What's he call himself?"

"The One," Freeze said.

"Whatever," Wanda said as she leaned over the desk looking for the message.

I'd seen her in a business suit and a big fuzzy robe, but if I had any remaining doubts about how fine Wanda had gotten, the black mini crushed them. Those beautiful legs led up to a near-perfect ass and that slim waist. Felicia Hardy crossed my mind. She had jumped back into law school and didn't seem to have a minute to talk anymore. Or maybe she was tryin' to tell me something.

"I'll see what he got," Wanda said. "You two gonna stay and watch the show with me?"

"No, I gotta roll. Doc said some niggas was tryin' to post up in his spot," Freeze said before I had a chance to say yes. Wanda looked momentarily disappointed, but she covered it up.

"Here it is," she said, handing Freeze a piece of paper.

"Derrick Washington?" Freeze said in surprise. "What Curl want?"

"I don't know. He just said to call him."

"Derrick Washington. I heard that name before," I said.

"You should have. You made him somebody when you killed Chilly," Freeze spit out.

"Chilly's lieutenant." I had been trying to put all that behind me, but I saw that wasn't happening.

"It's probably his boys that's tryin' to set up at Doc's. I'll be right back, Nick, then we going to Doc's." Freeze left the office, slamming the door behind him. I looked over at Wanda, who had taken a seat behind Bobby's desk. I expected her to say something about Chilly, but she didn't.

"You look tired, Nick."

"Yeah, maybe I need a vacation."

"Everything is taken care of with the police, so you might as well."

I laughed out loud. "I can't remember the last time I sat around somewhere with nothing to do all day."

"They tell me that's what people do on vacation. Try it, and let me know how it works out." Wanda laughed. "I haven't taken a vacation in years."

"Why don't you come with me?"

"Excuse me? Did you just invite me to take a vacation with you?" Wanda smiled. "What are you suggesting?"

"I didn't mean anything by it, Wanda. I was just sayin' that since you haven't taken one in years, you could probably use one too. I wasn't suggesting anything." I looked at Wanda, thinking that it wouldn't be such a bad idea.

"Well, thanks anyway, but I've got too much work to do. Where are you thinking about going?"

"I don't know. Maybe I'll go to the Bahamas, see Black. Meet our new queen." I regretted it as soon as I said it.

Wanda rolled her eyes. "That's a good idea. I know Black would like to see you. And when you get back, you and I need to sit down and go over some things."

"Like what?" I smiled and took a seat across from her.

"Business, Nick." Wanda smiled back.

"Business?"

"Just business. I don't know where your head is," Wanda paused, dropped her head, and quickly looked up. "I mean about what you wanna do now, but I know Black has some things he'd like to talk to you about."

"I've been thinkin' a lot about what I wanna do," I said suggestively.

"And what have you come up with?"

Just then, Freeze burst into the office. "Let's go, Nick," he barked.

I got up slowly.

"Good night, Nick. We'll finish our discussion when you get back," Wanda said suggestively.

"When you get back?" Freeze asked as we made our way down the stairs. "Where the fuck you going?"

"I'm going to meet Shy."

Chapter Twenty-eight

My cab pulled up in front of Black's Paradise, in Freeport, on Grand Bahama Island. I paid the cab driver and tipped him nicely. I opened my suitcase, and while the driver looked on in horror, I took my gun and extra clips out of the bag. I got out of the cab, put the gun in my waist and pulled my shirt down over it. I put the clips in my back pocket while I walked toward the door.

As I got closer, I could hear the sound of reggae music. I'd reserved a room at The Bahama Princess Hotel, but I decided to come to the club first. I went inside and wandered around looking for Black. Not seeing him anywhere I stepped to the bar to get a drink and ask for him. A very pretty bartender came over to see what I was drinking. "What can I get for you?" she asked.

"Johnnie Walker Black, straight up."

"Comin' up," she replied as she poured my drink. "Can I get you a menu?"

"Yeah," I said. "I heard the food was great here."

She handed me the menu and I glanced at it. "What do you recommend?"

"That depends. How hungry are you?"

"I haven't eaten all day, unless you call peanuts on the plane coming down here eating."

"Then you definitely want to try our Bahamian Platter. It's a taste of almost everything on the menu."

"Then that's what I'm having."

The bartender walked away to give the kitchen my order, but returned quickly. "Just got in, huh?"

"Yes," I said, taking a sip of my drink. "Just got in from New York."

"Really? I'm from New York."

"Oh yeah," I said, thinking that it figured that Black would hire somebody from New York to handle his money. "What part?"

"The Bronx."

"I'm from the Bronx. In fact, I came here to surprise an old friend. I was hoping he'd be here."

"Really? What's your friend's name?"

"Mike Black, is he here?"

"Who are you?"

"I'm sorry. My name is Nick Simmons."

The bartender smiled, "Well, it's a pleasure to finally meet you. I was beginning to think you were a figment of everyone's imagination."

"No, I'm for real." I paused. "You seem to have me at a disadvantage here. I mean, you seem to know me, but I haven't had the pleasure of making your acquaintance," I said, looking at the huge rock on her finger. *Why are all the really fine ones always married?*

"Oh, I'm sorry. My name is Shy. Mike Black is my husband," she said, extending her hand.

Not only is she married, but she's Black's wife. When will I ever learn? I shook her hand. "So, you're the famous Shy." She nodded and smiled. "Well, it is truly a pleasure to finally meet you, too. I've heard a lot about you, but I knew that you weren't imaginary. It took a real woman to get Black out of New York," I said finishing my drink. Shy poured me another and placed the bottle on the bar.

"It was Black's idea to move down here. It seemed like a good idea at the time. You know, fun and sun everyday. But to be honest with you, Nick . . ." Shy paused a second and looked around. "It's boring as hell here."

I laughed. "Really?"

"Yes, and it's too hot all the time. Some days I feel like David Ruffin, singing *"I Wish It Would Rain."* That is until it rains, I never knew it could rain so hard. And these women," Shy shook her head. "Let me stop."

"You just miss New York, that's all."

"You ain't told no lie there. But I guess you know that I'm a fugitive, so I can't go back to the city."

"Wanda hasn't been any help with that?" I asked.

"Not really. I mean, I give her credit. She did get the murder charges dropped, but she can't seem to be able to make no headway on the conspiracy to distribute. Sometimes I think she's glad I'm down here."

"Why do you think that?" I asked, thinking that she might be right.

"Come on, Nick. You've known her and Michael a lot longer than I have. Even though neither of them will say it and I've never asked either of them, I know at some point there was something going on between them. I know that whatever it was is over for Michael, but I think Wanda is still feelin' it."

"You sound a little jealous. Are you?"

"No!" Shy said quickly and louder than she needed to. "Well, maybe just a little. But I'm not worried about her. I got more than enough women to worry about on this boring ass island."

The cook brought my food before I could ask her what she was so worried about. Shy introduced me to the cook and told him that I was one of Black's best friends. "So the food better be good or he'll fire you." Shy laughed, sending the cook about his business with a very worried look on his face. I tore into the food like a man who hadn't eaten in weeks.

"Michael said you could eat. I'll let you eat in peace. I'll be back when you're done."

My mouth was too full to answer.

Once I finished eating, as promised, Shy returned and poured me another drink.

"So, I take it that Black's not here?"

"He's in New York."

"New York? Can't be. I just left there. Freeze dropped me off at Newark this morning. He can't be in the city and Freeze not know it." I laughed, then I thought better of it. *Suppose Black told her he was going to New York and went somewhere else?*

"No, he's there. Knowing those two, Freeze probably dropped you off at Newark and picked him up at Kennedy. You know how secretive they are."

I laughed, but I knew she was right.

Shy looked at me and leaned against the bar. "So, Black says you two have been friends since the first day you met."

"He said that?" I looked at Shy. Then it occurred to me that Black wouldn't have his wife bartending. I put my hand on my gun. "Is that what he told you?"

"Ain't that what happened?"

"No, we had a fight the first day we met."

"I'm glad you said that, Nick, 'cause I was gettin' ready to shoot your ass," Shy said then showed me the pump she kept under the bar. She reached for a glass and a bottle of Bacardi.

"I still might shoot you. Who won?"

"Come on, Nick." Shy smiled at me while she poured her drink. "You know you got your ass kicked."

I let go of my gun and laughed. "I'm glad you said that." I lifted my shirt to show her my gun. "So, why does Black have *you* bartending?"

"It's the manager's day off, so I'm just filling in for the regular bartender. He should be here by now."

For the next hour, Shy waited on customers while she and I talked and got better aquatinted. We talked a little this and that, Shy told me about how she and Black met, and about their adventures together. I talked about the old days running with Black, and about how I'd spent the last couple of weeks. And then the conversation turned. "Mind if I ask you a question?" Shy asked.

"Sure, go ahead."

"It's personal."

"Ask me whatever you want to know," I said, curious about what Shy wanted to know.

Shy took a deep breath, "What happened between you and Bobby? I know there's some drama with you two, but no one will ever say why."

"Did you ask Bobby?"

"No. Me and Bobby are cool, at least we are now, but I haven't felt comfortable enough with him to ask."

"And you feel comfortable with me?"

"Yes, I do."

I looked at Shy. "I know what Black sees in you."

"What's that?"

"It's your eyes."

"You do know him." Shy leaned against the bar. "He said I had beautiful eyes, very expressive eyes."

"Your eyes say, 'It's okay, Nick. You can tell me.'"

"Well?" Shy said.

She listened quietly while I told her the story. Once I finished, she said, "I understand why you're havin' such a hard time facing Bobby."

"You wanna share that wisdom with me?"

"You said it yourself. Betrayal. When you betrayed Bobby's trust, you said you felt like you betrayed everybody."

"And?"

"That includes you. You betrayed yourself. And that's what hurts you. So, now that you know the whole story, you're gonna have to forgive yourself for what happened. You were just a pawn in whatever game this woman was playing. Maybe when you forgive yourself, it will be easier for you to ask Bobby to forgive you."

I thought about what Shy said. "Maybe you're right. I dishonored myself and then ran away like a

coward. I have to move past that. Make peace with
Bobby and myself. Maybe then I won't feel like
such an outsider."

"That right," Shy said, then poured both of us another drink. "You know, you have very trusting eyes
too. Or maybe its because I feel like an outsider
sometimes too. I don't know. But I have to talk to
somebody or I'll go crazy." Shy took a sip of her
drink. "Black's not here because we had a fight last
night. He left the house and I haven't seen him
since. He may be in New York, or he may be right
here on this island. I don't know."

"What was the fight about?"

"You hit it dead center when you said I was
bored. I miss New York and I want to go home. I
really haven't made any real friends down here."
Shy leaned forward and whispered, "probably because I can't understand what they're sayin' half
the time." She laughed. "And these woman, oh
God. Why they all gotta fall all over my man. And
it's not just these island bitches. The tourists are
worse. Why do they have to have their half-naked
asses all up in his face, gigglin' over every word he
says while I'm standin' right there? I mean, Nick, I
try to rise above that 'cause I know he really ain't
like that anymore, but it's hard. Bitches ain't got
no respect."

"Sometimes gettin' bitches respect is overrated.
As long as Black shows you respect, fuck them
bitches. You're his wife."

"I know that, Nick. Michael shows me nothing
but love and respect. And I love him so much for
that. I know that's just something I got to get past.
I guess I'm just a jealous woman and I'm tired of it,
you know what I'm sayin'?" Shy poured herself an-

other drink, then she pushed the glass away. "But that's not the real issue. That was just something I threw in to spice things up a little, I guess." She laughed. "The fight was really about me wantin' to go back to New York."

"But you can't, because of the conspiracy charge," I said.

"He lost it when I told him that I would rather go home and do my time then stay down here. I don't want to be on the run for the rest of my life, Nick. I want to be free."

"I can understand that. I know what it's like to carry around a burden. Sometimes you got to face it, not run away from it," I said, knowing that I should take my own advice. Just then, I saw somebody I thought I knew sitting at a table by the door.

"Excuse me a minute, Shy. I'll be right back." I got up and walked over to him. "Roman. Roman Patterson?" I asked. The man didn't answer at first. He looked at the door then slowly at me.

"Nick Simmons?" he said quietly and looked back at the door. "What are you doing here?"

"I'm visiting some old friends." I started to sit down.

"Get away from me, Nick. I'm waiting for somebody," he said practically in a whisper.

"What?"

"I'm DEA, Nick. Get away from me," he said loudly enough for me to hear him this time. I turned quickly and walked away just as three men, one white and two Hispanic, entered the club and sat down at the table with Roman. I went back to the bar and sat down. Shy came over to me.

"What was up with that? You didn't know him?"

"He's DEA." I saw the expression on Shy's face. "Calm down. He's not here for you."

We looked on as the four men talked and laughed like old friends, until one of the Hispanic men glanced at me. The man stood up and looked directly at me, took out his gun, and shot the DEA agent in the head. Customers began running out the back door, turning over tables in their wake, while others dove on the floor. He turned and fired on me.

"Get down!" I yelled at Shy.

Shy ducked down behind the bar while I fired wildly then took cover behind a table. The other two men broke out semiautomatic weapons and began firing. They had me pinned down as they moved toward the door.

Shy reached for the pump. "Finally a little excitement on this rock." She rose up, took aim, fired at and dropped the Hispanic man with the semi. Shy took cover as the remaining two began shooting at her. This time it was me that came up blasting hitting the other Hispanic man who shot the agent. He went down.

Shy stayed low as she moved toward the end of the bar. She stood up and fired the pump just as the white man ran out the door. I came out from behind the table as Shy moved toward the door. With her back turned, she didn't see one of the men get up.

"Shy! Behind you!" I yelled and aimed my weapon, but it was too late. The man grabbed Shy and pointed his gun to her head.

"Drop it!" he yelled. Shy threw away the pump. "You too, drop it!" he yelled at me.

"Let her go!" I said, taking a step closer.

The man fired, barely missing Shy. "I'll kill her!"

I knew I should shoot the man in the head before he could get a shot off. And I was about to when the white guy burst though the door, firing that semi. It gave them enough time to get out the door. By the time I got outside, they were gone.

Now that the shooting had stopped, people started to get up off the floor and move around. The cook came out of the kitchen. "Go on and get out of here. I'll take care of things here," he said.

I grabbed a tablecloth and picked up the pump. I took my suitcase and left the club through the back door. I walked quickly and with my head down, past the crowd and along the beach until I reached the canal. Carefully, I wiped the pump clean and proceeded to smash it against the rocks. I picked up all the pieces and put them back in the tablecloth, then I walked down the canal and dropped broken pieces of the pump into the water. With all the pieces gone, I folded the tablecloth and put it in my suitcase. I made my way back to the main road and was able to flag down a cab. "Bahama Princess," I said as I got in the cab. "No, take me to the Lucayan Beach Hotel."

Once I arrived at the hotel, I checked in and went straight to my room. I opened the suitcase and took out the tablecloth and my gun. I put the gun on the nightstand and took the tablecloth down the hall to the laundry chute. I went back to the room and sat down on the bed. I tried but couldn't seem to make sense of what had just happened. I picked up the phone and called Freeze at Cuisine.

"Cuisine," Freeze answered.

"Freeze, it's Nick. Is Black there?"

"No, I thought he was down there with you. What's going on?"

"Some shooting went down at Black's club. And—"

Freeze interrupted. "Hold up, Nick. Wanda and Bobby are here. I'm gonna put you on speaker." *Great.* "Nick, you still there?"

"I'm here."

"Now, what happened?" Freeze asked.

"There was a shooting at Black's club. Bandits killed a DEA agent and took Shy with them when they left."

"What!" Freeze shouted.

"They took Shy."

"Took her where?" Wanda asked excitedly.

"I don't know."

"Start at the beginning, Nick. What happened?" Wanda asked.

"I saw a guy I knew. He turned out to be DEA. He wasn't there looking for Shy; he was just meeting somebody there. One of the people he met recognized me. When he saw me, he shot the agent and started shooting at me. Shy pulled out a pump from under the bar and started shooting back. One of them got behind Shy and grabbed her on the way out the door."

"Did you recognize any of them, Nick?" Wanda asked.

"No."

"What they look like?" Freeze asked.

"One Hispanic male, South American, I think. The other one was white. The Hispanic man's been shot."

"Damn!" Freeze said. "This is fucked up."

"What happened then, Nick?" Wanda asked. "What about the police?"

"I got out of there with Shy's pump and left the cook to deal with the cops."

"Okay, he's a good man. He knows how to handle the situation," Wanda said.

"That depends on who shows up," Freeze said.

"Where are you staying?" Wanda asked.

"Lucayan Beach."

"Okay, stay there. I'll call you back after I talk to the cook," Wanda said.

Before she disconnected the call, I heard Bobby say, "What's he been down there, four hours?"

End of Drug Related

Mike Black

Returns In

Payback

In Your Arms

A little something by roy glenn

Phase 1

It was just after ten o'clock when Marcus Douglas arrived at the Marriott Residence Inn. That afternoon he had his secretary, Janice, get a room for him in her name, in case Randa was looking for him. He walked down the long hall to his room and stuck the key card in the lock. He entered the room, dropped the key card on top of the television, and turned it on. While Peter Jennings reported the day's world news, Marcus wandered around aimlessly. This was his home now.

Marcus loosened his tie and took off his jacket. He reached in the pocket and pulled out a pack of cigarettes. It had been five years since he smoked his last Kool. He sat down on the couch and lit a cigarette, he took a long drag, and blew out the smoke. It hurt his chest and he coughed a little, but he hit it again. Today had been the worst day of his life.

If this was going to be his home for a while, there were a few things he'd need. "Soap, toothbrush and toothpaste. Deodorant would be a good thing. And I need to shave in the morning." He got up and started for the door. All he had were the clothes on his back. He would buy some clothes in the morning. "This is going to get expensive."

Marcus drove his 735i BMW down the street and turned into Krogers parking lot. It had been years since he had to shop for himself. Randa did all that for him.

He picked up a basket and headed for the pharmacy aisle. The store was quiet and empty for the most part. Marcus had picked up just about all the items he'd come for when the quiet was interrupted by the sound of high heels clicking against the tile.

His eyes were immediately drawn to the sound. There was a sense of urgency in her walk. Marcus glanced at her as she moved closer to him, and he had to take a closer look as she passed.

She stopped and tried on a pair of sunglasses and kept on walking. "I know her." He followed as she proceeded down the next aisle. When she stopped to pick up a box of hair color and some scissors, she turned and looked at him. Now he was sure. Although she turned away quickly, Marcus was sure that he knew her. "Yvonne Haggler." It had been nine years since he'd seen her. She looked good, even better then she did nine years ago. *If that's possible.* He remembered the day that she came to his office.

"Marcus."

"Yes, Janice."

"Your two o'clock is here."

"Give me five minutes then send her in."

Five minutes later, Yvonne Haggler was seated before him. She was an attractive young woman, barely twenty-one years old. She was simply but tastefully dressed. She didn't wear any makeup and her hair was pulled back in a ponytail. "Mrs. Haggler, tell me what I can do for you."

"Mr. Douglas, I need your help. My husband Richard died two months ago."

"I'm sorry to hear that."

"Thank you, Mr. Douglas." Yvonne spoke with the deep Mississippi accent that she hadn't managed to lose in the five years she'd been in Atlanta.

Yvonne was born and raised in Cold Water, Mississippi. The oldest of nine children, Yvonne was an average student in her junior year in high school. She met Richard Haggler when she was sixteen years old. He was twenty-eight. Richard was born in Cold Water as well, but his family moved away when he was ten. He came back to town to settle some personal matters for his recently deceased mother. When he met Yvonne, he fell deeply in love with the pretty young girl.

Two weeks later, Richard sought her mother's permission to marry Yvonne and take her back to Atlanta with him. Her father had died three years earlier and her mother was having problems making it by herself with nine children. Yvonne's mother had known Richard's family when they lived in Cold Water, and he seemed nice enough, polite, and respectful, and Yvonne did like him.

Richard had a good job and promised that he could make a better life for Yvonne in Atlanta. Cold Water was a small town, and her mother didn't have any money to send her daughter to college. She began to see this as an opportunity for her daughter to get away from there. Richard also promised he would be able to send Yvonne's mother some money every week to help out with the family. After very long and deep consideration, her mother consented for her daughter to be married.

They were married in a simple wedding a week

later, and that night they left for Atlanta. They
moved into Richard's mother's old house in Clarkston, a suburb of Atlanta. Richard was an old fash-
ioned man and insisted that Yvonne not work. He
told her she didn't have to finish high school if she
didn't want to, but Yvonne felt it was important
that she be the first in her family to graduate. Other
than going to school, she lived a quiet, somewhat
sheltered life as a housewife. She had a few girlfriends that she met in school, but Richard thought
it was inappropriate for a married woman to be
going to nightclubs and things like that, so Yvonne
made a very happy life for her and her husband.
She was totally dependent upon Richard for everything. She didn't mind, even though they didn't
have much money. Richard was a good man and
he treated her like a queen.

"Richard left a ten thousand dollar insurance
policy, and I gave it to the funeral people to pay
for his funeral. Well, my husband was a simple
man, and I thought he'd want to go out that way.
The whole thing came to a little less than seven
thousand dollars. They told me that they would
take care of things with the insurance company
and I'd get whatever was left over."

"That's pretty standard."

"But I still haven't got the money."

"Was there some problem with the policy?" Marcus asked as he took notes.

"I don't know. They wasn't tellin' me nothing.
Every time I called to find out what was going on,
they told me it would just be a few more days. Until
two days ago." Yvonne reached in her purse and

pulled out an envelope. She took out the letter and handed it to Marcus. "I got this in the mail. They said I could get my money after I signed it."

Marcus read over the letter while Yvonne continued talking. He glanced up at her and smiled. There was an innocence about her. She spoke without making eye contact. He thought that her accent was adorable.

"I showed that letter to my girlfriend Tyisha. Her mama died last year and she said she didn't have to sign nothing like this. She told me I should show it to a lawyer."

"Well, Mrs. Haggler, even though it doesn't come right out and say so, this letter is worded to give them power of attorney to settle your husband's estate."

"Estate? What estate, Mr. Douglas? Like I said, we're simple people. We got the house his mama left us. The house is paid for, but other than that, we ain't got nothing."

"It does seem a bit unusual to need power of attorney to settle an insurance policy. Have you spoken with the insurance company?"

"No, I just came to see you. Do you think I should sign it, Mr. Douglas?"

"No, Mrs. Haggler. I don't recommend you sign anything until you get some more information about why this is necessary. Would you like me to look into this for you, Mrs. Haggler?"

"Would you please, Mr. Douglas? Richard used to handle all the business for us. I'm not very good at talkin' to people like that."

"I would be happy to, Mrs. Haggler."

"Don't have much money. I been gettin' by on what money was in the checking account. But I just got a job at WalMart and I'm not making that much."

Marcus smiled at her as he got up and showed her to the door. "Don't worry about that now, Mrs. Haggler. For now all you need to do is see Janice before you leave. She has some paperwork for you to fill out. I'll look into it and get back with you in a few days."

Marcus was glad for something different to do. He had opened his own practice a year ago and dealt with the usual stuff. Accident cases, divorce, DUI's, but it would be nice for a change to actually help somebody. He would do it pro bono if he had to.

Marcus checked with the insurance company, and as he suspected, they informed him that they were waiting to receive power of attorney from her representative in order to settle Mrs. Haggler's claim. As it turned out, although Yvonne and Richard lived a simple life in their simple, paid for home in Clarkston, it wasn't because they didn't have any money.

Richard not only left her a ten thousand-dollar policy, there was also one for two hundred and fifty thousand. And that was just the tip of the iceberg. In addition to the insurance policies, there was a trust fund he had set up for her to receive once she turned thirty, worth another three hundred thousand. He also owned a number of properties in Georgia, Alabama, and Mississippi. Marcus estimated his estate to be worth well over a million dollars.

A week later, Marcus called Yvonne and asked her to drop by his office to discuss her case. She told him she was working that day and asked if he would mind staying late until she got off. "It's my first job, and I don't want to lose it."

He started to tell her that she could quit if wanted to, but he didn't want to tell her over the phone that she might stand to inherit quite a bit of money.

Yvonne arrived at the office a little after 7:30. "Thank you for waiting for me, Mr. Douglas. Did you find out something for me?"

"As a matter of fact, Mrs. Haggler, I have some very good news for you. Your late husband does have an estate to settle, and at this point, and mind you I've only made some preliminary inquires, but I estimate your husband's estate to be worth over a million dollars."

"Whaaat? You're kidding, right? That's not possible. Richard didn't have that kind of money. Where'd he get it?"

"I don't know at this time, but we'll find out." It was obvious to Marcus that Yvonne was taken completely by surprise by the revelation that she might be rich. "Do you know if your husband had a will?"

"Don't think so," Yvonne said as her smile widened.

"Have you gone through his things?"

"No, I haven't. I just didn't have the heart to. It just didn't seem right to start going through his stuff until he was resting peacefully. I was kinda waiting to settle this business first, and then I would go through his things."

"Do you know where your late husband worked, what he did for a living?"

"He worked as a property manager for Imperial Properties."

"That makes sense. He owns quite a bit of property. He might even own the company. Mrs. Haggler, what I want you to do is go home and go through your husband's things. See if you can find a will or any other legal documents. Have you been to his office to clean out his desk? Or had any contact with them at all?"

"No," Yvonne said with a shy smile. "I never even called them to say he was dead. They didn't call tryin' to find out why he didn't come to work. I just figured they didn't care."

Marcus smiled and let out a little laugh. "Call me in the morning and we'll make arrangements to go to Imperial Properties. But I don't want you to go there by yourself."

Yvonne went home and spent the rest of the night going through Richard's things. By 2:00 a.m. she had looked at every piece of paper in every file in Richard's office, but didn't find the will. However, if there was any doubt in her mind that Richard was much more financially well off than she was led to believe, none remained now. Yvonne found bank and dividend statements, and she knew she was going to be rich.

Yvonne left the office and headed for the closet in their bedroom. She stopped in front of the bed, realizing that this was the first time she had been in there since she found Richard dead of a heart attack.

Suddenly she felt tired. She'd gotten up early and had been on her feet all day, running the register. Yvonne took a deep breath and resumed her search. Still nothing. "Where else?" She wandered around the house, searching, and by 4:00, she was exhausted. She sat down in the living room and looked at their picture on the wall by the front door. That's when she saw it. "The hall closet." In a box on the shelf, Yvonne found a small metal box packed under a pile of old newspapers.

The metal box was locked, and for the next half an hour she tried to pick the lock with a hairpin. Finally, she went out to the garage and returned with a sledgehammer. The box surrendered its contents after her third swing. Yvonne picked up the papers and went through them. She found an envelope marked *Last Will and Testament*. She stood there awhile looking at the envelope, but she was afraid to open it. She put the envelope down on the coffee table, lay down on the couch, and went to sleep.

Once Marcus reviewed the will, the rest was simple. In addition to the insurance policies, the trust fund and the property, as expected, Richard was majority owner Imperial Properties and held stock in several companies. There was a provision in his will that in the event of his death, his partners would arrange financing to buy out his share of the company. The proceeds from that sale were to be given to his chosen heir, Yvonne Haggler.

When it was all said and done, Richard's estate was worth $2.2 million. Yvonne asked Marcus to liquidate his entire estate. Marcus was able to convince her to keep the stocks and make some investments that would provide her with an income from dividends.

After all the transactions were completed, Yvonne

moved to Los Angeles. Marcus received a letter from a lawyer named Tom Mack, informing him that he had been retained to handle her financial interests and that Marcus' services were no longer required. Marcus never saw or heard from her again. Until now.

Marcus moved closer to her as Yvonne read the label on the box of hair coloring she was holding. There was a certain sophistication about her now, no longer the innocent young girl he had turned into a millionaire. "Yvonne? Yvonne Haggler?" he said. She jumped when he spoke, and started to back away from him. Yvonne stopped and looked at Marcus. Then she smiled.

"Marcus Douglas. How have you been?"

"I'm doing okay," Marcus replied, knowing he was lying. Other then seeing her, he felt terrible. "How about you? You look great."

"Thank you, Marcus. Are you still practicing?"

She was even prettier than he remembered. She had lost her Mississippi accent in the last nine years. "Yes, I am. The practice is doing quite well. I've added a few new associates since I last saw you. Why?" Marcus smiled. "Do you need a lawyer?"

"No, Marcus, I don't think a lawyer is what I need right now," Yvonne replied as she walked to the registers. Once she paid for her hair color, she turned to Marcus. "It was great seeing you, Marcus. Maybe I'll see you again while I'm in town."

Marcus took out his wallet and gave Yvonne his card. "Give me a call and maybe we can have a dinner or a drink."

"I'd like that," Yvonne said. Nine years ago she

had what she called a schoolgirl crush on Marcus, but she knew she wouldn't be around long enough to take him up on his offer. She tucked his card in her purse. "Good night, Marcus." While the cashier scanned his items, Marcus watched Yvonne walk out of the store.

Yvonne started walking through the parking lot when she noticed two men standing by her car. She stopped dead in her tracks and looked around the lot. There was nobody in sight. She looked around again. When she saw Marcus coming out of the store, she walked toward him quickly. Just as he reached his car, she called out, "Marcus!"

"Hello again," Marcus said, his smile growing.

"I was wondering about your offer for that drink. Maybe I could take you up on it?"

"Sure. You've got my card. Just give me a call and we'll get together anytime you're free."

Yvonne looked back at the two men standing by her car. "Actually, I was talking about now. That is if you're not busy."

Marcus looked at Yvonne curiously. "No," he said slowly. "I'm not doing anything right now."

"Good," Yvonne said and walked around to the passenger side of the car.

"What about your car?"

"Ahh, it's not—it will be all right here for a while." She got in quickly. Marcus closed her door, shrugged his shoulders, and got in on the driver side. He started the car and started out of the parking lot.

As they passed her car, Yvonne dropped her purse and busied herself picking up the contents until they were well on their way. *I don't think they saw me,* Yvonne thought. She looked out the back window, and there didn't appear to be anyone following, although she couldn't be sure. Yvonne looked at Marcus and smiled as he drove, then she continued to look behind her.

"Is everything all right, Mrs. Haggler?"

"Huh? Oh, everything is fine. Where are we going?"

"There's a Bennigans not too far from here."

"Bennigans. Isn't there someplace a little more quiet? So we can talk and get reacquainted."

"I'm staying at a Residence Inn not too far from here. I think they have a bar."

"Sounds good to me. Mind if I ask why you're staying at a Residence Inn?"

"It's a long story, Mrs. Haggler."

"Yvonne. You can call me Yvonne."

"Okay, *Yvonne,* but it's still a long story."

"Okay, okay, I won't push it. You don't have to cop an attitude."

"I'm sorry. I didn't mean to snap at you." Marcus turned into the parking lot. "Maybe I do need a drink. Maybe two or three."

The hotel did have a bar, but it was closed. "That's okay, Marcus. We can talk in your room," Yvonne said and led Marcus away by the arm.

"My room," Marcus replied sheepishly.

"Don't worry. I promise I won't bite you. I haven't bitten anybody in years."

* * *

"Make yourself comfortable." Marcus said as they entered his room. Yvonne immediately walked from room to room and opened every door. "A little paranoid, are we?"

"Just a habit. I like to know where I am," Yvonne answered as she peeked out the window. She wasn't sure if she liked the fact that the room was on the first floor. She sat down.

"Don't just stand there, sit down. This is your room." Marcus sat down in a chair across from Yvonne. She made him feel nervous and uncomfortable. He tried not to show it, but it was too late.

"Am I making you feel uncomfortable, Marcus?"

"No, no, of course not. It's just that . . . well . . . you see . . ."

"Marcus."

"Huh?"

"Just relax and say what you're trying to say."

"Well, Yvonne, I ah, I left my wife today."

"Oh Marcus, that's too bad," Yvonne said. Her accent had suddenly returned, only now it sounded phony. "Or maybe it isn't."

"What do you mean by that?"

"You could be happy you left your wife."

"No, Yvonne, I'm not happy about it," Marcus said quietly and slumped down deeper in his chair.

"You wanna tell me how you feel about it?" Yvonne asked, kicking off her heels and curling up on the couch.

"I don't—wait a minute. I'm the one who is supposed to be on the couch."

"Oh, you mean like a shrink. I been in therapy before."

"You're not crazy, are you?" Marcus said with a smile.

"No, I was just depressed about some things. Therapy helped me deal. But you gotta really get into it. You know what I mean? Dig deep down and get in touch with the source. I know it sounds kinda dippy, but it worked for me."

"So what were you so depressed about?"

"Some things were happening to me, but that was just at the surface. What was really happening was I had never really dealt with what my mother did to me."

"What did she do?"

"Marcus, I was a sixteen-year-old virgin when I met Richard. I liked him, but I barely knew him. He arranged the whole marriage thing with my mother. They came to me after they had worked it all out, and she told me that I was going to marry Richard. That it was the best thing for all of us. She said that she couldn't afford to do anything for our family and Richard said he would send her money every week. She sold me to him."

"I didn't know that. I mean, I just thought that you were a young bride who moved to Atlanta with her new husband. I didn't know. I'm sorry."

"It all turned out all right. Richard was so sweet. He treated me good and I learned to love him with time. But she sold me, like I was a slave or something. Suppose Richard wasn't a good man. She didn't know him from a can of paint. Anything could have happened to me. She didn't care. I was just another mouth to feed, so I had to go. She did the same thing to my sisters when they got old enough. Found some old man, and sold them too. Beverly's husband wasn't bad. He just worked her like a slave, but so did my mother, so she was used to it. But Virginia, she wasn't that lucky. Denny was an animal. He stayed drunk most of the time. He treated her like dirt, beat her, and raped her when he felt like it. Forced her to have sex with his friends."

"My God. Is she still with him?"

"No."

"How did she get away from him?"

"The hard way. He hit her in the face with an iron because she wouldn't have sex with him. She ran out the house screaming and just by chance, the police were driving by. They took him to jail. She was so afraid of him. We had to beg her to press charges. They gave him ten years and I moved her out to L.A. with me."

"That's good."

"Not really, Marcus. She was pretty shot out when she got out there. Fell in with the wrong people, started smokin' crack. Let some nigga turn her out. He made her turn tricks to support their habit."

"Where is she now? Is she all right?"

"I don't know. I haven't seen her in years. I hope she's all right. I use to go looking for her when I hadn't heard from her in a while. The last time she disappeared, I never did find her."

"I'm sorry, Yvonne."

"Don't sweat it, Marcus. I've come to grips with all that. But we're supposed to be talking about you, not my dysfunctional family. Tell me about your wife."

"My wife." Marcus stood up and walked around the room. He picked up his jacket. "You mind if I smoke?" he asked, pulling the pack of Kools from the pocket.

"I am so glad you said that," Yvonne replied, digging in her purse for her pack of Benson and Hedges 100's. "I've been dying for a cigarette all night." They both lit up, inhaled deeply and exhaled, like a shared sigh of relief. "Now I need a drink."

"Are you sure that you don't want to go somewhere and have a drink?"

"No!" Yvonne said quickly and firmly. "I'm sorry, Marcus." She laughed. "Now, tell me about your wife."

"My wife, Randa. What can I say about my wife Randa?" Marcus returned to the chair and sat down. "She was a wonderful woman. She was beautiful, intelligent, and she had so much energy. She was always doing something for somebody. She volunteered at a retirement home a couple days a week. She had a teenage girl she was mentoring. We were very happy together. She was my best friend. We had so much in common and we would spend hours together just talking. That's the hardest part of dealing with this. I loved her, sure, but we were so close. I feel like I lost the best part of myself. We did just about everything together. People called us the poster children for the perfect relationship."

"Sounds like you guys had a good thing going. I mean, you do make her sound like she was just the little perfect woman." Yvonne rolled her eyes and took a drag.

"And like a fool, I bought into it, hook, line, and sinker. But she wasn't right. I was such a fool. I was so blind. How could I have been so blind?" Marcus leaned forward quickly in his chair. "I saw so much in her, but I guess I saw what I wanted to see. I put her on that pedestal; she was bound to fall off."

"What happened, Marcus?"

"What happened? You really want to know what happened to make this the worst day of my life?"

"I'll try not to take that personally."

"Please don't. Seeing you has been the only high point in an otherwise fucked up day. Excuse my language."

"That's all right Marcus. I'm a big girl now. All grown up. I've heard people curse before. I've been known to say a curse word or two myself. But you stop trying to change the subject. Tell me what happened."

"The day started out like any other. The alarm went off, we made love to each other, just like we did every morning."

Yvonne smiled. "I like it in the morning too. Makes the day go so much better," she said, seeming to purr like a kitten as she stretched. "I'm sorry, Marcus. Go on."

"We showered together and she cooked breakfast while I got ready to go to the office. Randa mentioned that she might go shopping with her girlfriend, Deloris. I asked her to pick me up a new tie."

"What color?"

"Black. Anyway, we ate breakfast and I left for the office, just like we do every morning. I had been working at home the night before, getting ready for a meeting with a client that I had this afternoon, and I left the paper at home. I called Randa to see if she could bring me the papers and we could have lunch together, but there was no answer. I needed those papers, so I went home to get them. When I got home, her Benz was in the driveway. I figured that Deloris came and picked her up, and she had gone shopping."

"I went inside and called her name a few times. She didn't answer. I went into the den and I couldn't find the papers, so I turned on the computer so I could print them. I had just picked up the papers off the printer when I thought I heard a noise. I stood still for a second, but I didn't hear anything else. So, I turned off the computer and headed for the door."

"I was out the house, Yvonne, and I was just about to close the door when I heard the noise again. I turned around and walked up the steps straight to the bedroom and opened the door. There she was. My wife. Pullin' her hair out, ridin' some man's dick. I stood there. I couldn't move. I stood there . . ."

"I guess it couldn't have been too long before I went back downstairs. I just walked outside I sat down on the steps. I don't know how long I'd been sitting there when I heard the door open and close and open again. When I looked up Randa was standing in front me." Marcus lit another cigarette with the one he was smoking.

"What did you say to her? Better yet, what did she say to you?"

"She asked me if I had been in the house. I just looked at her. I guess she got tired of me staring at her not saying anything, so she went back in the house. The two of them came out, got in the Benz I pay for, and left."

"Damn! The least she could have done was make the brother go home in a cab. Show you some respect. She needed to stay there and handle her business."

"I thought so too. But remember, I'm a fool. What makes it worse is after she leaves, the neighbor woman walks up to me."

"The neighbor woman?"

"The neighbor woman, that's what we call her."

"Okay."

"The neighbor woman says, 'I'm glad you finally woke up. And don't let her tell you that this was the first time.' Then she walked away. Now I felt embarrassed on top of feeling stupid. If the neighbor woman knew, the rest of the block did too. Maybe even the whole subdivision."

"I don't know what to say, Marcus." Yvonne stretched and repositioned herself on the couch. "Did Randa come back?"

"Yeah, she came back. While she was gone, I thought about all the things I would say to her. How could you, who is he, how long has this been going on?"

"Maybe you should have asked the neighbor woman." Marcus cut his eyes at Yvonne. "Sorry. Dagg, it was a joke."

"When she came back I couldn't say anything. She tried to explain, telling me that this was the first time, but the neighbor woman cleared that up. Told me how sorry she was. And she promised me if I forgave her it would never happen again. I couldn't say anything. I thought of a hundred things to say, but I was so mad, the words just wouldn't come out. I sat there for a minute or two, then I just got up and left."

"I'm so sorry, Marcus. I know that must have hurt." She yawned.

"Of course it hurt. You know what's funny about this whole thing?"

"What's that, Marcus?"

"I met her the day after you moved to L.A. I remember thinking that maybe I'd get lucky and find a woman as beautiful and as sweet as you."

"Oh, Marcus."

"I love her, Yvonne." Marcus stood up and began to wander around the room, talking while he paced back and forth. "But she betrayed all that. Not just me, but us. Everything about us, everything we meant to each other. She betrayed everything that we were. Everything we talked about. All of our plans. Our hopes. She betrayed our future. That's what hurt. We used to talk about growing old together, sitting on the porch watching our grandchildren run around. Grandchildren. We had been talking about having a baby. We had even gone out and started buying stuff we knew that we'd need for the baby. She betrayed all that. While I was building a future for us, she was tearing it down. I don't know what I'm gonna do without her."

Marcus stopped talking. "No comment from the peanut gallery?" He walked to the couch. "Yvonne? Yvonne?" She had fallen asleep. "Stop me if I bore you." Marcus took the spread off the bed then laid it over Yvonne and kissed her on the cheek. "Good night, Yvonne."

Phase 2

When Yvonne woke up the next morning, Marcus was already gone. He left a note on the television that read: *Gone shopping. Be back around noon. Please wait for me.* Yvonne smiled when she read it. Then she picked up the box of hair color and went into the bedroom. When she came out, she no longer had long, black hair. It was now short, and auburn.

She gathered her things and called for a cab to pick her up. When they asked what her destination would be, she hung up the phone. She put on her sunglasses and left the room through the sliding door and went into the lobby. She asked the desk clerk to get her a cab then told him she would be waiting in the bar.

Once the cab arrived, she offered the driver a fifty-dollar bill to take her where she wanted to go if he wouldn't call it in. The driver quickly promised, and they were on their way. Yvonne told him to drop her off at the Indian Creek Marta station. She would walk from there.

Yvonne walked down Redan Road and up South Hairston to the Main Street subdivision and the home of Tyisha, with whom she had gone to high school.

"Yvonne, I wasn't expecting you for a couple of days." Tyisha said, giving her a big hug. "Come on in out that heat, girl. It must ninety-five degrees out there. You're drenched. What, did you walk here from California?"

"No, girl. Just from the Marta station."

"Where's your car?"

"Don't ask. Did you get that package I sent you?"

"It came yesterday."

"Good."

Tyisha got the package and handed it to Yvonne.

"What's in there? You ain't in no trouble, are you, Yvonne?"

"Better if you don't know. I need one more favor from you, then I gotta go. And I want you to forget about this package and that you ever saw me."

"Whatever, girl."

"No, Ty. You never saw this box or me. Now, you promise me, Ty."

"Okay, okay, I promise. Now, what you need?"

"I need some clothes and I could use a shower."

"No problem." Tyisha got her some clothes and Yvonne disappeared into the bathroom, taking the package with her. She turned on the shower and began to get undressed then she sat down on the toilet and lit a cigarette.

Yvonne opened the box and removed its contents. The box contained a bag intended for a laptop. She opened the bag, took out a 9-millimeter automatic and laid it down on the vanity. She looked in the bag at the legal-size envelope and the money.

She shook her head and wondered how things could have gone so wrong. Yvonne opened the envelope, took out the papers and stared at them, wishing she knew what it said or what language it was. She returned the papers to the envelope and put it and the gun back in the bag. She finished undressing and got in the shower.

While she was in the shower, she thought about Marcus and Randa. She felt badly for him. And as much as she hated to involve him in all this, she needed an ally, and Tyisha wasn't the one. Marcus wasn't exactly James Bond, but he was all she had. Now he was the only one she could trust.

Yvonne asked Tyisha to call a cab for her, but she insisted that she could take her anywhere she needed to go. "All right, Ty. Take me to the New China Buffet."

"Are you hungry, Yvonne?" Tyisha asked on the way to open the door. "I could have made you something to eat."

"That's okay, Ty. I'm just meeting someone there." She hated having to lie to Tyisha. She was her best friend before Yvonne moved to L.A., and they managed to stay friends, real friends, in spite of the money. Once the word got around that Yvonne was to receive a large sum of money, most of her friends changed. But not Tyisha. She always kept it real, which was exactly why Yvonne wanted her to have no part in this.

When they arrived at the restaurant, they got out and Yvonne said good-bye to Tyisha. "Thanks for everything, Ty. You take care of yourself and remember, you never saw me."

Tyisha hugged her friend. "Girl, you too much. Why everything with you got to be some big secret?" she returned to her car. Yvonne stood at the door and watched Tyisha drive away. When she was out of sight, Yvonne came out and started walking down Memorial Drive, heading for the post office.

On the way, she made a mental note of the name of an apartment complex she passed.

Yvonne was hot and tired when she reached the post office. She went to the counter and asked the clerk for a box big enough to send a laptop and some tape to seal the box. Yvonne looked around the post office for a secluded spot where she wouldn't be seen by people or surveillance cameras and proceeded to pack the box. She took the gun out of the bag and taped it to the bottom of the box, then placed the bag with the papers and money on top of it. She sealed the box then retrieved Marcus's card from her purse. Yvonne addressed the box to herself in care of Marcus and marked it for next day delivery.

With that taken care of, Yvonne went to the pay phone and made arrangements to get a new fake ID and passport. Then she called a cab. She had the cab meet her at the apartment complex and take her back to the Residence Inn. When she arrived, she didn't see Marcus' car, so she let herself in through the sliding door. She turned on the television, lay down on the couch, and went to sleep.

Yvonne was awakened by a knock at the door. She started toward the door, but paused for a moment. *It might be his wife looking for him.* The peephole revealed nothing so Yvonne reluctantly said, "Who is it?"

"It's me, Yvonne. I forgot my key." Yvonne opened the door and was shocked to see the two men who had been waiting by her car in the parking lot the night before.

"Good to see you again, Yvonne," The first man said as he slapped her. Yvonne fell to the floor and tried to crawl away. The second man snatched her up from the floor. "Love what you've done to your hair." He slapped her too, then picked her up and threw her on the bed. "Where is it, Yvonne?" The first man asked pointing his gun at her.

"Where is what? I don't know what you're talking about." Her heart pounded. Tears rolled down her cheeks.

"Check the room. But don't make a mess." The other man searched the room and found nothing. "I'm not going to ask you again, Yvonne. Where is it?"

"I don't know what you're talking about!" she screamed. The man grabbed Yvonne by her hair and punched her in the eye. He drew back and was about to punch her again. "It's not here!" Yvonne yelled.

"Where is it?"

"I can't get it until tomorrow."

"I guess we'll just have to keep you company until then." He grabbed Yvonne by the hair again and pulled her to the door. "Now, we're going to walk through that lobby. If you scream or try to run, I'll kill you. It don't matter to me. I'll still get paid."

At 9:00 Marcus returned to his room, armed with a new wardrobe and a bottle of Hennessy. "Yvonne. You here?" He put down his packages and looked around. He had thoughts all day about Yvonne and hoped that she would be there when he got back, but she was gone. He sat down on the couch. He could smell the scent of Yvonne's perfume. It made him smile.

Throughout the day, Marcus allowed himself to slip into the fantasy of Yvonne standing by and supporting him through his divorce from Randa, and then they would get married. "Maybe she'll be back." He poured himself a glass of Henny. He stayed up, waiting for Yvonne to come back until he finally fell asleep after two in the morning.

The following morning, Marcus woke up and slowly came to the realization that he would never see Yvonne again. He tried to shrug it off as if it didn't matter. But it did. The truth of the matter was that nine years ago he had fallen in love with Yvonne. He thought that her coming back into his life on the very day that he left his wife was some kind of sign. He put his dream down and prepared to go to the office.

He arrived at his office after 1:00 to see his first client. After the client left, Janice told him, "this package came addressed to Yvonne Haggler. I was wondering why you seemed so happy today."

Marcus took the package from Janice and carried it in his office, closing the door behind him. He was overjoyed. He jumped up and down and danced around like a kid on Christmas morning. This meant he would see Yvonne again. He put the package in his desk and locked it.

At 4:00 Yvonne called.

"Hello, Yvonne. How—"

She had no time for pleasantries. "Did a package come for me?"

"It came about an hour ago."

"Marcus, I need you to bring it to me right now."

"What's wrong, Yvonne? Are you in trouble? Should I call the police?"

"Marcus, everything is fine. I just need that box as soon as you can," Yvonne said, trying to sound as calm as she could with someone listening on the other line and a gun pointed at her head. "I'm in the West End on Peters and Whitehall. There's a warehouse on the corner. Just come inside. I'll be waiting there for you. When do you think you can get here?"

Marcus looked at his watch. "I should be there in about an hour."

"Good, I'll see you then."

"Yvonne."

"Yes, Marcus."

"Maybe when you get finished with your business we can have dinner."

"Marcus," she said frantically. Then she calmed down. "I'd like that."

"Then it's a date. I'll see you in an hour." Marcus hung up the phone and called Janice. He told her to clear his calendar for the rest of the day. "For the rest of the week, Janice. I need some time off. Maybe I'll take a trip."

"Marcus, I know you're hurt. I know you want to get back at Randa for what she did, but give yourself a chance to heal."

"Thanks, Janice. Sometimes I don't know what I would do without you."

Marcus finished up his paperwork as quickly as he could in anticipation of seeing Yvonne. He drove downtown, stopping on the exit ramp to buy a red rose for Yvonne, wondering if she would like

to go to Aruba with him. *Won't that piss Randa off?*
Marcus thought and smiled. *Not that I care. She gets
what she gets now.*

He arrived at the warehouse and went inside.
When he came through the door, Yvonne came to
meet him. Marcus saw her swollen eye. "Yvonne,
are you alright?"

"Thanks for bringing this to me, Marcus," Yvonne
said loud enough for her new friends to hear. She
took the box from Marcus and whispered, "Wait for
me outside. Have the car running." She looked
over her shoulder. "Sorry I can't do dinner, but call
me tomorrow and we'll do lunch." She took the
rose and kissed him. "Please, Marcus, just go," she
whispered and turned away.

Yvonne looked back as Marcus walked quickly
to the door. Once he made it safely out of the
building, she tried to hand the box to the men.
"Open it."

They watched closely as Yvonne put the box
down on the table and opened it. She handed the
bag to them. The bag was opened. While one busied himself with the papers, the other smiled at
the money, and Yvonne removed the nine from
the box. She fired two shots, returned the papers
to the envelope, put them back in the bag, picked
up her rose and headed for the door.

When Marcus heard the shots coming from the
warehouse, it only served to increase his already
heightened sense of anxiety, to say the least. He
got out of the car and had just reached the door
when Yvonne came out. "What happened in there?"

"Not now Marcus. We gotta get outta here. Get

in the car and let's go!" Yvonne shouted as she walked quickly behind Marcus.

Marcus got in the car and drove away quickly. "What happened? Are you all right?" he asked as he looked in the rearview mirror.

"I'm fine, Marcus. Just drive."

"Where to?"

"I don't know. I'm making this up as I go. Just drive."

"Okay, we'll go back to my hotel."

"No, they know about that. That's where they found me."

"Who is they? What are you involved in?"

"Not now, Marcus, please. I need to think. Go to a hotel near the airport."

"Did you kill those men?"

"Yes, Marcus, I killed them. Now, please just let me think for a minute."

"Why, Yvonne? Why did you kill them?"

"They would have killed me and you too!" Yvonne yelled. "Is that a good enough reason for you?"

"It has something to do with that box, doesn't it? What have you got me mixed up in?"

"I don't know. I really just don't know what this is all about." Yvonne took a deep breath. "Please, Marcus. I'll tell you everything as soon as we get settled."

Marcus looked in the rearview mirror again. "Well, it doesn't look like the police or anybody is following us," he said, not really sure if he said it to reassure Yvonne or himself.

"This isn't a movie, Marcus. The police aren't on our tail."

He looked at the bag at Yvonne's feet. She had

just killed two men over that bag. Marcus said nothing else as he drove to the Hilton near the airport. As they entered the hotel, Yvonne stopped.

"What's wrong?" Marcus asked.

"Do you have cash?"

"No. I was going to put it on my credit card."

"No. Let's go to an ATM."

"There's one," Marcus said, pointing at the ATM in the lobby.

"No. They can track your credit card transactions. Go to a bank, and not one close to here either," Yvonne said. They left the Hilton and got back in the car. Marcus drove past three bank ATM machines before stopping at a First Union. With cash in hand, they returned to the Hilton. Once they got in the room, Marcus went straight to the mini bar. He poured a drink and downed it. He poured another drink.

"I'd like one too, if it's not too much trouble." Yvonne lay down on the bed and Marcus brought her a drink. "Thank you, Marcus. And thank you for my rose. It was sweet of you."

Marcus lit a cigarette and sat down on the bed. "You're welcome. It's not every day I give a woman a rose right before she kills somebody." Marcus posted an uneasy smile. Yvonne let out a little laugh. "What's going on, Yvonne?"

"Give me a drag of your cigarette." Marcus handed Yvonne his cigarette and she inhaled deeply and blew out the smoke.

"I'm a courier Marcus. Those men were assassins sent to kill me and recover the contents of that bag. There's a hundred thousand dollars and some papers in there. I don't know what's on the papers. It's in some language, I don't know which one. I think that just about covers it."

"A courier?"

"I travel to different places and pick up things from one person then deliver them to another."

"I know what a courier is, Yvonne. Why do you do it? Is it excitement?"

"No, I do it for money."

"Money?"

"Yes, Marcus, for money. Isn't that why most people do things?"

"I know that. But you've got money."

"I'm broke."

"Broke? What do you mean, broke? The way I had you set up, you should have been able to live comfortably."

"It's a long story."

"We seem to have plenty of time. We're not going anywhere."

Yvonne and Marcus lay on the bed quietly for the next two hours, sharing cigarettes, drinking and thinking. Marcus thought about how the events of the day would affect him. He was now an accessory to murder. Not only was he going to jail, but he would be disbarred. In two days, he had lost his wife, his career, and his freedom. He looked at Yvonne, eyes closed, smoking the cigarette he had just handed her.

She opened her eyes and noticed him staring at her. She handed him the cigarette and closed her eyes. Marcus desperately wanted to know what was going on, not only to satisfy his curiosity, but also begin planning their defense. If those men were actually trying to kill her, then their deaths were, in reality, self-defense. But Yvonne had shut down.

Yvonne, for her part, had just a bit more on her plate. Things were pretty cut and dried for Marcus, but her world was much more complicated. She felt badly for involving Marcus in her mess, but what's done was done. There was no turning back now. But he was entitled to an explanation.

"When I left here, I was set. I was twenty-one, rollin' a Benz, nice little condo in Northridge, and more money than I ever dreamed possible. And thanks to you, it just kept rollin' in. I was getting dividend checks just about every week from companies I'd never heard of. I just knew it would never run out. I was spending money, buying whatever I thought I wanted—clothes, mostly. Bought a house for Mama and sent my whole family money. And traveling. I loved to travel. I had never been anywhere, never seen anything. My eyes had opened up to a whole new world, and it was mine to command. I went everywhere, did everything I wanted. Even took my newfound fake friends on a cruise. All expenses paid by me, of course. I was a fool, a foolish young girl with money. I remember my papa tellin' me that a fool and his money are soon parted. Well, that's exactly what happened to me. I remember going to New York one day with this guy I met the night before. We had dinner at a French restaurant. After we left, we caught a cab to go back to the hotel, and we were talking about how the food wasn't that good and how the service was poor. He said, 'Too bad we can't have dinner in France.' I told the cab driver to take us to the airport. Next day we were in France having late supper with a view of the tower."

"You were out the box, Yvonne."

"A fool. A damn fool. After awhile I found that I was running out of money. The checks were still coming, but that wasn't enough."

"You could have changed your lifestyle."

"Marcus, that would have been too much like right. I had met this guy named Paris. He's the type who's into everything, knows everybody. You know the type. Anyway, we were hangin' out and I was tellin' him about my money problems, and he asked me if I would do some work for him as a courier. I told him no, so he introduced me to Tom Mack."

"The lawyer you gave power of attorney to."

"The same. He told me that if I let him make some investments for me that I would be set for life. I would be able to quadruple my money in less than a month. So, I gave him fifty thousand dollars. Three weeks later he wrote me out a check for two hundred thousand dollars."

"You want me to tell you what happened next?"

"Okay, go ahead."

"Old Tom Mack tells you that you could have the check or you could reinvest it, and since the market conditions are right, you could make half a million dollars."

"Yeah, how did you know?"

Marcus smiled. "Old scam."

"Yeah, well, the fool fell for it. Two weeks later he called me and said that we were close to flippin' that money, but he was on to something else that had the potential to be far more lucrative. I told him that I was just about broke, and that fifty I gave him was really all I had to invest. When I told him that—" Yvonne laughed. "I'll never forget that conversation. Marcus. It changed my life."

Tom Mack said, "Well, Yvonne, in another week you'll have half a million dollars. But I hate for you to miss out on this."

"I do too Tom, but there's nothing I can do until I get some more money."

"Well maybe there is."

"What's that?" Yvonne said greedily.

"Paris mentioned to me that you had some investments, that were providing you with a nice dividend income."

"Go on."

"If I had control of those investments I might be able to leverage those gains on this new deal and make it happen."

"What would you need?"

"Who controls those accounts for you?"

"My lawyer, Marcus Douglas in Atlanta."

"I would need you to fire him and give me power of attorney."

"I don't know, Tom. That money is all I'm living off now."

"I understand, Yvonne. Maybe it will come around again, but I doubt it. Anyway, I'll call you when I have some news for you."

"Wait a minute, Tom."

"Yes."

"Go ahead and draw up whatever you need. I'll be there an hour."

Three weeks later, Yvonne got a call from Tom Mack, letting her know that the market dropped and she had lost everything. With nowhere to go, she turned to Paris once again for help. He put her to work the next day as a courier. Yvonne's lifestyle was saved, and for the next five years she made the occasional trip, picking up and delivering whatever Paris asked her to.

Yvonne never knew what she was carrying and had convinced herself that she didn't care. "Better if I don't know. Yvonne would always tell Paris. If I knew what I carrying, I'd probably be scared shitless," Her plan was simple. She would only do it until she turned thirty, then she could collect on her trust fund.

"What went wrong, Yvonne?" Marcus asked.

"I don't know, Marcus."

"Well, what happened?"

"Paris sent me to Singapore. Everything was going fine. I picked up that bag and went back to my room. Then this man shows up at my door. He said that Paris sent him. That there was a change in plans and Paris wanted me to give him the bag and meet him back in L.A. in a week. I told him that I needed to call Paris to confirm. Paris always said that if there was a change in plans I would hear it from him. If it ever happened, I should kill whoever told me any different before they killed me.

"He stopped me from calling. Said that things were going on that I had no knowledge of, and my calling would put too many people at risk. I said I was calling Paris anyway. He grabbed me; we wrestled around for a while. I'm pretty strong for a Mississippi country girl. Anyway, I broke away from him and ran into the bedroom. I got to my gun and I shot him."

"You ever kill anyone before?"

"No. That was the first time I ever had to use it. Since I had to carry a gun, Paris made me learn how to use it. I was great on the range, but never thought that I would have to use it."

"What happened then?"

"I freaked out and I grabbed the bag and got out of there. I went straight to the airport and caught a plane to Hawaii and went to the drop-off point, but nobody showed up. I was really scared by then, so I called Paris. But I didn't mention anything about the man I shot. He said he didn't know what was going on and told me to come home and bring the bag to him. When I got back to my condo, there was somebody waiting for me."

"Did you shoot them too?"

"No I jumped off the balcony and ran to my car and took Interstate 10 out of town. I just kept driving until I was too tired to drive any further. I stopped for few hours in Picacho, Arizona to get some sleep, then I was gone again. I drove to El Paso, Texas. I was going to cross into Ciudad Juarez in Mexico, but I didn't want to use the fake ID and passport I had gotten from Paris, and I was in too much of a hurry when I left to get mine. So I went to FedEx and sent that box to Tyisha. And then I drove here."

"How did I get involved in this?"

"Those two men were waiting for me in the parking lot the night we met in the store. I didn't mean to get you involved, but they were at my car. You were the only way I could get away from there. I made arrangements for a new passport to get out of the country, then I sent that package to you. I figured that it was kind of an insurance policy. I was set, but I didn't want to leave without saying good-bye to you."

Marcus got up from the bed and paced back and forth thinking of a way out of their predicament. "Paris."

"I was thinking about Africa," Yvonne said.

"No, Paris is the key to it all. We'll go to L.A. and I'll return the bag. They shouldn't bother you after that."

"Are you crazy? For all I know Paris may kill me on sight and take the bag off my dead body."

"True, but we got to convince him that it's in his best interest to leave you alone."

"How you gonna do that?"

"Yvonne, I'm a lawyer. I'm a very good negotiator."

Marcus and Yvonne argued about what to do well into evening. He was convinced that talking to Paris and returning the bag was the only way. Yvonne, on the other hand, hated that plan. She just wanted to get away.

"I say we see the passport guy and go to Africa." She felt like she was talking to a brick wall.

Then it hit her. "You're right. Going back to L.A. is the only way out of this." Yvonne opened a new pack of Bensons and walked to the window.

"Good. I'm glad you finally see that." Marcus reached for the bottle on the nightstand and poured a drink. He took a sip. "We'll catch a flight and be in L.A. first thing tomorrow morning.

Yvonne sat on the bed and took the drink from Marcus in exchange for her cigarette. "We'll do it your way, Marcus." She yawned and lay down on the bed. Marcus gave back her cigarette. "We'll never be safe until we settle things with Paris." She curled into the fetal position. "And then it will be over."

Phase 3

The next morning, Marcus called Janice and told her where he was going then he and Yvonne set out for California. Yvonne insisted they fly into San Francisco, catch a flight to Santa Barbara and drive down the 101 into L.A. They checked into the Wyndham Hotel at the airport. As soon as they got to the room, Yvonne called and left a message for Paris to call her message service.

"Paris, this is Yvonne. I want to meet you somewhere tomorrow to return those items to you. And hopefully this will end our relationship without any further need for outside intervention."

She checked every half-hour to see if he returned her call. Hours dragged on. With nothing to do, they occupied themselves ordering room service and watching movies until it was almost 2:00. Marcus had fallen asleep hours earlier, but Yvonne kept up her thirty-minute vigil. At 2:30 Yvonne called again. Paris had left a message.

"Yvonne, it's good to hear your voice again. It's late and I'm tired. Be at my house in El Segundo at eleven."

"I don't think so." Yvonne called him back and left a message that Marcus would meet him at Bruce's Place, a bar and grill on West Grand at 11:00 and he would give him the bag. "One more thing, Paris. Come alone."

She started to wake Marcus, but he looked so

peaceful she didn't want to bother him. Yvonne turned off the lights and lay down next to Marcus. He stretched and put his arm around Yvonne. She smiled and went to sleep.

At 10:00 the next morning, they left the Wyndham to meet Paris. As Yvonne drove, she gave Marcus a description of Paris. "You can't miss him." She dropped him off on Main Street and West Grand, about a block from Bruce's Place. Marcus got out. "Wish me luck."

"Good luck, Marcus. I'll pick you up here when it's over."

Marcus started to walk away Yvonne got out of the car. "Marcus!" He turned around and walked back. "You know you've slept with me for the last three nights?"

"Yeah, and I haven't even kissed you," Marcus said as he leaned against the car.

"No, you haven't." She kissed him on the cheek then gently on the lips.

"I love you, Yvonne."

"I love you too, Marcus. When all this is over, I'll show you just how much."

"See you, Yvonne."

"See ya, Marcus."

Marcus walked down the street and entered Bruce's Place. He went into the bathroom and took the garbage bag out of the trashcan, placed the laptop bag in it and replaced the garbage bag. Then he took a seat in the back of the bar where he could see the door.

He checked his watch. It was 11:00. He tapped anxiously on the table. His tapping reminded him of the sound of Yvonne's heels clicking against the tile that first night at the store. He looked up and

Paris stood before him. Yvonne's description of Paris was dead on target. He was dressed in a dull gray suit, white shirt, opened at the collar, black Ray Bans and wet look hair.

"Marcus, I'll take it. Yvonne used to speak of you all time. You wouldn't mind standing up and opening your coat, would you?"

"I'm unarmed," Marcus said as he did as he was asked then sat down.

"May I sit?" Paris asked.

"By all means. Let's get this over with."

"Yes. This has been a very big misunderstanding. I never intended for any of this to happen. I don't know how much Yvonne told you, but—"

Marcus cut him off. "I'm just the delivery boy."

"When she didn't come see me, I simply had to take steps to recover the items. It was easy to track her movements, and it was obvious that she was heading for Atlanta. Unfortunately, I underestimated her abilities."

"Right."

"May I see the items?"

"Excuse me for a minute." Marcus went into the bathroom and returned with the bag. He handed it to Paris. "Here you go." Marcus stood over Paris and watched as he opened the bag and looked over its contents. Once he had satisfied himself that the items were intact, Paris got up and walked toward the door.

"Please tell Yvonne that I meant her no harm."

"She'll find that very comforting."

As soon as they were outside, Yvonne drove up quickly, and to Marcus' surprise, she fired one shot to Paris' head. Paris fell to the ground. Marcus started to pick up the bag.

"Leave the bag!" Yvonne yelled.

Marcus ran to the car. Once he was in, Yvonne drove away. "Why did you kill him? It was over. All he wanted was his shit back."

"How naïve are you, Marcus? As long as Paris was alive, it would never be over. Can't you see that? He would just keep sending people to kill us."

"Why'd we leave the bag?"

"I'm glad to be rid of it. Let the cops worry about what those papers mean."

Yvonne and Marcus drove back to Santa Barbara. They caught a flight back to San Francisco and bought tickets to Seattle. Yvonne knew someone there who could get them new passports, and would help her get out of the country. They sat at the gate waiting for their plane to begin boarding.

"You know it was the right thing to do, Marcus."

"I know, but you could have told me what you were going to do."

"If I told you, would you have gone along with it?"

"No."

"That's why I didn't tell you," Yvonne said with a smile. "Tomorrow we'll be safely out of the country, and I'll spend the rest of my life in your arms."

"You still could have told me." Marcus kissed Yvonne on the cheek. "I'm going to get some water." Marcus walked away. Yvonne watched him until a lady walked up and stood before her.

"Is anybody sitting there?"

"No, have a seat."

The lady sat down, slowly removing a .38 with a silencer from her purse. Yvonne looked at her and the lady shot her five times. The lady got up and walked away as Marcus returned. Yvonne struggled to her feet.

"Marcus." He caught her as she fell. Marcus looked around for the woman, but by then she had disappeared into the crowd. He held Yvonne in his arms and thought, *There is only one way out of the kind of life Yvonne was living.*

She died in his arms.